THE LIFE OF A USELESS MAN

MAXIM GORKI

The Life of a Useless Man

TRANSLATED

BY MOURA BUDBERG

DOUBLEDAY & COMPANY, INC.

GARDEN CITY, NEW YORK

1971

Library of Congress Catalog Number 71–144254

This Translation Copyright © 1971 by Baroness Moura Budberg

All Rights Reserved

Printed in the United States of America

Preface

THERE HAVE BEEN Russian writers in the past century whose style may have been considered better than that of Maxim Gorki's, but none enjoyed the popularity which Gorki received in his lifetime. The man remained a figurehead and popular mentor during one of his country's most fiery and devastating periods.

Gorki's popularity is in part due to his conception of a new language and a new hero. Much of traditional Russian literature was a phenomenon of the upper classes and consequently reflected their highly stylized literary conventions. Gorki introduced a new hero, the peasant, the workingman; the mode of language in his fiction was theirs. He was obsessed with social injustices and the plight of the common man. (The pen name, "Gorki," literally means "bitter"; his real name was Alexis Peshkov.) Unlike Dostoevsky, for example, for whom evil was a metaphysical problem, Gorki saw it as a result of class divisions, material conditions, political despotism, and social injustice.

Gorki's revolutionary activity reached its peak during the armed revolution against the Czarist regime in December 1905, when all of Russia was in chaos. This is the background of *The Life of a Useless Man*.

Not the least important factor in bringing about this uprising was the immensely unpopular Russo-Japanese War, begun in 1904, which revealed the unpreparedness and corruption of the government. The people drew up hundreds of petitions demanding that the autocracy be transformed into a parliamentary monarchy and the government responded with vague promises of constitutional reforms. On January 9, 1905, a famous Sunday subsequently entitled "Bloody," 150,000 workmen marched to the Czar's Winter Palace to present their petitions. This was met with armed police attacks, and a thousand demonstrators were killed. Street disorders subsequently became more violent and frequent. The following October there was a general strike and all public utilities, railroads, mail, and mills were shut down. As a result the government sought a compromise and the Czar issued a manifesto granting freedoms of speech, press, and assembly as well as the convocation of a State Duma, an elected legislative body.

Later, however, these privileges were rescinded. Many of the liberal factions had splintered and many of the peasants hesitated to completely renounce the Czar. The government recouped its physical power in the army and police force, whom the strikers had been unable to influence. The Revolution of 1905 did, however, serve as the dress rehearsal for that of 1917.

The Life of a Useless Man was written in 1907 and the first third of the novel appeared in a periodical, *Znanie*, in St. Petersburg in 1908. Gorki was prohibited by the government from publishing the remainder. It was, however, printed in its entirety in Berlin in Russian (without a date), but this edition and a French translation which appeared in 1910 were forbidden in Russia. The entire book was printed in Russia in 1914 but was not allowed to be published. The Central Committee of Foreign Censorship issued the statement that, "the author's purpose is to describe the odium of spying and persecution on the one hand and the noble character of the revolutionaries on the other. Such a tendency already makes it impossible to publish and as the author at every conceivable opportunity refers to the Czar and the intentions of the revolutionaries in regards to His Person and intimates that everything that is wrong in Russia is done at the Czar's orders and to His glory—it is clear that the book has to be banned and not only banned but forbidden to be secretly distributed."

The book was finally published with lacunae in 1917. This is the first full translation of the Russian text which Gorki completed and revised before his death.

THE LIFE OF A USELESS MAN

Chapter 1

YEVSEY KLIMKOV's father was shot dead by the forester when Yevsey was four years old, and his mother died suddenly in the field at harvest time when he was seven. The death was so strange that Yevsey was not even frightened when he saw her dead body.

Yevsey's Uncle Piotr, the blacksmith, put his hand on the boy's head, and said, "What are we going to do now?"

Yevsey glanced quickly at the corner where his mother lay upon a bench and answered in a low voice, "I don't know."

The blacksmith wiped the sweat from his face with his shirt sleeve, and after a long silence gently poked his nephew.

"You'll live with me . . . Get you into a school, shall I, so that you wouldn't be in the way? Ah, you funny little old man!" he said.

From that day on everyone called the boy Old Man. The nickname suited him perfectly. He was too small for his age, his movements were sluggish, and his voice was frail. A bird-like nose sadly stuck out from a bony face; his round pale eyes blinked anxiously; his sparse straw hair grew in tufts. At school they laughed at him and knocked him around, for his owl-like face somehow antagonized the other more healthy and lively children. He stayed aloof and lived alone, in the shade or in some hiding place or corner. From there, unnoticed, he stared with round unblinking eyes, like a frightened snail, upon the world outside. When his eyes grew tired he would close them, and for a long time would sit unseeing, gently swaying his frail, thin body.

Yevsey endeavored to escape notice even in his uncle's home, but here it was more difficult. He had to eat his meals in the company of the whole family, and when he sat at the table, Yakov, the uncle's youngest son, a fat, red-cheeked boy, played every trick on him, teasing him or trying to make him laugh. He made faces, stuck out his tongue, kicked Yevsey's legs under the table, and even pinched him. He never succeeded in making him laugh, but Yevsey would often jump with pain, his sallow face would turn grey, his eyes would open wide, and his spoon would tremble in his hand.

"What's the matter, Old Man?" his Uncle Piotr asked.

"It's Yashka," the boy explained in an even, uncomplaining voice.

If Uncle Piotr gave Yashka a box on the ear or pulled his hair, Aunt Agafya would pucker up her lips and mutter angrily, "Ugh, you little sneak!"

And Yashka would find him later and beat him mercilessly. Yevsey endured the hiding as something inevitable. It would have been unwise to complain, because if Uncle Piotr beat his son, Aunt Agafya would respond with even greater punishment upon her nephew, and her blows were more painful than Yashka's. So when Yevsey saw that Yashka was on the warpath, he would drop to the ground, curl up with all his strength, pull his knees up to his stomach, and covering his face and head with his hands, would silently yield his sides and his back to his cousin's fists. The more patiently he bore the blows, the angrier Yashka grew. Sometimes he even wept and shouted, while he kicked his cousin's body, "Scream, you filthy louse!"

Once Yevsey found a horseshoe and gave it to Yashka, knowing full well the boy would take it from him in any case. Mollified by the gift, Yashka asked, "Did I hurt you much when I beat you the other day?"

"Yes, you did," answered Yevsey.

Yashka thought for a while, scratched his head, and said, slightly embarrassed, "Don't worry; it won't last forever."

He went away, but somehow his words stirred something in Yevsey's heart, and he repeated hopefully in an undertone, "It won't last . . . forever."

Once Yevsey saw some women pilgrims massaging their tired feet with nettles. He followed their example and rubbed his

bruised sides with them and it seemed to soothe the pain. From then on he always rubbed his wounds with the coarse leaves of the sharp, unloved weed.

He was bad at his lessons because he came to school dreading the beatings, and left it overcome with a sense of injury. His fear of being wronged was written all over his face, and this provoked in all the others an unconquerable desire to bully the Old Man harder than ever.

The choirmaster discovered that Yevsey possessed an alto voice, and he made him sing in the church choir. Yevsey spent less time at home, but as if to balance this he met his schoolmates more often at the choir practices, and they all fought no less than did Yashka.

He liked the old village church. It had many dark corners and he was always curiously eager to peep into their snug, warm stillness, perhaps not consciously expecting to find something rare and good in one of them, something which would envelop him, caress him tenderly and talk to him the way his mother had once done, but the holy pictures, black with many years of soot, their expressions both kindly and stern, only reminded him of the dark-bearded face of his Uncle Piotr.

Inside the entrance to the church hung a picture representing a saint who had caught the devil and was beating him; the saint was a tall, dark, sinewy man with long hands, the devil a reddish, lean, embryonic creature who had the appearance of a small goat. At first Yevsey did not even glance at the devil—he even wanted to spit at him; but then he began to be sorry for the unfortunate little figure, and when nobody was around he gently stroked the goat-like chin disfigured in the picture by dread and pain. For the first time compassion was born in the boy's heart.

Yevsey liked the church for another reason; all the people, even the most notorious wrongdoers, behaved quietly and meekly. Loud talk frightened Yevsey; he wanted to run away and hide from excited faces and shouting. Once on a market day he had seen a group of peasants talking in loud voices. Then they began to shout and to jostle one another; one of them seized a club and waved it about and someone was struck. Terrible shouting and

clamoring ensued, and many of them started to run; they knocked
the Old Man off his feet and he fell on his face into a puddle.
When he jumped up he saw a huge peasant coming toward him
waving his hands, with a quivering, red blotch instead of a face.
This was so horrible that Yevsey yelled, and suddenly felt as if he
were falling into a black pit. He had to be doused with water before he came to his senses.

Yevsey was also afraid of drunkards; his mother had once told
him that a demon enters the drunk's body. The Old Man
imagined this demon prickly as a hedgehog and wet as a frog, with
a tawny body and green eyes, who settles in a man's stomach and
writhes about in there; this was what turned the man into a fiend.

Yevsey found many other good things about the church. Besides
the peace and quiet and the gentle twilight, Yevsey enjoyed the
singing. When he sang without the music he closed his eyes firmly,
allowing his clear alto voice to blend with the general chorus so
that it would not be heard above the others; he completely lost
himself in sheer delight as if overcome by a blissful sleep. In this
drowsy state it seemed to him he was drifting away from life and
approaching some other gentle, peaceful existence.

A thought took shape in his mind which he once expressed to
his uncle. "Could a person live so that he could go anywhere and
see everything, but nobody could see him?"

"Be invisible?" asked the blacksmith, and thought for a while.
"I should think it would be impossible."

Once all the villagers had begun to call Yevsey "Old Man,"
Uncle Piotr used "Orphan" instead. Though an odd man in every
respect, the blacksmith was never frightening, even when he was
drunk. He would merely remove his hat from his head and walk
about the street waving it, singing songs in a high, doleful voice,
smiling, and shaking his head. The tears would run down his face
more copiously than when he was sober.

Yevsey thought his uncle the wisest and kindest peasant in the
whole village. He could talk to him about anything. Though Uncle
Piotr often smiled, he hardly ever laughed; he spoke without
haste, in a quiet, serious tone. Not noticing his nephew at all or
simply forgetting about him—which particularly pleased Yevsey

—he would talk to himself at work, keeping up a continuous argument with some invisible opponent and scolding him without mercy.

"The devil take you," he would mumble, but without anger. "You greedy bastard! Don't I work hard enough for you? There, look, I've scorched my eyes, I'll be blind any day now. What more do you want? A thousand curses on this life of slavery! There is no beauty in it, no joy!"

There was something almost lyrical in the way he spoke, and Yevsey had the impression that his uncle could actually see the person he was talking to.

Yevsey once asked, "Who is it you're talking to?"

"Whom am I talking to?" repeated the blacksmith without looking at the boy. He answered then with a smile, "It's my own foolishness I'm talking to."

But it was rare for Yevsey to be able to speak with his uncle for he was seldom alone in the shop. Yashka often ran around the place like a top, drowning the blows of the hammer and the crackling of the coals in the furnace with his piercing shouts. When Yashka was there Yevsey did not dare to visit his uncle at all.

The blacksmith's shop stood at the edge of a shallow ravine, and Yevsey passed all his spare time in spring, summer, and autumn at the bottom among the willows. It was as peaceful here as it was in the church. The birds sang, the bees and drones hummed. The boy would sit there swaying his body from side to side, brooding, his eyes tightly shut. Or he would wander about in the bushes, listening to the noise from the blacksmith's shop. When he sensed that his uncle was alone, he would creep out and go and see him.

"What is it, Orphan?" would be the blacksmith's greeting, as he screwed up his watery little eyes.

"Is there an evil spirit let loose in the church at night?" Yevsey once asked.

The smith thought for a while and answered, "Why not? It could go anywhere. No problem for it."

The boy raised his shoulders, and with round eyes he searched the dark corners of the shop.

"You needn't be afraid of evil spirits," the uncle advised him.

Yevsey sighed and answered quietly, "I'm not afraid."

"They won't hurt you," the blacksmith explained with assurance, wiping his eyes with his black fingers.

Then Yevsey asked, "And how about God?"

"What about him?"

"Why does God let devils get into the church?"

"What's that to him? God isn't the church's keeper."

"Doesn't he live there?"

"Who? God? Why should he? His place, Orphan, is everywhere. The church is for the people."

"And the people, what are they for?"

"The people—it seems they are—well, for everything, I suppose! You can't get along without people, and that's a fact."

"Are they for God?"

The blacksmith looked with some suspicion at his nephew, and answered after a pause:

"Of course." Then, wiping his hands on his apron and staring at the flames in the furnace, he added, "I don't know much about this sort of thing, Orphan. You'd better ask the teacher about it. Or the priest, perhaps?"

Yevsey wiped his nose on his shirt sleeve.

"I'm afraid of them," he replied.

"It would be better for you not to talk about such things," Piotr gravely advised him. "You are only a boy. You should be playing and building up your strength. If you want to live you must be healthy. If you aren't strong, you can't work. Then you can't live at all. That's all the wisdom we know; we can't tell what God wants of us." He grew silent, and meditated without taking his eyes from the fire. Then, abruptly breaking his silence, he said earnestly, "On the one hand I know nothing, and on the other I understand nothing. They say all wisdom comes from him . . . But it's not by the size of the candle that you measure a man's worth . . ." He looked around the shop and his eyes fell on the boy in the corner. "Why are you crouching over there? I told you to go out and play." As Yevsey crept out timidly, the smith added, "a spark might fall into your eye, and then you'd be one-eyed, and who wants a creature with one eye?"

Long ago on winter nights Yevsey's mother had often told him stories. There had been stormy nights when the snow and wind had beaten against the walls of the little house, running along the roof, sweeping over everything as if searching in anguish for something, creeping down the chimney, then lying there moaning and whining in a hundred different notes. His mother told the tales in a quiet, drowsy voice that now and then broke down and her speech at times became confused; she often repeated the same words again and again. It seemed to the boy that she could actually see everything she described to him, but not clearly, as if in the dark.

Conversations with Uncle Piotr reminded Yevsey of his mother's stories. The blacksmith, too, it seemed, saw in the furnace-fire both God and the devil, and all the terrors of human life. Perhaps that was why he wept continually. Yevsey listened to his talk and remembered it. It set his heart quivering with an eerie feeling of expectation, the hope growing insensibly that some day he would see something different from life in the village, the drunken peasants, the cantankerous women, the noisy children —something lovable and serious, like the church service.

One of the neighbors had a blind child, Tanya, with whom Yevsey became friendly. He took her walking in the village, helped her carefully down the ravine, and talked to her in a low voice, his watery eyes as usual opening wide with fear. This friendship did not escape the notice of the villagers, and it pleased them. But once the mother of the blind girl came complaining to Uncle Piotr. She claimed that Yevsey had frightened Tanya with his talk, and now she could no longer be left alone. The girl either cried and could not sleep or she had disturbed dreams and often woke up screaming. It was impossible to extract from her what Yevsey had said. She kept babbling about devils, about the sky being black and having holes in it, about seeing fires through the holes with devils jumping about, mocking people. How could anyone tell such stuff to a small child?

"Come here," Uncle Piotr called to his nephew.

When Yevsey slowly left his corner, the smith put his rough, heavy hand on his head and asked, "Did you tell her all that?"

"I did."

"Why?"

"I don't know."

The blacksmith pushed back the boy's head without removing his hand, and looking into his eyes asked gravely, "Is the sky black then?"

"What else can it be if she can't see?" Yevsey muttered in a low voice.

"Who?"

"Tanya."

"Yes," said the blacksmith. After a moment's thought he asked, "and how about the fire being black? Why did you invent that?"

The boy dropped his eyes and was silent.

"Well, speak. Nobody is beating you. Why did you tell her all that nonsense, heh?"

"I was sorry for her," whispered Yevsey.

The blacksmith pushed him lightly to one side.

"You mustn't talk to her any more, do you hear?" he said. "Never! Don't worry, Aunt Praskovya, we'll put an end to this friendship."

"You ought to give him a whipping," said the blind girl's mother. "My little girl lived quietly, gave no one any trouble, and now someone has to be with her all the time."

After Aunt Praskovya had left, the smith took Yevsey's hand and led him into the yard without a word.

"Now talk sense. Why did you frighten the little girl?" he asked.

The uncle's voice was stern but not loud. Yevsey was frightened and quickly began to plead his cause, stuttering over his words.

"I didn't frighten her—I did it just—just—like that. She kept complaining—she said, 'I can see only black, while you can see everything'—so I began to tell her that everything was black so that she wouldn't be envious. I didn't mean to frighten her."

Yevsey broke into sobs, feeling himself wronged. Uncle Piotr smiled softly.

"You little fool! You should have remembered that she's been blind for only three years. She wasn't born blind, after all. She lost her sight after the smallpox. So she remembers different colors! Oh, what a stupid boy!"

"I'm not stupid. She believed me," Yevsey retorted, wiping his eyes.

"Well, all right. Only don't go around with her any more. Do you hear?"

"I won't."

"As for your crying; never mind. Let them think I gave you a beating." The blacksmith nudged Yevsey on the shoulder and added with a smile, "You and I, we're cheats, both of us."

The little fellow buried his head in his uncle's side, and asked tremulously, "Why is everybody against me?"

"I don't know, Orphan," answered the uncle after a moment's reflection.

The wrongs to which he was subjected now began to cause the boy a sort of bitter satisfaction. He began to be convinced that he was not like everybody else, and this was why everybody was against him.

The village stood on a little hill. On the other side of the river there lay a swampy marsh. In the summer after a hot day an oppressive, lilac-colored mist would rise from the swamp and a reddish moon would climb above the thin woods in the distance. The marsh exhaled putrid air over the village, sending swarms of mosquitoes. The air was humming with the insects' greedy bustle and dreary din; the people scratched, angry and pitiful, until blood showed on their bodies. Blue quivering lights flickered over the marsh at night. Believing them to be the homeless spirits of sinners, the villagers sighed sorrowfully and pitied them. But they had no pity for one another.

Yet it was possible for them to live in a different way, in friendship and happiness, as Yevsey was once to see.

One night the granary of the rich peasant Veretennikov caught fire. The little boy ran into the orchard, climbed up a willow tree, and watched the fire from there.

It seemed to him that the many-winged, supple body of a horrible smoke-black bird with a flaming beak was circling in the sky. It lowered its red blazing head earthward, tore greedily at the straw with its sharp fiery teeth, and gnawed at the wood. Its smoky body coiled and uncoiled playfully in the black sky and then fell upon the village, creeping along the roofs of the houses. It then soared up again majestically and lightly, without taking its scarlet head from the ground, its fierce jaws opening ever wider and wider.

Next to the fire the people seemed small and black. They sprinkled water on it, thrust long poles into the flames, and tore flaming sheaves from between its teeth and trampled on them. They coughed and spluttered and sneezed, gasping for breath in the greasy smoke. They shouted and yelled, their voices blending with the crackling and roaring of the fire. They approached nearer and nearer to it, surrounding its red head in a black living ring, as if tightening a noose around its neck. Here and there the noose broke, but they tied it again, more tightly, more firmly. The fire pitched savagely and leaped in the air, its body swelled, writhing like a snake, striving to free its head from the people holding it fast to the ground. Finally, enfeebled, exhausted, and sullen, it fell upon the neighboring granaries, crept along the orchards, and dwindled away, spent and faint.

"All together!" shouted the villagers, encouraging one another.

"Water!" rang out the women's voices.

The women formed a chain from the fire to the river, strangers and kinsmen, friends and enemies all in a row. And the buckets of water were passed swiftly from hand to hand.

"Quick, women! Quick, good women!"

It was strangely sweet and heartening to watch this friendly human activity in fighting the fire. The people encouraged one another, praised each other's dexterity and strength, and abused one another in kindly jest. There was no trace of malice in the shouting. It seemed as if in the presence of the fire everyone looked upon his neighbor kindly, and found pleasure in one another's company. When the fire was under control at last, the spirits of the villagers rose even higher. They sang songs and laughed, boasted of the work accomplished, and made jokes. The older people took vodka to drink away their exhaustion while the young stayed in the streets until almost dawn. Everything was as sweet as in a dream.

Yevsey did not hear a single malicious shout, nor did he notice a single angry face. During the entire time the fire was burning no one suffered pain or wounded feelings, nobody roared with the animal roar of savage wrath ready to do murder.

The next day Yevsey said to his uncle, "How wonderful it was last night!"

"Yes, Orphan, wonderful is the word! A little more, and the fire would have swept away half the village."

"I mean the people," the boy explained. "How they joined together as friends. If only they would live like that all the time, if only there were always a fire!"

The blacksmith reflected for a moment, then asked in surprise, "You mean that there should be fires all the time?" He looked at Yevsey sternly, and shook his finger. "You know-it-all, you, look out! Don't you start with such sinful thoughts. Just listen to him! He finds pleasure in fires!"

Chapter 2

WHEN YEVSEY CAME to the end of his school years, the blacksmith asked him, "What are we going to do with you now? There's nothing for you out here. You must go to the town. I have to get some bellows there, and I'll take you with me, Orphan."

"Will you take me yourself?"

"Yes. Will you be sorry to be leaving the village?"

"No, but I am sorry because I shall miss you."

The blacksmith pushed a piece of iron into the furnace, and arranging the coals with the tongs, said, wrapped in thought, "There's no reason to be sorry on my account. I can stand up to anything . . . . I'm just a peasant like everybody else."

"You're better than anybody else," Yevsey said in a low voice.

Uncle Piotr apparently did not hear the last remark, for he did not answer, but pulled the glowing iron from the fire, screwed up his eyes, and began to hammer, scattering red sparks around him. Then he suddenly stopped, slowly dropped the hand with the hammer, and said, smiling, "I ought to be giving you some advice, . . . how to live, . . . and all that . . ."

Yevsey waited eagerly to hear the advice, but the blacksmith put the iron back into the fire, wiped the tears from his cheeks, and gazed into the furnace, forgetting about his nephew. A peasant walked in with a broken wheel. Yevsey left and went down the ravine where he lay hidden in the bushes until sunset, waiting for his uncle to be alone, but there was always someone in his shop.

The boy was to remember little of the day he left the village.

He could only recall that when they drove out into the fields it was dark and the air was strangely oppressive. The cart jolted horribly, and on both sides rose black motionless trees. The farther they went the wider and the brighter the world became. His uncle was sullen the whole way, and reluctantly gave brief and unintelligible answers to Yevsey's questions.

They drove the whole day, stopping for the night in a small village. During the night Yevsey could hear an accordion being played beautifully for a long time; a woman wept, and occasionally an angry voice cried, "Shut up!" and swore abuse.

They continued on their way the following night. Two dogs followed them, racing wildly in the dark around the cart and barking shrilly. As they left the village a bittern called sullenly and plaintively in the forest to the left of the road.

"Pray God it's for luck!" mumbled the blacksmith.

Yevsey fell asleep, and awoke with his uncle tapping him lightly on the legs with the stock of the whip.

"Look, Orphan, look!"

To the sleepy eyes of the boy the town appeared like a huge field of buckwheat. Thick and speckled, it seemed to stretch endlessly, with the golden church steeples standing out like yellow flowers, and the dark burrows of the streets like fences between patches of land.

"Oh, Lord in Heaven!" said Yevsey after another look.

As they approached, the town became more and more varied in coloring. It glittered with green and red and golden lights, as the rays of the sun and the gold of the church steeples were reflected from the countless windowpanes. It kindled a dim expectation of something unusual. Kneeling in the cart with his hand on his uncle's shoulder, Yevsey eagerly looked ahead while the smith said, "This is how you must live—do whatever you're told to do, then keep to yourself. Beware of bold men. One bold man in ten succeeds, and nine break their necks."

He spoke with indecision as if doubting himself whether what he was saying was the right thing to say. Yevsey listened gravely, intently, expecting to hear some particular warning about the dangers of a new life.

The blacksmith drew a deep breath and continued more firmly, with more assurance, "One day, Orphan, they came near to beating me with rods in the district office. Yes, I was just going to get married, it was time to go to the altar—and there they were, whipping me. It was all the same to them, they're not concerned with other people's affairs. And there was another time—I even lodged a complaint with the governor—they kept me for three and a half months in prison, to say nothing of the beatings. I got terrible whippings, even spat blood, and it's from that time that my eyes keep watering. There was one policeman, a short, red-haired fellow, who kept going for my head."

"Uncle, dear," Yevsey said quietly, "don't speak of these things . . ."

"What else is there to speak about?" cried Uncle Piotr with a smile. "There's nothing else, Orphan."

Yevsey's head drooped sadly.

They passed one house after another, dirty houses, wrapped in heavy smells which seemed to suck the horse and cart and its passengers deeper and deeper into their tangled web. Chimneys stuck out like warts on the red and green roofs, puffing blue and grey smoke. Some chimneys grew straight out of the ground, monstrously tall and filthy, and threw out clouds of thick black smoke. The heavily trodden ground seemed steeped in black grease; heavy, alarming sounds filled the air on all sides, there was humming, whistling, howling, and the angry clanging of iron.

Uncle Piotr said, "This isn't the town yet. These are factories." They pulled into a wide street lined with wooden houses. Painted in various colors, old and squat, they looked peaceful and snug, particularly the pleasant houses that had gardens, which they wore like clean, green, cheerful aprons.

"We'll soon be there," said the smith, turning the horse into a narrow side-street. "Don't be frightened, Orphan."

He drew up at the open gate of a large house, jumped down and disappeared into the yard. The house was old and crooked, the beams protruded under small, dim windows. In the large, dirty yard there were a number of carriages; four peasants were standing around a white horse, patting it with their hands and shouting. One of them, round and bald-headed with a long, yellow beard

THE LIFE OF A USELESS MAN

and a rosy face, waved his hands wildly when he saw Uncle Piotr, and cried, "Aaaaah!"

They drank tea in a narrow, dark room. The bald man laughed and shouted till the dishes rattled on the table. It was close in the room and there was a strong smell of hot bread. Yevsey wanted to sleep, and he kept looking into the corner where he could see a wide bed with many pillows behind dirty curtains. Large black flies buzzed, lighting on his forehead, crawling over his face, irritating and tickling his perspiring skin; but he was too embarrassed to drive them away.

"We'll find a place for you!" the bald man shouted to him, nodding his head gaily. "Natalya, did you send for Matveyich?"

A plump woman with dark brows, a small mouth, and full breasts, answered clearly, "How many times have you asked me already?"

"Piotr, my friend, look at Natalya! Droppings from the honeycomb!" shouted the bald man deafeningly.

Uncle Piotr laughed softly, as if fearing to look at the woman, who pushed a hot rye cake filled with curds in Yevsey's direction, and said, "Eat, eat more. In town people have to eat a lot."

Yevsey felt faint from all he had to eat, but he did not dare to decline and humbly tackled everything set before him.

"Eat!" cried the bald man, and continued his story to Uncle Piotr. "I tell you, it's sheer luck. It's only a week since the horse trampled the little boy to death. He was going to the inn to fetch some boiling water, when suddenly . . ."

A man entered unnoticed and unheard by the others. He, too, was bald, but small and thin, with dark spectacles on a large nose and a long tuft of grey hair on his chin.

"What is going on, you people?" he asked in a low voice.

Their host jumped up from his chair, uttered a cry, and then laughed aloud, but Yevsey was suddenly seized with alarm.

In addressing Uncle Piotr and his host as "people," the man had seemed to set himself apart from them.

The man sat down some distance from the table, then moved even farther away from the blacksmith and looked around, slowly moving his thin dry neck. Just over his forehead over his right eye was a large lump. His little pointed ears clung closely to his skull, as if to hide themselves in the short fringe of grey hair. He had a dusty grey appearance. Yevsey tried in vain to have a peek at his eyes under the glasses and the inability to see them disturbed him.

The bald host cried, "Do you understand, Orphan?"

"What a stroke of luck!" remarked the man with the bump. He sat with his thin dark hands leaning on his sharp knees and spoke little. Occasionally Yevsey heard him utter some peculiar words. Finally he said, "And so that is settled."

Uncle Piotr moved heavily in his chair. "Now, Orphan, you have a job. This is your master."

The man with the bump on his forehead adjusted his glasses, glanced at Yevsey, and said, "My name is Matvey Matveyich."

Turning away, he took a glass of tea and drank it without a sound. He then rose and with a silent nod walked out.

Yevsey and his uncle went to the yard and sat in the shadows near the stables. The blacksmith spoke to Yevsey cautiously, as if trying to express something beyond his grasp.

"You'll surely be happy with him. He's a quiet old man. He's come to terms with his destiny and left his sins behind him. Now he lives taking little bites, and he grumbles and purrs like a satisfied tom-cat."

"Isn't he a sorcerer?" asked the boy.

"Why should he be? I should not think there are any sorcerers in the towns." After reflecting a few moments, the blacksmith went on. "Anyway, it's all the same to you. A sorcerer is a man, like anybody else. But remember this, a town is a dangerous place; it can destroy people. It once happened that the wife of a man went away on a pilgrimage and he took a woman to cook for him in her place and he had his fun with her . . . But the old man will not be setting you an example like that. That's why I say you'll be well with him. You will live with him as behind a bush, just sitting and watching."

"And if he dies?" Yevsey inquired warily.

"That probably won't be soon . . . You'd better smear your head with oil to keep your hair from sticking out."

Uncle Piotr told Yevsey to bid farewell to their hosts, and went back with him to the center of town. Yevsey took in everything with his owl-like eyes, pressing close to his uncle's side. The doors of the shops slammed, pulleys squeaked, carriages rattled, carts rumbled heavily, traders shouted, feet scraped and trampled. These sounds, all jumbled together became tangled up into a stifling, dusty cloud. People walked quickly, hurrying across the streets under the horses' noses as if they were afraid of being too late for something. This constant bustle tired the boy's eyes. Now and then he closed them, stumbled, and said to his uncle, "Come, let's go faster!"

Yevsey wanted to find some corner where it was not so unnerving, nor so noisy and hot. At last they arrived at a little open square hemmed in by a narrow fringe of old houses which seemed to support one another solidly and firmly. In the center of the square was a fountain, which cast damp shadows on the ground around it. It was more tranquil here, and the noise more subdued.

"Look," said Yevsey, "there are only houses without any hedges around them at all . . ."

The blacksmith answered with a sigh, "Read the signs. Where is Raspopov's shop?"

They walked to the center of the square and stopped at the fountain. There were many signs; each house was covered with them like a beggar's coat with motley patches. When Yevsey saw the right name, a shiver ran through his body and he examined it carefully without saying a word to his uncle. The sign was small and eaten by rust and stood over a door leading down into a dark basement. In front of the door was a hole in the pavement fenced around by a low iron railing. The house where the shop was, a dirty yellow house with falling plaster, had three floors. The front had a blind look, crafty and unfriendly.

They went down some stone steps—five of them—and the blacksmith raised his cap and peered cautiously into the shop.

"Come in," said a clear voice.

The proprietor was sitting at a table by the window drinking tea, wearing a black silk cap without a peak.

"Take a chair, peasant, and have some tea. Boy, fetch a glass from the shelf."

The man pointed to the other end of the dark shop. Yevsey looked in the same direction, but saw no one there. He turned toward Yevsey.

"Well, what's the matter? Aren't you a boy?"

"He's not used to it yet," said Uncle Piotr quietly.

The old man waved his hand again.

"The second shelf on the right. A master must be halfway understood. That's the rule."

The blacksmith sighed. Yevsey groped for the glass in the dim light, and stumbled over a pile of books on the floor in his haste to hand it to his new master.

"Put it on the table. And the saucer?"

"Oh, you nitwit!" exclaimed Uncle Piotr. "What's the matter with you? Have you forgotten the saucer?"

"It will take a long time to teach him," said the old man, glancing knowingly at the blacksmith. "Now, boy, go around the shop and memorize where everything stands."

Yevsey felt as if something had entered his body which dictated his every move. He shrank into himself, drew in his head, and straining his eyes began to look around the shop, all the while listening to what his master was saying. It was cool and dusky in the shop. It was narrow and long as a grave and closely lined with shelves holding books in neat rows. Large piles of books cluttered the floor at the end of the room and barricaded the back wall, rising almost to the ceiling. Apart from the books, Yevsey could only make out a ladder, an umbrella, some galoshes, and a white pot that had lost its handle. There was a great deal of dust which he felt probably accounted for the heavy smell.

"I'm a quiet man, I live all alone, and if he suits me maybe I will make him perfectly happy. I have lived an honest and straightforward life, and I will not excuse dishonesty. If I notice anything of that nature I'll hand him over at once to the court. Nowadays they sentence minors, too. They have founded a prison for that very thing; it's called the Colony for Junior Criminals—for little thieves, you know."

The man's colorless drawl enveloped Yevsey tightly, evoking in him a timorous desire to oblige the old man promptly and to please him.

"Well, it's time to say good-bye. The boy must get to work."

Sighing, Uncle Piotr rose. "Well, Orphan, so you'll live here now. Obey your master. He won't want to do you any harm. Why should he? Now don't be downcast, will you?"

"Nah," Yevsey said.

"You ought to say 'No,' not 'Nah,'" his master corrected him.

"No," repeated Yevsey, quickly.

"Well, good-bye," said the blacksmith, putting his rough hand on the boy's shoulder, and giving his nephew a little shake, he walked out as if he had suddenly become vaguely alarmed.

Yevsey shivered, oppressed by a leaden sadness, and went to the door. Then he turned, his round eyes questioning the yellow face of his master. The old man twirled the grey tuft on his chin while looking down on it, and Yevsey thought he could discern large, dim black eyes behind the glasses. As the two stood thus for a few minutes each apparently expecting something from the other, the boy's breast began to beat with a terror he had never known before. But the old man merely took a book from a shelf, and pointed to the cover.

"What number is this?"

"1873," replied Yevsey, lowering his head.

"That's right."

The master touched Yevsey's chin with his dry finger.

"Look at me."

The boy straightened up and quickly mumbled, his eyes closed, "I shall always obey you. I shall." His heart sank within him and he could see nothing.

"Come here."

The old man sat on a chair, his hands resting on his knees. He removed his cap and wiped his bald spot with his handkerchief. His spectacles slid to the end of his nose, and he peered over them at Yevsey. He seemed now to have two pairs of eyes, the real eyes were small, unmoving, dark grey with red lids.

"Have you been beaten often?"

"Yes, often," Yevsey replied in a low voice.

"Who beat you?"

"The boys."

The master drew his glasses up to his eyes, made a chewing movement with his dark lips and said, "The boys are quarrelsome here, too. Don't have anything to do with them, do you hear?"

"Yes, oh, yes."

"Be on your guard against them. They are rascals and thieves. I want you to know I am not going to teach you anything bad. I am a good man. You could become fond of me. If you can get along with me, you'll have a good time here, you understand?"

"Yes."

The master's face assumed its former expression. He rose, and taking Yevsey by the hand, led him to the farther end of the shop.

"You see these books? The date is marked on every book. There are twelve books for every year. I want them arranged in order. How are you going to do it?"

Yevsey thought awhile, and answered timidly, "I don't know."

"Well, I am not going to tell you. You can read and you ought to be able to find out for yourself."

The old man's dry even voice seemed to lash Yevsey. Restraining his tears, he began to untie the parcels. Each time a book dropped to the floor with a thud he started and looked around. The master was sitting at the table writing; his pen scratched slightly. As people went by in the street their feet flashed for a moment and their shadows jerked across the shop. Tears rolled from Yevsey's eyes one after another, and they frightened him. He wiped them quickly from his face with his dusty hands, and full of a dark dread he set anxiously to work on sorting out the books.

At first he found it difficult, but in a few minutes he had drifted off into that familiar state of thoughtlessness and emptiness which took such a powerful hold of him when, after beatings and insults, he sat alone in some corner. His eye caught the date and the name of the month, his hand mechanically arranged the books in a row, and all the while he sat on the floor swaying his body and becoming more and more lost in that tranquil half-conscious state that is the denial of reality. As always at such moments the dim hope, the expectation glowed in him of something different, unlike what he saw around him. Sometimes the all-embracing words glimmered in his memory, "It won't last forever."

The promise hinted in these words warmed his heart in a moment. The boy's hands involuntarily began to move more quickly, and he ceased to notice the passage of time.

"You see, you knew how to do it," the master said.

Yevsey, who had not heard the old man approach, was startled from his dreams and glanced at his work.

"Is it all right?" he asked.

"Perfect. Do you want tea?"

"No."

"You ought to say, 'No, thank you.' Well, keep on with your work then."

He walked away. Yevsey, following him with a glance, saw an elderly man carrying a stick enter the shop. He had neither beard nor mustache and wore a round hat pushed back on the nape of his neck. He sat down at the table and began to rearrange some small black and white objects on it. Yevsey started to work again, and every once in a while he heard abrupt sounds from his master and the newcomer.

"Castle."

"King."

The confused noises of the street filtered wearily into the shop, and the strange words within were like the croaking of frogs in a marsh.

"What are they doing?" thought the boy anxiously, and he sighed. He had the feeling that from all directions new, unusual things were crowding in on him, but they were not what he had timidly expected. The dust tickled his nose and eyes, and set his teeth on edge. He recalled his uncle's words, "You will live with him as behind a bush."

It grew dark.

"King and checkmate!" cried the guest in a thick voice. Clucking his tongue, the master called out loudly, "Boy, close the shop!"

The old man lived in two small rooms on the third floor of the same house. The first room had one window, and in it stood a large chest and a wardrobe.

"This is where you will sleep," said the master.

The two windows in the second room looked over the street, affording a view of endless rows of uneven roofs and a rosy sky. In the corner, in front of the ikons, flickered a little light in a blue glass lamp. In another corner stood a bed covered with a red blanket. On the walls hung gaudy portraits of the Czar and various generals. The room was stuffy but clean, and smelled like a church.

Yevsey stayed at the door surveying his new dwelling. Standing beside him, the old man remarked, "Note the arrangement of everything here. I want it always to be the same as it is now."

Against the wall stood a heavy black sofa, a round table, and around the table were three chairs, also black. This corner had a mournful, sinister aspect.

A tall, white-faced woman with eyes like a sheep's entered the room and asked in a low singing voice, "Shall I serve supper?"

"Bring it in, Rayissa Petrovna."

"A new boy?"

"Yes. His name is Yevsey Vlimkov."

The woman walked out.

"Close the door," ordered the old man. Yevsey obeyed, and he continued in a lower voice. "She is the landlady. I rent the rooms from her with dinner and supper. You understand?"

"I understand."

"But you have only one master—myself. You understand?"

"Yes," replied Yevsey.

"That is to say, you must listen only to me. Go into the kitchen and wash."

While washing in the kitchen Yevsey tried to catch a glance of the landlady. The woman was preparing the supper, arranging plates, knives, and bread on a large tray. Her large round face had thin brows; she seemed kind. Her smoothly combed dark hair, her unwinking eyes, and her broad nose made the boy think, "she seems to be gentle . . ."

Noticing that she, in her turn, was looking at him, her thin red lips pursed tightly together, Yevsey grew confused and spilled some water on the floor.

"Wipe it up," she said, but without anger. "There's a cloth under the chair."

When he returned, the old man looked at him and asked, "What did she say to you?"

But Yevsey had no time to answer before the woman brought in the tray, put it on the table and said, "Well, I'll be going now."

"Very well," replied the master.

She raised her hand to smooth the hair over her forehead—her fingers were long and tapering—and then she left the room.

The old man and the boy sat down to their supper. The master ate slowly, noisily munching his food and at times sighing wearily. When they began to eat the finely chopped roast meat, the old man said, "You see how good the food is? I never have anything but good food."

After supper he told Yevsey to carry the dishes into the kitchen, and showed him how to light the lamp.

"Now, go to sleep," he said. "You will find some felt in the wardrobe, a pillow, and a blanket. They belong to you. Tomorrow I'll buy you some decent new clothes. Go along now."

When he was half asleep, worn out after the day's confusing impressions, the master came in to Yevsey and asked, "Are you comfortable?"

Though the chest made a hard bed even with the felt, Yevsey answered:

"Yes."

"If it is too hot, open the window."

The boy at once opened the window, which looked out upon the roof of the next house. He counted the chimneys; there were four, all alike. He looked at the stars with the longing gaze of a timid animal in a cage. But the stars said nothing to his heart. He flung himself on the chest again, drew the blanket over his head, and closed his eyes tightly. He began to feel stifled, thrust his head out, and listened without opening his eyes. In his master's room he could hear a dry, clear voice, "Behold, God is mine helper; the Lord is with them that uphold . . ."

Yevsey realized that the old man was reciting the Psalms; listening attentively to the familiar but incomprehensible words of King David, the boy fell asleep.

Chapter 3

YEVSEY'S LIFE ran smoothly and evenly. He wanted to please his master for he felt this could only be to his advantage; he behaved with a watchful calculation, but without any warmth in his heart for the old man. His fear of people made him try to oblige them; defending himself against some imaginary attack, he was ready for all kinds of services. The constant expectation of danger developed keen powers of observation in him which deepened his mistrust of people still more.

He observed the strange life that went on in the house without really understanding it. From the basement to the roof people lived packed in together, and every day from morning until night they crawled about in the tenement like crabs in a basket. They worked here more than the people did in the village, and, it seemed, were imbued with keener bitterness. They lived restlessly, noisily, and hurriedly, as if to get through all their work as soon as possible like preparing for a holiday on which they wanted to meet as free people, washed, peaceful, and tranquilly happy. The boy's heart continued to sink within him, and the silent question kept repeating itself in his mind, "Will it last forever?"

But the holiday never came. The people spurred one another on, wrangled, and sometimes fought. Scarcely a day passed on which they did not speak ill of one another.

In the mornings the master went to the shop while Yevsey stayed behind to tidy their rooms. He washed afterwards, went to the public house for boiling water, and then to the shop where he drank his morning tea with his master. The old man almost invariably asked him, "Well, what next?"

"Nothing."

"Nothing isn't much," the master said.

Once, however, Yevsey had a different answer. "Today the watchmaker told the furrier's cook that you receive stolen goods."

Yevsey was surprised at himself for saying this, and was instantly seized with a fit of trembling. He bowed his head. The old man laughed softly and said in a drawling voice, but without anger, "The s-scoundrel!" His dark, dry lips quivered. "Thank you for telling me. Thank you!"

After that Yevsey began to pay closer attention to every conversation and promptly repeated everything he heard to his master, speaking in a quiet voice and looking straight into his face. Several days later while tidying his master's room, he found a crumpled paper ruble on the floor, and when at tea the old man asked him, "Well, what next?"

Yevsey replied, "I found a ruble."

"You found a ruble, did you? I found a gold piece," said the master, laughing.

Another time Yevsey picked up a twenty-kopek coin in the entrance to the shop, and he gave this also to the master. The old man slid his glasses to the end of his nose, and rubbing the coin with his fingers looked into the boy's face for a few seconds without speaking.

"According to the law," he said thoughtfully, "a third of what you find, in this case six kopeks, belongs to you." He was silent, sighed, and stuck the coin back into his vest pocket. "But you're a strange boy." Yevsey never got the six kopeks.

Quiet and unnoticed, and when noticed, obliging, Yevsey Klimkov rarely drew attention to himself, though he followed people doggedly with his all-seeing owl-like eyes. If his staring was observed at all, it was immediately forgotten.

The silent, quiet Rayissa Petrovna fascinated him from the beginning. Every evening she put on a dark, rustling dress and a black hat, and left the house. She was still asleep in the morning when he tidied the rooms. He saw her only in the evening before supper, and then not every day. There was something mysterious about her life, and she herself, silent, with her white face and un-stirring eyes, kindled in him a faint awareness of something un-usual. He was secretly convinced that she lived better and knew more than everybody else. A warm feeling which he did not under-stand sprang up in his heart for this woman. Every day she seemed to him to grow more beautiful.

One day he awoke at dawn and went into the kitchen for a drink. Suddenly he heard someone entering the front door. He rushed to his room in fright, lay down, and covered himself with the blanket, trying to press himself into his bedding as closely as he could. In a few minutes he stuck his ear out and heard heavy steps in the kitchen, the rustle of a dress, and Rayissa Petrovna's voice, "Oh, you, oh, you . . . !" she was saying.

Yevsey rose, walked to the door on tiptoe, and looked into the kitchen. The woman was sitting quietly at the window, taking off her hat. Her face seemed whiter than ever and tears streamed from her eyes. Her large body swayed and her hands moved slowly.

"I know your tricks" she said, shaking her head. She rose to her feet and leaned on the windowsill.

The bed in the master's room creaked. Yevsey quickly jumped back onto his trunk, lay down, and wrapped himself up.

"They've hurt her," he thought, and was inwardly glad of her tears. They brought this quiet woman who lived a secret, noctur-nal existence closer to him.

Someone seemed to flit past him with stealthy steps. He raised his head and suddenly jumped up, as if scorched by the shrill an-gry shout, "Ugh! Go away!"

The master hastily came out of the kitchen, stooping in his nightgown, then stopped and said to Yevsey in a whistling voice, "Go to sleep! Go to sleep! What's the matter with you? Go to sleep!"

The next morning in the shop the old man asked him, "Were you frightened last night?"

"Yes."

"She was in her cups. It happens to her sometimes."

Yevsey wanted to ask more about her, but he didn't dare.

"Does she attract you?"

"Yes," Yevsey replied faintly.

"You ought to know," added the master sternly, "that she's an extremely shrewd woman. She is silent, but wicked. And a sinner too. She plays the piano, you know. A person who plays the piano is called a pianist. Do you know what a house of ill-fame is?"

Yevsey already knew something about it from the talk of the furriers and the glaziers in the yard, but wishing to learn more, he answered, "I don't know."

The old man gave him a cryptic, but vivid explanation. He spoke with heat, occasionally spitting and wrinkling up his face to express his disgust of such abomination. Yevsey looked at the old man, and for some reason did not believe in his disgust though he believed everything he told him about the houses of ill-fame.

"She plays there every night and dissolute women dance with drunken men to her music. The men are all crooks, maybe even murderers . . . Don't you trust her, d'you hear? She's sly and mean, oh yes!"

All that the master said about the woman only served to increase Yevsey's mistrust of him (and raised Rayissa in his estimation).

Besides Rayissa there was someone else who aroused Yevsey's curiosity, Anatol, the glazier Kuzin's apprentice, a thin, snub-nosed boy with tousled hair who was always jovial and steeped in the smell of oil. He had a high ringing voice which Yevsey loved to hear when he shouted, "Wi-i-ndow pa-anes replaced!"

It was he who first spoke to Yevsey. Yevsey was sweeping the staircase when suddenly he heard the loud question from below, "Say there, you, what district are you from?"

"From this one," answered Yevsey.

"I am from the district of Kostroma. How old are you?"

"Thirteen."

"I am, too. Why don't you come with me?"

"Where to?"

"To the river, to bathe."

"I have to stay in the shop."

"Today is Sunday."

"That makes no difference."

"Well, go to the devil then."

The glazier's boy disappeared, but Yevsey was not offended by his outburst.

Anatol was out the whole day carrying a box of glass around the city, and he usually returned home just as the shop was being closed. Then his unflagging voice, his laughter, his whistling, and singing would rise from the yard below for nearly the entire evening. Everybody scolded him, but they all loved to play with him and laugh at his jokes. Yevsey was amazed at the boldness with which the ragged, snub-nosed boy behaved with the adults, but he felt a certain envy when he saw the girls who sold gold-embroidery running around the yard in pursuit of the mischievous boy. His admiration for him served as a powerful magnet. When Yevsey sank into his vague dreams of a pure, quiet life, the shaggy-haired little daredevil now had a place of his own in them.

After supper, Yevsey would ask the master, "May I go down in the yard?"

The old man agreed reluctantly. "There's nothing good for you in that yard."

Yevsey ran down the staircase quickly, and sat down somewhere in the shadow to watch Anatol. The small yard was hemmed in on all sides by high houses. Workmen and workwomen rested on the piles of junk against the walls. Anatol was giving a performance in the middle of the yard.

"The furrier Zvorykin going to church!" he shouted.

To his astonishment Yevsey could actually see the little stout furrier with his hanging lower lip and his eyes screwed up as if in pain. Thrusting out his belly and leaning his head to one side, Anatol struggled toward the gate with short steps, reluctance showing in his every movement. The audience laughed and shouted approval.

"Zvorykin returning from the public house!"

Now Anatol staggered through the yard, his feet dragging feebly, his arms hanging limp. There was a glazed look in his wide-open eyes, his mouth gaped hideously, yet comically. He stopped, beat himself on the chest, and said in a wheezy voice, "God—how satisfied I am with everything and everybody! Lord, how good and pleasant everything is to Thy servant, Yakov Ivanich. But the glazier Kuzin is a bad one, a rogue in God's eyes, a fool in the people's—that's the truth, oh God . . ."

The audience roared, but Yevsey did not laugh. He was oppressed by a twofold feeling of astonishment and envy. The desire to see this boy frightened and wronged mingled with anticipation of his next tricks. He felt annoyed because the glazier's boy failed to portray man as something dangerous, but merely as something laughable.

"Here comes glazier Kuzin!"

In front of Yevsey there suddenly materialized the gaunt, red-faced, red-bearded peasant who was always half-drunk. The sleeves of his dirty shirt were rolled up. His right hand was thrust in the breast of his apron, his left hand stroked his beard with deliberation. Frowning and surly, he moved slowly; looking sideways he screeched in a cracked, hoarse voice, "Carrying on again, you heretic? How long am I to listen to this nonsense? You damned, impertinent devil!"

"Now the miser Raspopov!" announced Anatol.

The smooth, sharp little figure of Yevsey's master crept past him moving on noiseless feet. His nose twitched comically as if he were smelling something; he nodded his head quickly, and kept tugging at the tuft on his chin with his little hand. There was something revolting but pathetic and laughable in this imitation. Yevsey found himself becoming increasingly annoyed. He knew well that his master was not really as the young glazier represented him.

Anatol then began to mimic members of his audience. Inexhaustible, he continued till late at night like a little tinking bell and made everyone roar with good-natured laughter. Sometimes the man who was the object of his innocent performance would rush at him and there would be a sudden noisy chase about the yard. Yevsey sighed with envy again.

Anatol, catching sight of Yevsey, pulled him by the hand into the middle of the yard where he introduced him to the audience.

"Here he is—all sugar and soap. Miser Raspopov's little toad-stool of a cousin."

Turning the boy's slim body in all directions, he poured out a great stream of strange comic words about Yevsey's master, about Rayissa Petrovna, and about Yevsey himself.

"Let me go!" Yevsey shouted, timidly trying to tear his hand from Anatol's strong grip, yet all the while listening attentively, trying to understand the filthy innuendoes. When Yevsey struggled harder to tear himself away, the audience, usually the women, lazily said to Anatol, "Let him go."

For some reason their attempts to assist him irritated Yevsey. It exasperated Anatol, too, and he began to push and pinch his victim, challenging him to a fight. Some of the men urged the boys on.

"Well—go on, fight, then! See who is the stronger!"

The women objected, "No, don't."

And again these words sounded unpleasantly in Yevsey's ears. Finally Anatol pushed Yevsey scornfully aside. "Oh, you idiot!"

One morning after just such a scene Yevsey met Anatol outside the house carrying his box of glass, and suddenly, without intending to do so, he said to him, "Why do you always mock me?"

The glazier's boy looked at him. "What of it?" he asked.

Yevsey was unable to reply.

"Do you want to fight?" asked Anatol again. "Come to our shed, or wait until tonight." He spoke calmly and in a business-like way.

"No, I don't want to fight," replied Yevsey quietly.

"Then you don't have to! I'd lick you anyway," said the glazier's boy, adding with assurance, "I certainly would."

Yevsey sighed. He could not understand this boy, but he wanted to. So he asked a second time, in the same low voice, "I want to know why you make fun of me."

Anatol seemed strangely embarrassed. He winked with his lively eyes, smiled, and suddenly shouted angrily, "Oh, go to the devil! What are you bothering me for? I'll give you such a . . ."

Yevsey quickly ran into the shop, and felt the undeserved insult tugging at his heart for the rest of the day. It did not put an end to his admiration for Anatol, but it forced him to leave the yard whenever Anatol noticed him, and he dismissed the glazier's boy from his dream world.

Soon after this unsuccessful attempt to get close to a human being Yevsey was awakened one evening by the sound of loud talking in his master's room. He listened and thought he recognized Rayissa's voice. To convince himself that he actually did, he rose, quietly slipped over to the tightly closed door, and lowered his eyes to the keyhole.

His sleepy glance fell first upon the light of the candle and it momentarily blinded him. Then he saw the large, prominent body of the woman on the black sofa. She way lying face upward, naked; her hair was spread over one breast while her long fingers slowly wove it into a plait. The light quivered over her white body. Clean, vivid, it seemed as light as a cloud. It was very beautiful. She was talking but Yevsey could not catch the words; he heard only the singing, tired, plaintive voice. The master was sitting in his nightgown on a chair by the sofa, pouring wine into a glass with a trembling hand. The tuft of grey hair on his chin also trembled. He had removed his glasses and his face was loathsome.

"Yes, yes, yes! Hm! What a woman you are!" he said.

Yevsey moved away from the door, lay down on his bed, and thought, "They're married now."

He pitied Rayissa; why did she have to become the wife of a man who spoke ill of her? and also how cold it must be for her, lying naked on the leather sofa. A wicked thought flashed through his mind, confirming the words of the old man about her, and Yevsey anxiously drove it away.

The next evening Rayissa brought in the supper as always and said casually, "I am going now."

The master spoke to her in his usual dry and careless manner. Nothing seemed to have changed between them. Yevsey began to believe that he had seen the naked woman only in a dream.

Once Uncle Piotr appeared unexpectedly, for no apparent reason. He had become grey, wrinkled, and shorter.

"I am getting blind, Orphan," he said, sipping tea noisily from a saucer and smiling with his watery eyes. "I can't work any more, so I'll have to go begging. Yashka is beyond control. He wants to go to the town and if I don't let him, he'll run away. That's the sort of person he is."

Everything the blacksmith said was unpleasant to hear. He

looked guilty, and Yevsey felt awkward and ashamed for him in the presence of his master. When he got ready to go, Yevsey quietly pushed three rubles into his hand, and saw him to the door with relief.

After a while the bookshop seemed to resemble in the boy's mind a tomb tightly packed with dead books. All were ragged, man-handled, and gave off a moldy, putrid odor. Few were sold, and this did not surprise Yevsey. What stirred his curiosity was the attitude of his master to the purchasers and to the books themselves.

The old man would take a book in his hand, carefully turn over its musty pages, stroke the covers with his dark fingers, smile softly, and nod his head. He seemed to fondle the book as though it were alive, to play with it as with a kitten or a puppy. Reading a book, he would carry on a quiet querulous conversation with it, like Uncle Piotr had done with the forging furnace. His lips moved in a sarcastic smile, his head would nod, and now and then he mumbled.

"So, so—yes—hmm—see—what's that? Ha, ha! Oh, the impudence—I understand, I understand—it'll never come about—no-o-o—ha, ha!"

These strange exclamations coming from the old man as if he were arguing with somebody both astonished and frightened Yevsey. It pointed to the secret duplicity in his master's life.

"Never read books," the master once said to him. "Books are lechery, the product of a prostituted mind. They deal with everything, they excite the imagination and create useless disturbance. There was a time when we used to have good historical books, stories written by quiet people about the past. But nowadays every book wants to lay bare a man's soul; he would be far better off living in secret in the flesh, and in the spirit as well, if he's ever going to protect himself from the demon of curiosity and from an imagination which destroys faith. Only in old age can books no longer harm a man."

Though Yevsey did not understand this sort of talk, he retained it in his mind and it all confirmed the sense of mystery shrouding his master's life.

When the old man sold a book, he almost seemed to regret it, and he would smell the buyer and talk to him in a strange voice, either extremely loud and rapid, or else lowered to a whisper. His dark glasses would fix themselves upon the face of the customer. Often when seeing a student who had bought a book to the door, he would follow him with a smile; once he shook his finger at the back of a boy who had just left, a short, handsome youth with little black whiskers on a pale face. Most of the customers were students, but sometimes old men would come. They would rummage a long time among the books and haggle sharply over the prices.

An almost daily visitor was a man who wore a bowler hat and a large gold ring set with a stone on his right hand. He had a broad blotchy nose on a fat, flat, clean-shaven face. His name was Dorimedont Lukich. Playing chess with the master, he sniffed loudly and tugged at his ear with his left hand. He often brought books and paper parcels with him. The master would nod his head approvingly, smile at them, and then hide them in the table or in a corner on a shelf behind his back. Yevsey never saw his master pay for these books, but he did see him sell them.

One of the students took to visiting the shop more frequently than the others. He was a tall, blue-eyed young man with a reddish mustache and a cap stuck back on his neck, leaving his large white forehead bare. He spoke in a thick voice and always bought many old periodicals.

Once the master offered him a book that Dorimedont had brought. While the student silently turned the pages the old man said something to him in a quick whisper.

"Interesting!" exclaimed the student, with a smile. "Ah, you old sinner, aren't you afraid, eh?"

The master sighed and answered, "If one feels absolutely convinced that it's the truth, one ought to help it along in whatever little ways one can."

They whispered for a long time. Finally the student said, "Write down my address."

The old man took the address down on a piece of paper. The next time Dorimedont arrived and asked, "Well, what's new, Matveyich?" the master handed him the paper and said with a smile, "Here's a new one."

"S-so—Nikodim Arkhangelsky," read Dorimedont. "That sounds like business. We'll look up this Nikodim."

A few days later when they sat down to play chess, he announced to the master, "That Nikodim of yours turned out to be a fish with plenty of roe. They found a lot of stuff in his place."

"Let me have the books back," murmured the master, moving a pawn.

"Of course I will."

The student with the blue eyes never appeared again. The short young man with the black mustache also disappeared. All of this increased the boy's suspicions and pointed to some secret, some enigma.

Books held no interest for him. He attempted to read but never succeeded in concentrating on a book. Overcrowded as it was with new impressions, Yevsey's mind dwelt too much on details which dissolved and finally disappeared, evaporating like a thin stream of water on a sun-warmed stone. When he worked and moved about he was incapable of thinking; the motion, as it were, tore the cobweb of his thoughts. The boy did his work slowly and accurately, but automatically, without bringing anything personal into it.

When he was free he sat without moving, and was often carried away by a pleasant sensation of flight in a transparent mist which enveloped the whole of life and softened everything, transforming intrusive reality into a sweet slumber.

When Yevsey was in this mood the days passed with lightning speed. His life was monotonous and his brain became unnoticeably clogged with the dust of the working day. He seldom went into the town. He did not like it, its ceaseless movement tired his eyes, and the noise filled his head with a heavy, paralyzing confusion. The town seemed like a monster in a fairy-tale, displaying a hundred greedy mouths and bellowing with hundreds of insatiable throats.

In the morning when he tidied his master's room, Yevsey pushed his head out of the window and peered down to the bottom of the deep, narrow street. He saw the same people everywhere, and he already knew what each of them would be doing in an hour or the next day or forever; the shop boys, all of whom he knew and did not like, seemed almost menacing to him with their pranks. Everyone seemed chained to his work like a dog to his kennel. Occasionally, something new flashed by or resounded in his ear, but it was difficult for him to understand it in the mixture of all that was familiar, ordinary, and distasteful.

Even the churches in the town were not to his liking. They were too bright, heavy with the strong odor of incense and oil. Yevsey could not bear strong smells, they made him dizzy.

Sometimes the master closed the shop on a holiday and took Yevsey for a stroll around town. They walked a long time, slowly, and the old man pointed out the houses of the rich and the great, and told Yevsey about their lives. His stories were full of figures, of women who ran away from their husbands, of dead people, and of funerals. He talked about them in a dry, solemn voice, critical of everything. He grew animated only when telling how and from what this or that man died; he spoke then as if matters concerning death were the most edifying and wise of all earthly subjects.

At the end of every walk he treated Yevsey to tea in a public house where a music box played, and everybody knew the old man and behaved toward him with timid respect. Yevsey, tired and lost in a cloud of heavy smells, would fall into a drowsy torpor under the rattle and din of the music.

Once, however, the master took him to a house packed with innumerable beautiful things, marvelous weapons, and garments of silk and brocade. Suddenly his mother's forgotten tales began to stir in the boy's breast, and a new, winged hope trembled in his heart. He walked silently through the rooms for a long time, blinking in bewilderment and expectation. When they returned home he asked the master, "Whose are they?"

"They are state property—the Czar's," the old man explained impressively.

The boy put a different question. "Who wore such coats and sabers?"

"Czars, boyars, and other imperial people."

"There are no such people today?"

"How so? Of course there are. You couldn't do without them. Only now they dress differently."

"Why differently?"

"More cheaply. Russia used to be richer than it is now. It has been plundered by various foreign peoples, Jews, Poles, Germans."

Raspopov talked for a long time explaining that nobody loved Russia, that everybody robbed it and wished it every kind of harm. When he spoke at any length Yevsey ceased to believe him or understand him. But he still asked, "Do I belong to the Czar, too?"

"Of course you do. In our country everything belongs to the Czar. The whole earth is God's earth, and the whole of Russia belongs to the Czar."

Yevsey imagined handsome, stately figures in glittering dress circling in a bright, multicolored saraband, conjuring up a new and fabulous life. The thought remained with him after he lay down to sleep. He saw himself in this other life dressed in a sky-blue robe embroidered with gold and wearing red boots of Morocco leather. Rayissa was there, too, in brocade and adorned with precious gems.

"So this will not last forever!" he thought.

Once again hope for a different future lit up his heart.

On the other side of the door he heard the dry even voice of his master, "Except the Lord build the house, they labor in vain . . ."

Chapter 4

ONE DAY, when Yevsey and his master had just closed the shop and were coming out into the yard, they heard a shrill, ringing scream. It was Anatol.

"I won't do it again, uncle, never!"

Yevsey started, and instinctively exclaimed in quiet triumph, "Aha!"

It felt good to hear a cry of fear and pain coming from the lips of such a cheerful boy, one who was everybody's favorite.

"May I stay here in the yard?" Yevsey asked the master.

"It's time for our supper. But I'll stay and have a look, too, and see just how they punish the young devil!"

People had gathered at the door of the brick shed beyond the porch; the sound of heavy blows and Anatol's wailing voice came from there.

"I didn't do it, uncle. Oh, God! I won't do it, I won't! Stop, for Christ's sake!"

"That's right! Give it to him!" said the watchmaker Yakubov, puffing at his cigarette.

The squinting embroiderer Zina supported the tall, yellow-faced watchmaker. "Perhaps we shall have some peace after this. You couldn't have a quiet moment in the yard."

Raspopov turned to Yevsey, and asked, "They say he's a wonder at imitating people?"

"Oh, yes, he is," confirmed the furrier's cook. "He's a little rascal! He makes fun of everybody."

A dull, shuffling sound came from the shed, as if a sack filled with something soft were being dragged over the old boards of the floor. At the same time was heard the hoarse, panting voice of Kuzin and the cries, growing more feeble and less frequent, of Anatol.

"Help!—Oh, God!"

His words began to flow together into a faint, choking groan. Yevsey trembled, remembering the pain of the beatings he used to receive himself. The comments of the onlookers awakened a confused feeling. It was strange to stand among people who only the day before had been eager and happy to enjoy the boy's antics, and now looked on with the same pleasure while he was being beaten. But now these surly, unhealthy people, worn out with work, seemed more comprehensible to him; he believed in his heart that none of them were pretending as they watched the torture of a human being with genuine curiosity. He felt a little sorry for Anatol, yet it was not unpleasant to hear his groans. The thought flashed through his mind, "now he will be more quiet, more friendly with me."

Suddenly Nikolai the furrier appeared, a short black curly-headed man with long arms. Impudent as always and respecting nobody, he thrust the people aside, walked into the shed, and from there he shouted loudly, "Stop! Get out!"

Everybody suddenly moved away from the door. Kuzin bolted out of the shed, sat on the ground, clutched his head with both hands, and opening his eyes wide, bawled hoarsely, "Police!"

"Let's get away from this evil, Yevsey," said the master.

The boy retreated to a corner by the porch and stood there looking on.

Nikolai came out of the shed. The little trampled body of the glazier's boy hung limply over his arm. The furrier laid him on the ground, straightened himself up and shouted, "Water, women, you wretched sluts!"

Zina and the cook ran off for water.

Kuzin throwing his head back snorted heavily. "Murder! Police!"

Nikolai turned to him and gave him a kick on the chest which laid him flat on his back.

"You filthy dogs!" he shouted, the whites of his black eyes flashing. "A child is being killed, and it's just a show to you! I'll smash in every one of your ugly faces!"

He was met with a shower of abuse, but nobody dared approach him.

"Let's go," said the master, taking Yevsey by the hand.

As they walked away they saw Kuzin, bent over, run noiselessly to the gates.

When Yevsey was alone again he felt that he was no longer jealous of Anatol. He strained his slow mind to explain to himself what he had seen and arrived at the conclusion that people seemed to like Anatol only because he amused them. In fact it was not so. All people enjoyed fighting, looking on while others fought, enjoyed being cruel. Nikolai had interceded for Anatol because he liked to beat Kuzin, and he actually did beat him up on almost every holiday. Bold and strong, he could lick any man. In his turn, though he was beaten by the police. The moral is, Yevsey concluded, whether you are quiet or daring, you'll be beaten and insulted whatever you do.

Several days passed. The rumor spread among the tenants in the yard that the glazier's boy, having been taken to the hospital, had gone insane. Then Yevsey remembered how the boy's eyes had burned when he gave his performances, how violent his gestures had been, and how quickly the expression of his face had changed, and he thought with dread that perhaps Anatol had always been insane. He soon forgot about him.

On the rainy nights in autumn broken sounds came from the roof under Yevsey's window, preventing him from sleeping and filling him with anxiety. On one such night he heard the angry exclamations of his master.

"You vile woman!"

Rayissa answered as usual in a low singing voice, "I cannot allow you, Matvey Matveyich."

"You low creature! Look at the money I am paying you!"

The door to the master's room was half-open, and the voices could be easily heard. The fine rain sang a tearful song outside the window. The wind crept over the roof, sighing like a large homeless bird weary of the inclement weather, softly flapping its wet wings against the panes. The boy sat up in bed, clasped his hands around his knees, and listened, shivering.

"Give me back the twenty-five rubles, you thief!"

"I do not deny it. Dorimedont Lukich gave me the money."

"Aha! You see, you hussy!"

"No, permit me—when you asked me to spy on the gentleman . . ."

"Sh . . . sh . . . Not so loud . . ."

They closed the door, but even through the wall Yevsey could hear his master shouting.

"Remember, you vile woman, that you are in my hands. And if I find out that you're having fun with Dorimedont . . ."

The woman's voice was warm and flexible, it coiled itself like a cat around the old man's angry words, wiping them from Yevsey's memory.

The woman must be right. Her composure, his master's whole attitude to her, convinced the boy that she was. Yevsey was now in his fifteenth year, and the attraction this gentle and beautiful woman exercised on him began to be enhanced by a pleasurable excitement. Since he never met Rayissa for more than a minute or two, he merely gazed into her face with a secret feeling of timid joy. She spoke to him gently and this roused a certain grateful emotion in him; it drew him to her more and more powerfully.

He had learned the harsh truth of the relations between man and woman while still in the village. The town dressed up this truth with splashings of mud, but it did not affect the boy. Of a timorous nature, he did not dare to believe what was said about women, and such talk aroused no temptation in him, only a deep disgust. Now, sitting up in bed, Yevsey remembered Rayissa's kind smile, her soft words; carried away by these memories, he had hardly time to lie down when the door to the master's room opened and she stood before him, half dressed, her hair loose, her hand pressed to her breast. He grew frightened and lay very still. She was smiling as she shook a threatening finger at Yevsey and disappeared into her own room. He fell asleep at once.

In the morning as he was sweeping the kitchen floor he saw Rayissa at the door of her room. He straightened himself up with the broom in his hands.

"Will you come and have coffee with me?" she asked.

Happy and embarrassed, the boy replied, "I haven't washed yet. Just a second."

In a few minutes he was sitting at the table in her room, seeing nothing but the white face with the fine brows and the kind eyes with the sparkling smile in them.

"Do you find me attractive?" she asked.

"Yes," replied the boy.

"Why?"

"You are beautiful and good."

He answered as in a dream. It was strange to listen to her questions, her eyes must surely know everything that went on in his soul.

"And do you like Matvey Matveyich?" Rayissa asked in a slow undertone.

"No," Yevsey answered simply.

"Is that so? He, on the other hand, loves you. He told me so himself."

"No," repeated the boy, shaking his head.

Rayissa raised her brows, moved a little nearer to him, and asked, "Don't you believe me?"

"I believe you, but I don't believe my master, not at all!"

"Why? Why?" she asked twice in a quick whisper, moving still nearer to him. The warm gleam of her eyes penetrated the boy's heart, and stirred within him a swarm of thoughts which he had never experienced before. He quickly shed them while with her.

"I'm afraid of him. I'm afraid of everybody except you."

"Why?"

"You, too, have been wronged . . . I saw you cry. You were not crying then because you had been drinking. I understand. I understand a lot! Only I do not understand everything put together. I can see a thing by itself clearly to the tiniest wrinkle, and then I can see alongside it something different, not even vaguely like it, and somehow I can understand this as well. But what does it all mean? The one is quite separate from the other. There seems to be one way of life and then another one beside it."

"What are you talking about?" Rayissa asked in amazement.

"It is the truth."

For several moments they looked at one another in silence. The boy's heart beat fast, and his cheeks grew red with confusion.

"You'd better go now," Rayissa said in a low voice, getting to her feet. "Go, or else he will ask you why you were away so long. Don't tell him you were with me. You won't, will you?"

Yevsey walked away filled with the tender sound of the lilting voice, warmed by the tenderness in the eyes. The woman's words rang in his memory the whole day and enveloped his heart in a wave of quiet joy.

That day was strangely long. A murky cloud hung over the roofs of the houses and over the square. The day, weary and dull, seemed to have become entangled in its greyness and remained suspended there. After dinner two customers came into the shop: one a lean, stooping man with a handsome greyish mustache, the other a man with a red beard and spectacles. Both carried out a long and careful search among the books. The lean one whistled softly and his mustache stirred all the time, while the one with the red beard talked with the master.

Yevsey arranged in a row the books the customers had selected and listened to what old Raspopov was saying. He knew in advance what his master would say, knew how he would say it and in his impatience for the evening to come he tried to relieve the tedium by testing his knowledge of the old man.

"You are buying these books for a library?" the old man inquired with exaggerated courtesy.

"For the Teachers' Association's library," replied the man with the red beard. "Why do you ask?"

"Now he'll flatter him," thought Yevsey, and he was not mistaken.

"You show extremely good judgment in your choice. It is good to see books appreciated in the right way."

"Good?"

"Now he'll smile," thought Yevsey.

"Yes, indeed," said the old man, smiling graciously. "You can become familiar with good books like these, so that you come to love them. They aren't just dead wood, you see, but products of the mind. When one sees a customer who like oneself has a respect for books, it comes as a pleasant surprise. The average customer is an odd fellow. He comes and asks, 'Have you an entertaining book, by chance?' It's all the same to him. He seeks amusement, a toy, but nothing to improve his mind. And then from time to time someone will suddenly ask for a prohibited book."

"What do you mean by prohibited?" asked the man, screwing up his small eyes.

"One published abroad, or secretly in Russia."

"And are there books like these for sale?"

"Now he will lower his voice." Again Yevsey found himself anticipating his master's next move.

Fixing his spectacled gaze upon the face of the red-bearded man, the master lowered his voice almost to a whisper.

"Why not? Sometimes one buys up a whole library, and one can find anything there, yes, anything."

"Have you any such books here now?"

"Yes, I have a few."

"Let me see them, please," the red-bearded one asked.

"Only I must ask you to keep this to yourself. You see, it's not for profit's sake, merely as a courtesy. One likes to do a favor now and then."

The stooping man stopped whistling, adjusted his spectacles and scrutinized the old man.

Today the master had seemed particularly loathsome to Yevsey, and he watched him with a cold, gloomy anger. Now when Raspopov went over to the corner of the shop to show the red-bearded man some books hidden away there, the boy suddenly said in a whisper to the stooping customer, "Don't buy those books."

The moment he had said these words Yevsey began to tremble with terror. A pair of bright, small eyes peered into the boy's face from behind the spectacles.

"Why not?"

With a great effort Yevsey answered after a pause, "I don't know."

The customer readjusted his spectacles, moved away from him, and began to whistle louder, studying the old man out of the corner of his eye. Then he raised his head, which seemed to make him look straighter and taller, stroked his grey mustache, and walked unhurriedly up to his companion, from whom he took the book; he looked at it and then dropped it on the table. Yevsey followed his movements, expecting some calamity to befall himself. But the stooping man merely touched his companion's arm, and said quite simply and calmly, "Well, let's go."

"But the books?" exclaimed the other.

"Let's go. I'm not buying any books here."

The red-bearded man glanced at him and then at the master, his small eyes winking rapidly. Then he walked to the door and out into the street.

"You don't want the books?" demanded Raspopov.

Yevsey realized by his tone that the old man was surprised.

"I don't," answered the customer, his eyes fixed upon the master's face.

Raspopov shrank, stepped back, and suddenly said with a wave of his hand in an unnaturally loud voice which Yevsey had never heard before, "As you please, of course. Still—you must excuse me, but I don't quite understand."

"What don't you understand?" asked the stooping man, smiling.

"You rummaged among the books for two hours, agreed upon a price, and then suddenly—but why?" cried the old man anxiously.

"If only because I remembered your loathsome face. You haven't given up the ghost yet, I see."

The stooping man pronounced his words slowly, not loudly, yet quite distinctly and left the shop unhurriedly, but with a heavy echoing tread.

For a minute the old man's eyes followed him; then immediately he pattered up to Yevsey.

"Follow him, find out where he lives," he said in a rapid whisper, clutching the boy's shoulder. "Go! You mustn't let him see you, you understand? Be quick!"

Yevsey would have fallen if the old man had not held him firmly on his feet. His master's words crackled drily in his breast like peas in a baby's rattle.

"Why are you trembling, you little idiot?"

When Yevsey felt his master's hand release his shoulder, he ran to the door.

"Wait you fool!" Yevsey stood still, paralyzed by the scream. "I shouldn't have asked you! You'd never be able to do it—oh, my God!"

Yevsey darted into a corner. It was the first time he had seen his master so violent. Yevsey realized that his anger was tinged with fear, a feeling he understood only too well; and yet, though his own soul was desolate with it, it pleased him to see Raspopov's alarm.

The dusty little old man darted about the shop like a rat in a trap. He ran to the door, thrust his head out into the street, craned his neck and turned back again into the shop. His hands trembled helplessly, awkwardly groped about his body; he mumbled and hissed, shaking his head till the glasses leaped from his nose.

"Um . . . the dirty blackguard—oh! Yes, you filthy blackguard, I'm still alive!" Minutes later he shouted to Yevsey, "Close the shop!"

The old man then went into his room, crossed himself, drew a deep breath, and flung himself heavily on the black sofa. Usually so sleek and so smooth, his skin had suddenly grown wrinkled; his face had shrunk and his clothes hung in folds on his agitated body.

"Tell Rayissa to give me some peppered vodka, a large glassful." When Yevsey brought the vodka his master rose, drank it down at a gulp, and, with an open mouth, stared for a long time into Yevsey's face.

"Do you understand that he insulted me?" he asked.

"Yes."

The old man raised his hand and silently shook his finger.

"I know him," he said in a broken voice.

Removing his black cap, he rubbed his naked skull with his hands, peered about the room, touched his head again with his hands, and then returned to the sofa.

Rayissa brought in the supper.

"Are you tired?" she asked as she set the table.

"I don't feel too well. I've got a touch of fever, I think. Give me another glass of vodka. Sit down with us awhile. It's too early for you to go."

He talked rapidly, ordering her about. Rayissa sat down; the old man raised his spectacles and scanned her suspiciously from head to foot. Then at supper he suddenly raised his spoon in the air and said, "I don't want to eat."

Bending over the plate, he was silent for a while.

Yevsey tried and tried again to understand what had happened in the shop that day. He felt as if he had unexpectedly struck a match and its tiny flame had suddenly set something aflame and had almost consumed him in its sudden angry blaze. Somehow it seemed that everyone was bound together, enmeshed by unseen threads—if one of these threads were accidentally pulled, a man would twist and turn in helpless anger.

Suddenly in a low suspicious tone, looking at Yevsey, the old man asked, "What are you thinking about?"

Yevsey rose and answered in embarrassment, "I am not thinking."

"Well, then, away with you. You've had your supper. Clear the table and go."

Determined to irritate his master, Yevsey was intentionally slow in clearing the table.

"Go, I tell you!" the old man screamed in a squeaking voice. "You idiot!"

Yevsey went to his room and sat down on the chest. He left the door slightly ajar for he wanted to hear what his master was going to say.

"What are you sitting there for?"

The boy turned around, and saw the master's head poked through the door.

"Lie down and go to sleep."

The door was then tightly closed. Yevsey undressed and lay down.

The dry words of the old man could be heard fluttering, like autumn leaves, behind the door. Now and then the old man grew angry and shouted; this kept the boy from being able to either think or sleep.

The next morning Rayissa called him to her room again.

"What happened in the shop yesterday?" she asked with a smile when he had sat down.

Yevsey told her everything in detail, and she laughed content-edly and happily. Then suddenly she drew her brows together and asked quietly, "Do you realize what he is?"

"No."

"An informer," she whispered, her eyes growing wide with fear.

Yevsey was silent. She got up and came over to him.

"What a strange boy you are!" she said thoughtfully, gently stroking his head. "You don't understand anything. What was all that stuff you were telling me the other day? About some other life?"

Her question brought him back to reality; he wanted so much to talk about it. Looking into her face with the fathomless stare of unseeing eyes, he began to speak.

"Of course there's another life. Where else would the fairy-tales come from? And not only the fairy-tales, but . . ."

The woman smiled, and rumpled his hair with her warm fingers.

"You little fool! They'll get you," she added seriously, almost sternly, "they'll lead you wherever they want you to go, and do whatever they want to do with you. That is all that life is!"

Yevsey nodded his head, silently agreeing with every word Rayissa said.

She sighed and looked through the window at the street. When she turned again to Yevsey, her face surprised him. It was red, and her eyes had become smaller and darker.

"If you were smarter," she said in an indolent, hollow voice, "or more alert, maybe I would tell you something. But you're such an odd one that there's no telling you anything. As for your master, he ought to be strangled. There, now you can go tell him what I've said—you who tell him everything."

Yevsey rose from the table, feeling as if a cold stream of insult had been poured over him, and murmured, "I'll never tell anything about you—to anybody. I love you very much, and—even if you strangled him, it wouldn't change anything. That's how I love you."

He shuffled listlessly to the door, but the woman's hands caught him like warm white wings and turned him back.

"Did I hurt you?" he heard her say. "Well, forgive me . . . If you only knew what a monster he is, and how much I hate him."

She pressed him closely to her breast, and kissed him twice. "So you love me?"

"Yes," whispered Yevsey, feeling as though he were swept into a hot whirlpool of unknown bliss.

Laughing and fondling him, she said, "Ah, you little baby!"

He smiled to himself as he went down the stairs and listened to her laughter. His head was spinning, his body was filled with a sweet lassitude. He walked slowly and cautiously, as if afraid of spilling the ardent joy that was in his heart.

"Why have you been so long?" asked the master.

Yevsey looked at him, but saw only a dim, formless blur.

"I have a headache," he answered slowly.

"And I, too. What can it mean? Is Rayissa up yet?"

"Yes."

"Did she speak to you?"

"Yes . . ."

"What about?" the master asked hastily.

The question was like a slap in Yevsey's face. He braced himself, however, and answered indifferently, "She said I hadn't swept the kitchen properly."

And then Yevsey heard the old man's low, gloomy words, "That woman is a dangerous creature! Oh, yes, yes! She wants to find out everything, and worms out of you whatever she wants to know."

Chapter 5

THE DAYS PASSED rapidly in a jumbled mass, as if joy were lying in wait somewhere ahead. Yet every day grew more and more disturbing.

The old man became sulky and taciturn. He peered about strangely, would suddenly burst into a fury, shout, and then howl dismally, like a sick dog. He complained constantly of ill-health, nausea; at meal times he smelled the food suspiciously, crumbled the bread into small pieces with trembling fingers, and held the tea and the vodka up to the light. His nightly scoldings of Rayissa and his endless threats to ruin her entirely became more and more frequent. She answered all his outbursts softly, with composure.

Yevsey's love for the woman waxed stronger, while hatred for his master increased and oppressed him.

"Do you think I don't understand what you're up to, you worthless creature?" raged the old man plaintively. "Where does my sickness come from? What is it you are poisoning me with?"

"Now, now,—you mustn't get such ideas!"

The woman's calm voice sounded reassuring. "It's old age that makes you sick."

"You lie! You lie!"

"And fear is another reason . . ."

"You miserable woman, hold your tongue!"

"And it's time you thought of death."

"Aha! That's what you want! You lie! You hope in vain! I'm not the only one that knows all about you. I told Dorimedont Lukich all about you. Yes!" He burst again into a loud tearful whine. "I know he's your lover. It's he who talked you into poisoning me. You imagine you'll have it easier with him, don't you? Well, you won't, you know you won't!"

One night, after a similar scene, Rayissa left the old man's room with a candle in her hand, half-dressed, white-skinned, voluptuous. She walked as if in a dream, swaying from side to side and treading the floor uncertainly with her bare feet. Her eyes were half-closed, and the fingers of her outstretched right hand clawed the air convulsively. The flame of the candle inclined toward her breast, the smoky red tongue almost touching her blouse, lighting up her tired, parted lips and glowing on her teeth.

She passed Yevsey without noticing him, and he instinctively followed her to the door of the kitchen where the sight that met his gaze numbed him with horror. She had left the candle upon the table and stood holding a large kitchen knife in her hand, testing its sharp edge with her finger. She then bent her head, her hand moved to her round neck, just by the ear, where she seemed to be searching for something with her long fingers. Then she drew a long sigh and slowly put the knife back on the table. Her hands fell to her sides.

Yevsey clutched the doorpost. At the sound the woman started and turned to him.

"What do you want?" she asked in an angry whisper.

Yevsey answered breathlessly.

"He'll die soon . . . Why are you doing that to yourself?"

"Hush!"

She stopped him and touched him with her hand as if seeking support. Then she walked back into the old man's room.

Soon the master became unable to leave his bed. His voice grew feeble, and a rattle often sounded in his throat. His face grew dark, his weak neck failed to support his head, and the grey tuft on his chin stuck out incongruously. The doctor came every day and each time Rayissa gave the sick man his medicine, he groaned hoarsely, "With poison, eh?"

"If you don't want it, I'll throw it away," she replied quietly.

"No, no! Leave it! Tomorrow I'll call the police. I'll ask them what you are poisoning me with."

Yevsey would stand at the door, sometimes his eye, sometimes his ear close to the crack. He marveled, almost to tears, at Rayissa's patience. His compassion for her swelled powerfully in his breast, and together with it grew a desperate longing for the old man to die.

The bed creaked. Yevsey could hear the thin tinkle of a spoon knocking against glass.

"Mix it, mix it! You scum!" mumbled the master.

One day he ordered Rayissa to carry him to the sofa. She picked him up in her arms as if he were a child. His yellow head lay upon her pink shoulder, his dark, shriveled feet dangled limply in the folds of her white skirt.

"God!" wailed the old man, sprawling on the broad sofa. "God, why hast Thou given over Thy servant into the hands of the wicked? Are *my* sins more grievous than *their* sins, O Lord?" He lost his breath and his throat rattled. "Get out!" he went on in a wheezing voice. "You have poisoned one man already—it was I who saved you from hard labor, and now you are poisoning me —ah, ah! You liar!"

Rayissa slowly moved away. Now Yevsey could see his master's dry little body. His belly rose and fell, his legs twitched; his face was grey and on it the lips twisted convulsively, as he opened and closed them, greedily gasping for air, licking them with his thin tongue, revealing the black hollow of his mouth. His forehead and cheeks glistened with sweat, his little eyes, now large and sunken, followed Rayissa's every movement.

"I have nobody, no one close to me on earth, no true friend. Why, O Lord?" The voice of the old man wheezed and broke. "You wanton woman, swear before the ikon that you are not poisoning me!"

Rayissa turned toward the corner and crossed herself.

"I don't believe you, I don't believe you," he muttered, clutching at the sheets, at his chest, at the back of the sofa.

"Drink your medicine. You'll feel better," Rayissa suddenly almost shrieked.

"Better?" the old man repeated. "My dearest, my only one, I will give you everything, my own Ray . . ."

He stretched his bony arm toward her and beckoned to her to come closer, moving his dark little fingers.

"Oh! I can bear you no longer, you loathsome creature!" Rayissa cried in a stifled voice. Snatching the pillow from under his head, she flung it at the old man's face, threw herself upon it with her whole body, and muttered, "The devil take you now! Go, go!"

Yevsey heard the stifled rattle, the muffled blows; he realized that Rayissa was fighting the old man, smothering him, and that his master was beating his legs upon the sofa. He felt neither pity nor fear. He merely wished that the end would be quick. He covered his eyes and ears with his hands and sank to the floor.

The sudden push of the opening door brought him to his feet. Rayissa stood before him arranging her hair which was hanging about her shoulders.

"Well, did you see?" she asked gruffly.

Her face was flushed but calm and her hands did not tremble.

"I did," replied Yevsey, nodding his head. He moved closer to Rayissa.

"Well, you can inform the police—if you want to . . ."

She turned and walked into her room, leaving the door open. Yevsey remained at the door, trying not to look at the sofa.

"Is he dead, really dead?" he asked in a whisper.

"Yes," answered the woman distinctly.

Then Yevsey turned his head, and glanced indifferently at the little body of his master. Flat and dry it lay upon the sofa as if glued to it. He looked at the corpse, then at Rayissa, and breathed a sigh of relief.

In the corner near the bed the clock on the wall sounded softly and hesitatingly, one stroke, then a second. At each stroke the woman started; she went up to the clock and stopped the halting pendulum with an uncertain hand. She sat down on the bed, her elbows on her knees and her head pressed between her hands. Her hair fell down again, covering her face and hands as with a dense, dark veil.

Barely touching the floor with his toes so as not to break the stern silence, Yevsey went over to Rayissa, gazing at her white round shoulders, and said in a low voice, "It's what he deserved."

"Open the window," said Rayissa gruffly. "Wait a moment. Are you afraid?" she added softly.

"No."

"How is that? You are a timid boy."

"When you are here, I'm not afraid."

"Are you sorry for him?"

"No."

"Open the window."

The cold night air streamed into the room, and circling round it, blew out the lamp. Shadows flickered on the walls. The woman shook her head, tossing her hair back on her shoulders and straightened herself to look at Yevsey with her huge eyes.

"Why am I pursued by ruin?" she asked, perplexed. "All my life it has been this way. From one pit to another, and each one deeper than the one before."

Yevsey went and stood beside her; they were silent for a long time. Finally she put her soft, cold hands around his waist, and pressing him to her asked in a low voice, "Listen to me, are you going to tell?"

"No," he answered, closing his eyes.

"You won't tell? Not a soul? Never?" the woman asked pensively.

"Never!" he repeated quietly but firmly.

"Don't tell. I'll help you along," she promised, stroking his cheek. She rose, looked around her, and said briskly, "Put on your clothes. It's cold. And the room must be tidied up a little. Go and get dressed."

When Yevsey returned he saw the master's body completely covered with a blanket. Rayissa remained as she had been, half-dressed, her shoulders bare. This touched him. Taking their time, they put the room in order, and the boy felt that all the silent turmoil in the stuffy room during the night bound him more closely to the woman, who, like himself, knew what fear meant. He tried to remain as near to her as possible and avoided looking at the master's body.

The day began to dawn.

"Now, go, lie down and sleep," Rayissa ordered. "I will wake you soon and give you a note to take to Dorimedont Lukich." She felt the bedding with her hand as she accompanied him to his trunk and said, "Oh, how hard it must be!"

When he lay down, she sat down beside him, and stroking his head with her soft smooth hand, spoke in a low voice, "If anyone asks you how it happened, tell him you don't know. Tell him you were asleep and didn't see anything."

Yevsey could hardly keep his eyes open.

"No . . ." she went on. "You'd better say . . ."

She gave her instructions calmly, firmly, and her caresses awakened memories of his mother. He felt happy. He smiled.

"Dorimedont Lukich is an informer, too," he heard her lulling voice. "You must be on your guard. If he gets it out of you, I'll say you knew everything and that you helped me. Then you'll be put in prison, too." Now she, too, smiled and repeated, "In prison, and then hard labor. Do you understand?"

"Yes," Yevsey whispered happily, looking into her face and already half asleep.

"You are falling asleep. Well, sleep then." Happy and grateful, he heard the words as he drifted away. "Will you forget everything I have told you? What a pathetic little soul you are! Go to sleep!"

Yevsey fell asleep, but almost immediately it seemed a stern voice was waking him.

"Boy, get up! Quickly! Boy!"

He sprang up and out of bed, stretching out his hands. At his bedside stood Dorimedont Lukich holding a stick.

"Why are you sleeping? Your master has died, and here you are, sleeping."

Rayissa stood at the kitchen door, her hat on, a parasol in her hand.

"He's tired. We haven't slept the whole night!"

"Tired? On the day your benefactor dies, you should be weeping, not sleeping! Get dressed!"

The spy's flat, blotched face was stern. His words seemed to pull at Yevsey, like reins steering a docile horse.

"Run to the police station. Here's a note, don't lose it."

Yevsey dressed listlessly and went out in the street. He forced his eyes open as he ran along the pavement bumping into passers-by.

"I wish we'd get him buried soon!" he thought to himself anxiously. "Dorimedont will frighten her and she'll spill the whole story . . . Then I'll go to prison, too . . . If I'm together with her it's all right, I won't be frightened . . . She didn't wake me, she let me sleep, she went herself to fetch him . . . Or maybe she's afraid? How am I going to live now?"

When he came back he found a black-bearded policeman and a greying old man in a frock coat already sitting in the room. Dorimedont was talking to the policeman in a firm, commanding voice. "You heard what the doctor said, Ivan Ivanich? It was cancer, you see? . . . Ah, there's the boy! Go and bring half a dozen bottles of beer, Yevsey! Quick."

Rayissa was busy in the kitchen preparing eggs and coffee. Her sleeves were drawn up, her white arms darted about swiftly, efficiently.

"I'll give you some coffee when you come back," she promised Yevsey, with a smile.

Yevsey was kept running the whole day. He had no time to notice what was happening in the house but felt that things were going well for Rayissa. That day she was more beautiful than ever, everybody found pleasure in looking at her.

At night, when almost sick with exhaustion he lay down in bed with an unpleasant, sticky taste in his mouth, he heard Dorimedont tell Rayissa in a hard, pressing voice, "We mustn't let him out of our sight, you understand? He's stupid."

Then he and Rayissa came into Yevsey's room. The spy put out his hand with an important air, and said sniffling, "Get up! Tell us how you're going to live now?"

"I don't know."

"If you don't know, who is to know?" The spy's eyes were swollen, his face and nose grown purple. He breathed hotly and noisily, like an overheated stove.

"You will live with us, with me," said Rayissa kindly.

"Yes, you will live with us, and I will find a good job for you." Yevsey was silent.

"Well, what's the matter with you?"

"Nothing," said Yevsey, after a pause.

"You ought to be thanking me, you little fool," Dorimedont explained condescendingly.

Yevsey felt that the small grey eyes seemed to rivet him implacably to a spot.

"We'll be better to you than relatives," Dorimedont continued, walking away, leaving behind him the heavy odor of beer, sweat, and grease.

Yevsey opened the window and listened to the grumbling and stirring of the town sinking into sleep. He lay down and peered into the darkness with frightened eyes. Wardrobes and trunks slowly moved around in it like large black blocks; the walls, barely visible, seemed to vacillate and all this filled him with a mounting terror, as if pushing him into a stifling, inescapable trap.

In Rayissa's room the spy guffawed.

"That's nothing . . . hm . . . It'll soon pass! You'll get used . . ."

Yevsey thrust his head under the pillow but a minute later, unable to breathe, he jumped out of bed. The dry shadowy feet of his master seemed to flash before him, his little red sickly eyes flared up. Suddenly in the darkness Yevsey let out a short shriek and ran to Rayissa's door, his arms outstretched. He pushed against it and cried out piteously, "I'm frightened."

Two large white bodies bounded across the room. One of them bawled in a startled, angry voice, "Get out of here!"

Yevsey fell on his knees and sank down on the floor at their feet like a frightened lizard.

"I'm frightened! he squeaked softly.

The following days were taken up with preparations for the funeral and with the moving of Rayissa to Dorimedont's quarters. Yevsey floated about like a small bird in a cloud of dark fear. Only occasionally did the timid thought flicker in his mind like a will o' the wisp, "what will become of me?" It scalded his heart with yearning, and awoke in him the desire to run away and hide. But everywhere he met the eagle eyes of Dorimedont and heard his dull voice, "Here, boy, quickly!"

The command would echo somewhere within Yevsey, and push him this way and that, day in, day out. In the evening he fell asleep empty and exhausted, his sleep heavy and dark and full of terrible nightmares.

Chapter 6

YEVSEY AWOKE one day from this existence to find himself in a dusky corner of a large room with a low ceiling, sitting at a table covered with a dirty green oilcloth, and holding a pen in his trembling hand. Before him lay a thick book full of notes and a few pages of blank ruled paper. He had no idea what he was supposed to be doing with all these things and stared about him helplessly.

There were a number of tables in the room with two or four people at each table. They sat there, tired and ill-tempered, moving their pens rapidly, smoking uninterruptedly, and now and then exchanging curt words with one another. A pungent blue smoke floated to the windows; a deafening, incessant clamor came from the street. A multitude of flies buzzed about the men's heads and crawled over the tables and over the notices on the walls; they knocked against the window panes and in their senseless bustle seemed to imitate the people who filled this stifling, filthy cage.

Policemen stood at the doors; people came and went, exchanged greetings, smiled obsequiously, and sighed. Their rapid, plaintive talk hung in the air, interrupted by the stern calls of the officials.

Yevsey sat in his corner, his neck stretched over the table scrutinizing the room and the various clerks, trying to remember their faces and to find among them someone who would help him. Because of his strengthened instinct of self-preservation he concentrated all his oppressed feelings, all his broken thoughts into single-mindedly adapting himself to this place and to these people as soon as possible, simply to make himself anonymous among them.

All the clerks, both young and old, had a certain seedy and shabby appearance in common. All were equally irritable and shouted, gesticulating and baring their teeth. Many were elderly and bald-headed men; several had reddish and two grey hair. Of these two, one was tall, wore his hair long, had a thick mustache, and looked like a priest who'd had his beard shaved off; the other was red-faced with a huge beard and a shaved skull. It was the latter who had placed Yevsey in a corner, laid a book in front of him, and, tapping it with his finger, had ordered him to copy certain parts of it.

Now an elderly woman dressed entirely in black stood before this old man, and whined in a plaintive tone, "Gracious sir . . ."

"You disturb me in my work," shouted the old man without even looking at her.

Some people came to complain, to make requests, to justify themselves; they stood up and spoke humbly, tearfully. Others, sitting down, shouted back at them, angrily, scornfully, or wearily. Paper rustled, pens squeaked; and across all this noise came the soft weeping of the girl.

"Aleksey," the man with the grey beard called aloud, "take this woman away from here." His eyes lighting on Yevsey, he walked briskly up to him and asked gruffly, as if surprised, "What's the matter with you? Why aren't you writing?"

Yevsey hung his head and was silent.

"Hmm, another fool given a job," said the old man, shrugging his shoulders. "Hey, Zarubin!" he shouted as he walked away.

A thin youth with a low forehead and restless eyes and black curls on a small head sat down beside Yevsey.

"What's the trouble?" he asked in an undertone, nudging Yevsey with his elbow.

"I don't understand what I am supposed to do," Yevsey explained, overcome with terror.

The youngster let out a hollow, broken sound, as though from the depths of his stomach. "Ugh!" Then, as if imparting a great secret, he whispered, "I'll teach you, and you'll give me half a ruble when you get your pay. Agreed?"

"Agreed."

The boy pointed out the names that had to be copied from the book.

"Call me when you've finished and I'll see if you've made any mistakes. My name is Yakov Zarubin."

Something again seemed to break inside the boy's body. "Ugh!" He disappeared, gliding nimbly between the tables, stooping as he went, his elbows pressed to his sides, his wrists to his breast. He turned his shaggy black head in all directions, and his narrow little eyes darted about the room. Yevsey, after watching him for a minute, reverently dipped pen in ink and began to write. Soon he sank into a blissful and familiar state of complete oblivion of his surroundings, became absorbed in work which required no thought, and in it lost his fear.

Yevsey quickly became accustomed to his new position. Instinctively conscientious, he always was ready to serve anyone in order to be rid of him the sooner. Meek and submissive with everyone, he cleverly took refuge from the cold curiosity and the cruel pranks of his fellow clerks in his work. Silent and reserved, he built for himself an existence in his corner that escaped all notice, without finding any meaning in the noisy, motley days that passed before his round, fathomless eyes.

He went on hearing the complaints, the groans, the frightened exclamations, the stern voices of the police officers, the irritated grumbling and the malicious snubs of the clerks. Often people were slapped on the face and dragged out the door by the scruff of their necks. Not infrequently was blood drawn. Sometimes policemen brought in men bound with ropes, beaten up and bellowing with pain. The thieves looked embarrassed but smiled at everybody, as at familiar good old friends, and the street women also smiled ingratiatingly and always rearranged their dress with one and the same gesture. Those who had no identity papers kept a sullen or dejected silence and observed the world with cowering glances. The political offenders under police supervision came in carrying their heads high; they argued and shouted, greeted nobody, and behaved with quiet contempt or pronounced hostility. This type of offender provided the office with a great topic of conversation; they were an object of scorn and sometimes anger. But beneath the ridicule and hostility Yevsey felt a hidden interest and something like a reverent awe for these people who behaved with such an independent spirit.

The so-called political spies, these men of elusive appearance, so stern and silent, were the people who aroused the greatest interest among the clerks. The clerks talked with a keen envy of the huge sums of money they made. With fear in their voices they affirmed that these people knew everything, that nothing was hidden from them, that their power over the lives of other people was immeasurable. It was not beyond them to arrange it so that every man, no matter what he did, would finally end up in prison.

Klimkov imperceptibly gathered experience, which, though his weak, clumsy mind was incapable of fusing it into a harmonious whole, gradually acquired a shape. It sharpened his curiosity because of its importance, and sometimes it suggested ideas and possibilities to him that frightened him by their very boldness.

No one near him showed pity for anybody else. Nor did Yevsey feel sorry for other people. It began to seem to him that they were all pretending, even when they cried and groaned from beatings. In everybody's eyes he saw something concealed, something distrustful, and more than once his ear caught the threatening, though subdued, cry, "Wait, one day our turn will come."

In the evening, when he sat in the large room almost alone and recalled the impressions of the day, everything seemed superfluous and unreal—none of it made sense. Everybody appeared to know that they ought to live quietly and without malice, but for some reason no one wanted to disclose the secret of a different life. No one trusted his neighbor; everyone lied and made everyone else lie. The general irritation caused by life was very plain to see. All complained aloud of its burden, each looked upon the other as upon a dangerous enemy, and dissatisfaction with life could only be matched with mistrust of the others.

At times Yevsey was seized by a heavy, debilitating sense of boredom. His fingers seemed to have no strength; he put the pen aside and rested his head on the table, staring without blinking into the murky twilight of the room while trying to discover something essentially necessary to him in the depths of his own soul.

Then his chief, the old man with the shaven head, would shout to him, "Klimkov, have you fallen asleep?"

Yevsey would seize the pen and repeat to himself with a sigh, "This cannot last."

But he could not decide whether he still really believed in these words, or perhaps had already ceased to believe in them and was merely trying to find consolation.

It was more tedious, more difficult at home than in the police station. In the morning, Rayissa, half-dressed, with a crumpled face and dim eyes, would give Yevsey his coffee without uttering a word. Dorimedont coughed and spluttered in her room; his dull voice began to sound louder and more authoritative than ever. At dinner and supper the man munched noisily, licked his lips, thrust his thick tongue far out, bellowed, and examined the food greedily before starting to eat. His red blotched cheeks were shiny and his small grey eyes glided over Yevsey's face like two cold beetles, unpleasantly tickling his skin.

"I know how to distinguish the important from the unimportant in life, brother," he said. "I know what a pound of good and what a pound of bad is worth to a man, yes, I do. You, I may say, you were lucky to come to me when you did. Here, you see, I have given you a position, and I am going to push you farther and farther just as high as you can go—if you aren't foolish, that is."

He swayed his bulky body as he spoke, and the chair under him groaned plaintively. Yevsey felt that this man could force him to do anything he wanted.

From time to time the spy would boast, glowing with self-satisfaction, "I received thanks again today from Filip Filoppovich. He even gave me his hand."

One evening at supper Dorimedont, pulling his ear, told a story.

"I was sitting one day in a restaurant and I saw a man eating a cutlet. He kept looking around and looking at his watch. Now you should know, Yevsey, that an honest man with a clear conscience doesn't keep glancing in all directions; people do not interest him, and he knows what the time is. The only ones who are known to observe other people are the agents of the Security Department and criminals. So of course I noticed this gentleman. The suburban train pulls in, another gentleman comes into the restaurant, a dark fellow with a little beard, a Jew to judge by appearances, with two flowers in his buttonhole, a red and white one—a sign, a secret sign in fact. I see them greet each other with their eyes. 'Aha!' I think to myself. The dark man orders something to eat, drinks a glass of soda water, and walks out. The one who has been in the restaurant first follows him casually and I go after them."

Dorimedont puffed out his cheeks and then blew a great breath stinking of meat and beer into Yevsey's face. Yevsey staggered in his chair, and the spy burst out laughing. Then he belched noisily and continued, raising his thick finger in the air.

"For a month and twenty-three days I courted these two men. Finally I reported them! I said I was on the track of doubtful characters. We started the hunt, to find out who they were. The fair-haired fellow who had eaten the cutlet said, 'It's none of your business.' But the Jew gave his real name and we nabbed him. Along with him we took a woman—it was the third time she had fallen into our hands. We went to various other places, gathering people up like mushrooms. But it was all small fry, people we already knew. I was considerably put out until yesterday when the fair-haired man finally gave us his name. He turned out to be an important gentleman escaped from Siberia . . . Yes . . . And so there you are, on New Year's Day I can expect a reward."

Rayissa listened, looking somewhere over the spy's head; she slowly chewed a crust of bread, biting off little pieces at a time.

"You catch them, and you keep on catching them, but still there are always some left," she said lazily.

The spy smiled, and answered pompously, "You don't understand politics, that's why you talk nonsense, my dear. We don't want to exterminate these people at all. They serve as sparks to show us where the fire really starts. That's what Filip Filippovich says, and he himself was once a political offender, moreover, a Jew. Yes, yes. It's a very subtle game."

Yevsey's gaze wandered gloomily around the square, airless room. The yellow-papered walls were hung with portraits of czars, generals, and naked women, reminding him of sores and wounds on the body of a sick man. The furniture was pressed close against the walls, as if to withdraw from people, and the air was permeated with vodka and warm, greasy food. The lamp burned under a green shade and cast dead shadows upon their faces.

The spy stretched his hand across the table and pulled Yevsey's hair. "When I speak, you must listen."

Dorimedont often beat Yevsey. Though his blows were not painful, they were particularly insulting, as if he struck not the face but the soul. He was especially fond of hitting Yevsey on the head with the heavy ring he wore on his finger; he would bend the finger and knock against the boy's skull producing a strange, dry, crackling sound. Each time Yevsey was struck Rayissa would say, contemptuously, moving her brows, "Stop, Dorimedont Lukich, don't do that."

"Why? This won't break him. He has to be taught."

Rayissa had grown thinner, blue circles had appeared under her eyes, and her gaze had become duller, more immobile. On the evenings when the spy was out she would send Yevsey out for vodka, which she gulped down in little glassfuls. Then she would begin to talk in a deliberately even voice; what she said was confused and unintelligible, and she frequently stopped and sighed. When she finally relaxed she gradually undid one button after the other, unlaced herself, and half-dressed, sprawled in the armchair like a lump of sour dough.

"I am bored," she would say, shaking her head, "so bored! If you were handsomer, or even older, you might help to distract my thoughts. Oh, how useless you are!"

Yevsey hung his head in silence. The coldness of the insult seared his heart.

"Well, why are you looking so wan, so gloomy?" he heard her sad complaints. "Others at your age would have started making love to girls long ago; they live, they are alive."

Sometimes when she had been drinking, she drew him to her and tousled his hair, awaking in him a complex feeling of fear, shame, and a sharp but timid curiosity. He shut his eyes tightly, and yielded himself silently, automatically to the power of her coarse, shameless hands. His poor weak spirit was crushed by a debilitating premonition of disaster.

"Go to bed, go! Oh, my God!" she exclaimed, pushing him away in disgust.

Yevsey left her to go to the anteroom where he slept. He withdrew from her more and more, gradually losing the undefined soft feeling he had had for her.

As he lay in bed filled with a sense of both injury and sharp unpleasant excitement, he heard Rayissa singing in a thick cooing voice—always the same sad song—and heard the clink of the bottle against the glass.

But one dark night when thin streams of autumn rain lashed violently against the window by his bed, Rayissa succeeded in arousing in the adolescent the feeling she had needed.

"There, now," she said, smiling a drunken smile. "Now you are my lover. You see how good it is? You see?"

He stood by the bed breathless, his feet trembling, his heart pounding. He gazed at her large, soft body, at her broad face spread in a smile. He was no longer ashamed, but his heart was overcome with a strange sense of loss, and it sank within him, outraged. For some reason he wanted to weep. But he was silent. He felt with a growing sadness that this woman was a stranger to him, unwanted and undesired; that all the good, tender feelings he had harbored for her had been swallowed up in one gulp by her greedy body, and had vanished into it without leaving a trace, like a belated drop of rain into a muddy pool.

"You and I together, we'll show Dorimedont, the pig, how we can deceive him—come closer to me!"

He did not dare refuse her, but now she was no longer able to overcome his distaste for her. She toyed with him a long time and laughed at him impudently, then roughly pushing his bony body away from her, she swore at him, and went away.

When Yevsey was left alone he thought in despair, "Now she will ruin me. She'll hold this against me; she won't forget it, and I'm lost."

He looked through the window. Something formless and frightened throbbed and quivered there in the darkness. It wept, lashed the window with a doleful howl, scraped along the wall, jumped on the roof and fell down into the street with a moan.

A cautious, alluring thought stole softly into his mind. "Suppose I let it out that she strangled the old man!"

The idea frightened Yevsey, but he was unable to put it out of his mind for a long time.

"One way or another she will ruin me," he answered himself. Yet the idea was strongly fascinating and did not desert him.

In the morning, however, it seemed to him that Rayissa had forgotten about the sad fury of the night before. She gave him his bread and coffee lazily, with an air of indifference. As always, she felt sick from the previous day's drinking, but by neither word nor look did she hint of their changed relationship.

He left for the office somewhat reassured, and from that day on he stayed in the office working at night and then walked home very slowly so as to arrive as late as possible. It was difficult for him to remain alone with the woman. He was afraid to speak to her, dreading that she would remember the night when she had destroyed his feeling for her, for weak as it had been, he had dearly cherished it.

Yakov Zarubin's and Yevsey's chief, Kapiton Ivanovich, the man with the grey mustache whom everyone called Old Pipe behind his back, remained in the office at night more frequently than did the others. The chief's shaven face was covered with a network of thin, red veins, so that although at close range it looked as if it were criss-crossed with tiny twigs, at a distance it had a rosy appearance. His unsmiling eyes gleamed angrily from under grey brows and eyelids that drooped wearily. He spoke in a grumble and smoked thick yellow cigarettes uninterruptedly. Clouds of bluish smoke always hovered above his large white head distinguishing him from all the other men.

"What a self-important person he is," Yevsey once said to Zarubin.

"He's a bit weak in the head," the black haired little Yakov answered. "He spent almost a whole year in a lunatic asylum."

Yevsey saw that sometimes Old Pipe took a small black book from the pocket of his long grey jacket, brought it close to his face, and mumbled something through his moving mustache.

"Is that a prayer book?"

"I don't know."

Zarubin's swarthy face twitched spasmodically. His small eyes flared up, he leaned over toward Yevsey, and whispered hotly, "Do you go with girls?"

"No."

"Why?"

Yevsey answered shyly, "Haven't the courage . . ."

"Ugh! Come with me. All right? We can get it for nothing. We need only twenty-five kopeks for a couple of beers. If we say we are from the police, they'll let us in free, and give us girls for nothing. They are afraid of us police officers." In a still lower voice, but with even more fire and greed, he continued. "And what girls they are! Large, warm, like downy feather-beds. Girls are the best thing in the world, my word they are! Some fondle you the way your own mother would, . . . stroke your hair until you fall asleep . . . It's fine!"

"Have you got a mother?"

"Yes, but I live with my aunt. My mother is a bitch. She lives with a butcher who keeps her. I don't go to see her, the butcher won't allow it. I went there once, and he gave me such a kick on the backside! Ugh!"

Zarubin's little mouse-like ears quivered, his narrow eyes rolled strangely upwards, he tugged at the black down on his upper lip with a convulsive movement of his fingers, throbbing all over with excitement.

"Why are you so quiet? You ought to be bolder or they'll kill you with work. I was frightened, too, at first, and they almost drove me to death. Come, let's be friends for the rest of our lives!"

Yevsey did not like him and his restlessness unnerved him, but he said, "All right."

"Your hand on it. There, it's done! So tomorrow we'll go to the girls?"

"No, I won't go."

They did not notice Old Pipe coming up to them.

"Well, who's got the upper hand?" he growled.

"We're not fighting," said Zarubin, sullenly and disrespectfully.

"You're a liar," said Old Pipe. "You, Klimkov, don't you give in to him, do you hear me?"

"I do," said Yevsey, standing up in front of him.

A feeling of respectful curiosity drew him to the man. One day, he surprisingly summoned up enough courage to speak to Old Pipe.

"Kapiton Ivanovich!"

"What is it?"

"I want to ask you, if you please . . ."

"Come on, come on . . ."

"Why do people lead such bad lives?" asked Yevsey, finishing his sentence with an effort.

The old man raised his heavy brows. "What business is it of yours?" he rejoined, looking into Klimkov's face.

Yevsey was taken aback. The old man's question stood before him in all the power of its simplicity.

"Ah!" said the old man softly. Then he drew his brows together, whipped the black book from his pocket, and tapping it with his finger said, "The New Testament. Have you read it?"

"Yes."

"Did you understand it?"

"No," answered Yevsey timidly.

"Read it again." Moving his mustache, the old man hid the book in his pocket. "Three years since I started reading it. No one understands it. It's a book for children, for the pure in heart . . ."

His grumbling was encouraging, and Yevsey wanted to ask more questions, but could not formulate them. The old man lit a cigarette; the smoke enveloped him, and it seemed he had forgotten his questioner. Yevsey moved away cautiously. He felt more and more drawn toward Old Pipe and found himself thinking, "It would be nice to sit nearer to him."

Henceforth this became his dream. But Yakov Zarubin's dream was different.

"You know what, Klimkov?" he said in a hot whisper. "Let's try to get into the Security Department as political spies. Then what a life we'll lead! Oho!"

Yevsey was silent. Political spies frightened him with their stern eyes and the mystery surrounding their dark lives, their dark work.

Chapter 7

A DISASTER TOOK place at home. Dorimedont appeared one day late at night in torn clothes, without hat or stick, his face bruised and smeared with blood. His bulky body shook, and tears ran down his swollen cheeks. He sobbed and said in a hollow voice, "We must go away—to some other town . . . quickly!"

Rayissa silently wiped his face with a towel dipped in vodka and water. He writhed and groaned.

"Not so rough! The beasts! What a beating they gave me, with clubs, just think of it! Men—with clubs? . . . Take care . . . it hurts . . ."

As he removed the spy's shoes, Yevsey listened to his groans, watched his tears and his blood with secret satisfaction.

"Who was it?" asked Rayissa when Doremidont got to bed.

"They followed me, to the suburbs . . . I'll ask for a transfer to another town. They'll kill me if I stay here."

They began to argue when Yevsey retired.

"I won't go," said the woman in an unusually firm voice.

"Hold your tongue! Don't upset a sick man!" the spy exclaimed with sadness in his voice. "I'll make you go!"

In the morning Yevsey could see from Rayissa's stony face and the spy's angry irritation that the two had not made peace. At supper they began to quarrel again. The spy cursed and swore; his swollen, blue face was horrible to look at, his right hand was in a sling, and he shook his left one menacingly. Rayissa, pale but imperturbable, rolled her round eyes, following the swinging of his red hand, and abruptly and stubbornly repeated, scarcely varying her words, "Never, I'll never go."

"Why not?"

"I don't want to."

"No, of course you'll go."

"I won't."

"We shall see. Who are you anyway? Have you forgotten?"

"All that makes no difference."

After supper the spy wrapped his face in a scarf, and went away somewhere, while Rayissa sent Yevsey for vodka. When he had brought her a bottle of it and another bottle of some dark beverage, she poured some of the contents of each into a cup, drank it down, and remained standing a long time with her eyes closed, rubbing her neck with the palm of her hand.

"Do you want some?" she asked, nodding toward the bottle. "Have a drink. You'll have to drink some time, it might as well be now."

Yevsey looked at her hanging breasts, her small mouth, her dim eyes, and remembering what she had been only such a short time ago, he felt a wave of dismal pity for her rise inside him.

"Ah, Yevsey," she said, "if one could only live one's whole life with a clean conscience."

Her lips twitched spasmodically. She filled another cup and offered it to him.

"Drink it!"

He shook his head, refusing it. She laughed.

"You little coward! Life is hard for you—that I understand. But what you are living for—that I don't understand. What is it for?"

"Just like that," answered Yevsey gruffly. "What else is one to do?"

Rayissa glanced at him, and said tenderly, "I think you'll hang yourself one day."

Yevsey sighed, upset by this remark and settled down more firmly in his chair.

Rayissa paced up and down the room, moving lazily, noiselessly. She stopped in front of the mirror, and looked at her face for a long time without blinking. She felt her full white neck with her hands, her shoulders quivered, her arms dropped heavily, and she began again to pace up and down the room, her hips swaying. She hummed a tune without opening her mouth, her singing resembled the groans of a man suffering from toothache.

A lamp covered with a green shade was burning on the table. Through the window the round disc of the moon could be seen in the empty sky. The moon, too, looked green, it hung there, a bad omen, motionless like the shadows in the room.

"I am going to bed," said Yevsey, rising from his chair.

Rayissa did not answer, and did not look at him. Then he stepped to the door, and repeated in a lower voice, "Good-night. I am going to sleep."

"Go, then, I'm not keeping you. Go!"

Yevsey realized that Rayissa was sick of her life. He wanted to say something to her.

"Is there anything I can do?" he inquired, stopping at the door.

She looked into his face with her tired, sleepy eyes. "Go to hell!" she answered softly.

She kept pacing up and down the room. Her skirts rustled, the bottles tinkled. Now and then she coughed.

Her calm words had remained stuck in Yevsey's mind, "I think you'll hang yourself one day . . ."

In the middle of the night the spy rudely awoke Klimkov. "Where is Rayissa?" he asked in a loud whisper. "You don't know? You fool!"

Dorimedont went into the other room, then thrust his head through the door, and asked sternly, "What was she doing?"

"Nothing."

"Was she drinking?"

"Yes."

"The pig!"

The spy pulled at his ear, and vanished.

The lamp made a sputtering noise. The spy swore under his breath, then began to strike matches which flared up, frightening in the darkness, and then went out again. Finally a pale ray of light from the room reached Yevsey's bed. It quivered timidly, and seemed to seek something in the narrow entrance. Dorimedont came back into Yevsey's room. One of his eyes was closed by the swelling, the other, clear and restless, rapidly swept the walls, and stopped on Yevsey's face. "Did Rayissa say anything?"

"No."

"The fool . . ."

Yevsey raised himself in his bed.

"Stay where you are!" said Dorimedont, and sat down on the bed at Yevsey's feet.

"If you were a year older," he began in an unusually gentle tone, "I would get you into the Security Department as a political agent. It's a very good position. The salary is not large, but if you are successful, you are well rewarded . . . And free to do as you like . . . Rayissa is a beautiful woman, isn't she?"

"Yes, beautiful," agreed Yevsey.

The spy gave a strange smile. He kept touching the bandage on his head with his left hand, and pinching his ear. "Woman! You can never have enough of her, the mother of all temptation and sin. —Where do you think she went?"

"I don't know," Yevsey answered softly, a vague fear mounting in his heart.

"She has no lover . . . Look out, Yevsey, don't be in a hurry with the women. They're an expensive lot. I've earned many thousands of rubles—and where are they?"

Heavy, unwieldy, covered with bandages, he swayed before Yevsey's eyes, and seemed ready to fall to pieces. His dull voice sounded uneasy, his left hand constantly felt his head and his breast.

"What a lot of time I've wasted on them!" he said, peering suspiciously into the dark corners of the room. "It's a restless pursuit, but there's nothing better in the world . . . Some say cards are better, but they, too, can't get along without women . . . Nor does hunting protect you from women . . . Nothing does."

In the morning Klimkov saw the spy sleeping in his clothes on the sofa. The lamp was still lit, the room was filled with smoke and the smell of paraffin. Dorimedont was snoring, his large mouth wide open, his sound hand dangling above the floor. He was repulsive and pitiful.

Dawn came, and a pale square piece of sky peeped through the window. The flies awoke in the room, and buzzed, darting about on the grey background of the window pane. Together with the smell of paraffin the room was penetrated with some other smell, thick and sinister.

Yevsey put out the lamp, washed distractedly in a great hurry, dressed, and started for the office.

It was about noon that Zarubin shouted to Yevsey, "Klimkov, Rayissa Fialkovskaya is your master Lukich's mistress, isn't she?"

"Yes. What about it?" asked Yevsey hastily.

"She's cut her throat."

Yevsey rose to his feet, stung in the back by a sharp blow of terror.

"They've just found her in the storeroom. Let's go and have a look."

"I'm not going!" said Yevsey, sinking back into his chair.

Zarubin ran off, announcing to the clerks on his way, "I told you she was Dorimedont Lukich's mistress."

He shouted the word "mistress" with particular emphasis and zest.

Blankly Yevsey watched him go, and there rose in the air before him a vision of Rayissa, her heavy beautiful hair streaming round her. Her face was green, her lips tightly clenched and she had dark stains in the place of eyes. The dead face stared at him and Yevsey was unable to chase it away.

"Why don't you go to lunch?" asked Old Pipe.

Scarcely anybody had remained in the office. Yevsey sighed and answered, "My landlady has cut her throat."

"Ah, I see! Yes! Well, then go to the public house."

Old Pipe moved away. Yevsey jumped up and seized his arm. "Take me with you."

"Where to?"

"Take me to stay with you altogether."

Old Pipe bent toward him.

"What do you mean by 'altogether'?"

"To your rooms—to live with you—always."

"Let's get our lunch first . . . Let's go . . ."

A shrill canary was singing uninterruptedly in the public house. The old man silently ate fried potatoes but Yevsey was unable to eat, looking into his companion's face expectantly, imploringly.

"So you want to live with me? Well you'd better come then."

When Yevsey heard these words, he felt instantly that they somehow sheltered him from a terrible life. Encouraged, he said gratefully, "I will clean your shoes for you."

Old Pipe thrust his long foot in a torn boot from under the table and said, looking at Yevsey, "You needn't do that . . . What about your landlady? Was she a good woman?"

The old man's eyes fell gently on the boy and seemed to beg, "Tell me the truth."

"I don't know," said Yevsey, dropping his head, feeling for the first time that he used these words too often.

"So!" said Old Pipe.

"I don't know anything," said Yevsey, feeling deeply dissatisfied with himself. Suddenly he grew bolder. "I see this and that, but what it is all about, what for and why, I cannot understand. There must be some other life."

"Another one?" repeated Old Pipe, screwing up his eyes.

"Yes. It would be impossible otherwise."

Old Pipe smiled softly, then knocked his knife against the table, and shouted to the waiter, "A bottle of beer! So it would be impossible otherwise? That's curious."

"Please, let me come and live with you . . ." Yevsey repeated, "May I come today?"

"Yes, yes, come along . . ."

He began to drink his beer in silence.

When they returned to the office, Yevsey was met by Dorimedont. His bandages had loosened, the one eye was suffused with blood; he hastened up to Yevsey and asked, in a mysterious whisper, "Have you heard about Rayissa? It was drink that did it, there's no doubt about that."

"I'm not going back there any more," said Yevsey. "I am going to live with Kapiton Ivanovich."

Suddenly appearing disturbed, Dorimedont looked around and whispered, "You'd better be careful! He's not in his right mind. They keep him here only out of pity. He could even be dangerous. Be careful with him. Keep your mouth shut . . ."

Yevsey had expected the spy to fly into a passion. He was surprised at his whispering, and listened attentively to what he said.

"I am going to leave this town. So this is where we part! I will speak to my chief about you, and when he needs a new man, he will remember you, you can be sure. Take your things away from the house, today, do you hear? I'll be moving in to a hotel. Here are five rubles, they'll be useful. And keep your mouth shut!"

He continued to whisper rapidly for a long time, his eye darting suspiciously all around him, and when the door opened he leapt from his chair as if to run away. The smell of some sort of ointment emanated from him. He seemed to have grown less bulky and smaller in stature, to have lost his self-importance.

"Good-bye," he said, placing his hand on Yevsey's shoulder. "Live carefully, never trust anybody and especially women. Remember the value of money. Buy with silver, save the gold, don't scorn copper, defend yourself with iron—that's a Cossack saying. I'm a Cossack, you know!"

Yevsey found it hard and tedious to listen to him. He did not believe one word the spy said and, as always, he was afraid of him. He felt relieved when he walked away, and he turned eagerly to his work, trying to lose himself in it and so shut out memories of Rayissa and everything else that troubled him. Something altered in his life and stirred within him that day. He felt he was standing on the threshold of another life, and all the time he followed Old Pipe from the corners of his eyes. The old man bent over his table in a cloud of grey smoke. Yevsey thought involuntarily, "Everything seems to happen at once. She has cut her throat, and now I . . ."

He did not quite know what was going to happen and anxiously waited for the day to end.

In the evening he walked along the street with Old Pipe and saw that almost everybody noticed the old man, some even stopping to have a look at him. He walked not rapidly, but with long strides, swinging his body and thrusting his head forward like a crane. He stooped, holding his hands behind his back, the sides of his open jacket flying out and flapping against his body like broken wings. The attention which the old man attracted seemed in Klimkov's eyes to stress his special place in the world.

"What is your name?"

"Yevsey."

"Ivan is a good name," observed the old man, smoothing his crumpled hat with his long hand. "I had a son named Ivan."

"Where is he?"

"That doesn't concern you," answered the old man calmly. After several steps he added in the same tone, "If I say 'had' that means I have him no longer, he's no longer here." He stuck out his lower lip, scratched it with his little finger, and said softly, "We shall see who'll get the better of whom." Then he moved his neck to one side, bent his head and looked into Klimkov's eyes. "Today a friend will be coming to see me," he said solemnly, shaking his finger in the air. "I have a friend—only one! What we talk about and what we do is no concern of yours. What you know I do not know, and what you do, I do not want to know. The same applies to you. Absolutely."

Yevsey nodded his head.

"Make this a general rule. Apply it to everybody. No one knows anything about you. And you do not know anything about others. The path of human destruction is knowledge sown by the devil. Happiness is ignorance. That's quite clear."

Yevsey listened attentively, peering into his face. Observing this the old man mumbled, "There is something human about you, I see." And added, "There's something human also in a dog."

They climbed a narrow wooden staircase to a stifling attic, dark and smelling of dust. Old Pipe gave Yevsey a box of matches and told him to strike them while he crouched and fumbled for a long time opening the door which was covered with torn oilcloth and ragged felt. Yevsey held up the matches and they scorched the skin of his fingers.

The old man lived in a long, narrow white room, with a ceiling resembling the lid of a coffin. A wide window shone dimly opposite the door. A little stove stood in the corner to the left of the entrance. A bed extended along the left wall, and opposite it sprawled a sagging reddish sofa. The room smelled strongly of camphor and dried herbs. The old man opened the window, and heaved a deep sigh.

"It's good to have fresh air," he said. "You will sleep on the sofa. What is your name, did you say? Aleksey?"

"Yevsey."

He raised the lamp from the table, and pointed to the wall. "There's my son Ivan."

A portrait drawn in thin pencil strokes and set in a narrow white frame hung inconspicuously upon the wall. It was a young face, with a wide forehead, a sharp nose, and stubbornly compressed lips. The lamp shook in the old man's hands, the shade knocked against the glass, filling the room with a gentle, plaintive sound.

"Ivan," he repeated, setting the lamp back on the table. "A man's name means a great deal."

He thrust his head through the window, breathed in the cold air noisily, and without turning to Yevsey told him to prepare the samovar. While the boy busied himself by the oven a hunchbacked man came in, removed his straw hat in silence, and fanned his face with it.

"It's close, even though it's autumn already," he said in a beautiful deep voice.

"Aha, you are here!" said Old Pipe.

They began to talk in low voices standing by the window. Yevsey realized that they were talking about him, but he could not distinguish any words.

The three then sat down at the table. Old Pipe began to pour the tea. From time to time Yevsey stole a look at the guest. His shaven face was tinged with blue, and he had a wide, thin-lipped mouth and dark eyes sunk in two hollows under a high smooth forehead. His head, bald to the crown, was angular and large. He drummed softly on the table with his long fingers.

"Well, read," said Old Pipe.

The hunchback pulled out a packet of papers from his coat pocket and unfolded it. "I'll skip the titles." He coughed, and half closing his eyes began to read. " 'We, the undersigned, people known to nobody and already arrived at a ripe age, now fall slavishly at your feet with this distressing statement of our grievances which wells from the very depths of our hearts, our hearts shattered by life but not robbed of sacred faith in the mercy and wisdom of Your Majesty.' Well, is it all right?"

"Continue," said Old Pipe.

"'For you are the father of the Russian people, the source of blessed wisdom, and the only power on earth capable—'"

"Better say, 'the only power on earth endowed with authority,'" suggested Old Pipe.

"Wait, wait! 'The only power capable of restoring and maintaining justice in Russia—' Here we ought to put in another word for the sake of style, but I don't quite know which."

"Be careful with words," said Old Pipe, sternly but not loudly. "Remember that they convey a different meaning to every man."

The hunchback looked at him, and adjusted his glasses.

"Yes, indeed . . . But we'll see to it later . . . 'Great Russia is falling into ruin. Evil is rampant in our country and horror prevails. People are oppressed by poverty and want. Hearts have become perverted with envy. The patient and gentle Russian people are perishing, and a heartless tribe ferocious with greed is being born, a race of man-wolves, cruel beasts of prey. Faith is destroyed, and outside her holy fortress the people stand perturbed. Persons of depraved minds aim at the defenseless, lure them with satanic shrewdness, and entice them on to the road of crime against all thy laws, curate of our lives.'"

"'Curate'? That's too ecclesiastic," grumbled Old Pipe. "We must put it in some other way. And we must say outright that a spirit of revolt has sprung up among people, 'and therefore thou, who art called by God—'"

The hunchback shook his head disapprovingly.

"We may point out. We have no right to advise."

"'Who is our enemy, and what is his name? The atheist, the socialist, and the revolutionary, a trinity. The destroyer of the family, the robber of our children, the forerunner of the anti-Christ.'"

"You and I don't believe in the anti-Christ," said the hunchback softly.

"That doesn't matter. We are speaking for the masses. They believe in the anti-Christ. We must point out the root of the evil. And where do we see this? In the doctrine of destruction . . ."

"He knows it himself."

"Who is there to tell him the truth? Nobody cast the noose of insanity around his children. On what are their teachings based? On general poverty and the bitterness caused by it. And we ought to say to him straight out, 'Thou art the father of the people and thou art rich. Then give the riches thou hast accumulated to thy people. Thus thou wilt cut down the root of the evil, and everything will have been saved by thy hand.'"

The hunchback's mouth spread into a wide, thin crack, and he said, "They'll send us to hard labor for that."

Then he looked into Yevsey's face and at Old Pipe. Klimkov listened to the reading and the conversation as to a fairy-tale, and felt that all the words entered his head and imprinted themselves forever in his memory. With parted lips and eager eyes he looked at one and the other, and did not drop his gaze even when the dark look of the hunchback fastened upon his face. He was fascinated by the proceedings.

"I confess," said the hunchback, "this is a little embarrassing . . ."

"What are you up to, Klimkov?" asked Old Pipe glumly.

Yevsey's throat went dry, and he did not answer at once. "I am listening."

Suddenly he realized by their faces that they did not believe him, that they were afraid of him. He rose from the table, and becoming confused, blurted out, "I won't say anything to a soul — please let me listen. —Why, I myself said to you, Kapiton Ivanovich, you remember, that things ought to be different."

"You see?" said Old Pipe crossly, pointing at Yevsey. "You see, here's an example. A mere boy, yet he, too, wants things to be different. That's where they get their strength."

"Yes, yes," said the hunchback.

Yevsey grew shy. Old Pipe, his brows stern, bent toward him. "You should know that we are writing a letter to the Czar. We ask him to take more rigorous measures against those who are under supervision for political unreliability. Understand?"

"I understand."

"Those people," the hunchback began clearly and dictatorially, "are agents of foreign governments, chiefly of England. They receive huge salaries for stirring up the Russian people to revolt and for weakening the power of our government. The English do it so that we should not take India from them."

They spoke to Yevsey in turn. When one had finished, the other carried on. He listened attentively, trying to remember their complicated language and became almost intoxicated with the unaccustomed taxing of his brain. It seemed to him that he was on the point of understanding something overwhelming which would illuminate the whole of life and all people, and all their misfortunes. It was inexpressibly pleasing for him to recognize that two wise men were talking to him as to an adult, and he was powerfully gripped by a feeling of gratitude and respect for these men, needy, poorly dressed, and yet so preoccupied with the construction of a new and better life. But soon his head grew heavy, as if filled with lead, and oppressed by a painful sensation of his heart overflowing, he involuntarily closed his eyes.

"Go, go to bed," said Old Pipe.

Klimkov rose obediently, undressed with care and lay down on the sofa.

A warm, fragrant moisture wafted through the window with the breath of the autumn night. Thousands of bright stars quivered in the dark sky, soaring higher and ever higher. The flame of the lamp flickered, and it too tried to climb upwards. Two men, bending toward each other, spoke in grave, low voices. Everything around Yevsey was mysterious, awe-inspiring, and awakened in him a joyful aspiration for something new, something good.

Chapter 8

YEVSEY HAD BEEN living with Kapiton Ivanovich only a few days when he began to feel already that he was a person of some consequence. Before, when addressing the police officers who served in the office, he spoke in hushed and respectful tones. Now he summoned the old man Butenko to his table in a stern voice, and rebuked him, "Look, there are flies in my inkstand again!"

The grey-haired soldier covered with crosses and medals began a casual but verbose explanation.

"There are all in all thirty-four inkstands here, and thousands of flies. The flies want to drink and they crawl into the inkstands. What else are they to do?"

In the bathroom before the looking glass Klimkov carefully examined his grey and angular face, with its sharp little nose and narrow lips, searched for signs of a mustache, and looked into the watery, uncertain eyes.

"I must have my hair cut," he decided after failing to smooth the thin tufts of hair upon his head. "And I ought to wear starched collars; my neck is too thin."

The same evening he got his hair cut, bought two collars, and felt that he was even more a man.

Old Pipe was attentive and kind with Yevsey, but there often was a sarcastic gleam in his eyes which disconcerted and confused the boy. Whenever the hunchback came the old man's face assumed a preoccupied expression, and his voice sounded stern. He disagreed violently with almost everything the other said. "It's not that—it's not so—no—your brain works like a gun that doesn't shoot straight, it scatters thoughts all over the place. One ought to be able to shoot so that one hits the target fair and square."

The hunchback shook his heavy head and answered, "Good work is not done in a day."

"Time passes and the enemy grows."

"By the way, I have been watching a man," said the hunchback one day, "who has taken lodgings not far from mine. He is a tall man, with a pointed beard, screwed-up eyes, and he walks with a quick stride. I asked the yardman where he was working. He told me the man had come to look for a job. I sat down and wrote a letter to the Security Department immediately. This is it."

Old Pipe interrupted his talk with a wide sweep of his arm.

"That sort of thing is of no importance. If the house is damp, obviously there'll be cockroaches in it. You won't get rid of them just like that. It's the house that must be made dry. I am a soldier," he said, beating himself on the chest. "I commanded a company, and I understand life. All people should be thoroughly familiar with the laws and regulations—this produces unanimity. What is it that hinders understanding of the law? Poverty. Stupidity is only a result of poverty. Why doesn't he fight poverty? Want is the root of human folly and of all the hostility toward him, the Czar."

Yevsey took in the old man's words greedily, and trusted him: the root of all human misfortune is poverty. That is clear. Hence come envy, malice, cruelty. Hence also greed and the fear of life common to all people, and fear of one another. Old Pipe's plan was simple and wise. The Czar was rich, the people poor. Let the Czar give the people his riches and then they would all be content and kind.

Yevsey's attitude toward people began to change. He remained as obliging as before, but began to look upon others with a certain condescension, with the eyes of a man who has solved the secret of life and can show others the way to peace and contentment.

One day, eating in the public house with Yakov Zarubin, he felt the need to boast of his knowledge and proudly expounded everything he had heard from the old man and his hunchback friend.

Zarubin's narrow eyes flashed. He fidgeted in his seat and rumpled his hair, thrusting the fingers of both hands through it.

"It's perfectly true, it is, by God!" he exclaimed in an under-tone. "What the devil, in fact! He has thousands of millions, and here we are perishing. Who taught you all that?"

"Nobody," said Yevsey firmly. "I thought of it myself."

"No, tell me the truth. Where did you hear it?"

"I tell you, I came to it myself."

Yakov looked at him with approval.

"If it's true," he said, "you must have a good head. But I believe you're lying."

Yevsey felt affronted.

"It's all the same to me whether you believe me or not."

For some reason Yakov burst out laughing, heartily rubbing his hands.

Two days later the assistant police inspector and a grey-eyed gentleman with a round close-cropped head and a bored, yellowish face, came up to Yevsey's table.

"Klimkov, you're to go straight to the Security Department," said the police inspector in a low and ominous voice. "Is your desk locked?"

"No . . ." Yevsey rose, but his legs trembled, and he dropped back into his chair again. The cropped-hair man pulled out his table drawer and took out all the papers.

Paralyzed with fear and unable to understand what was hap-pening, Klimkov came to his senses in a half-darkened room at a desk covered with green felt. A wave of anguish rose and fell in his breast, the floor heaved and billowed under his feet, and the walls of the room, with a green cast, swayed this way and that. Above the table rose a man's white face framed in a thick black beard, wearing shiny blue spectacles. Yevsey gazed unfalteringly at the glasses, at the blue bottomless darkness; it drew him like a magnet and seemed to suck the blood from his veins. He told in detail and to the point all he knew about Old Pipe and his hunch-back friend as if he were shedding a layer of skin from round his heart.

A shrill voice which pierced his eardrum interrupted him. "So these asinine creatures say the Emperor the Czar is to blame for everything?"

"Yes . . ."

The man with the blue glasses slowly stretched out his hand, raised the telephone receiver to his ear, and asked in a scornful tone, "Belkin, is that you? Yes? See to it, my good fellow, that a search is made tonight in the rooms of two scoundrels and have them arrested. One is a clerk in the police department, Kapiton Reussov, and the other an official of the chancery of the exchequer —Anton Driagin. Well, yes, of course."

Yevsey seized the edge of the table with his hand.

"So, my friend," said the man with the black beard, throwing himself back in the armchair. He smoothed his beard with both hands, played with his pencil, flung it on the table, and thrust his hands into his trousers' pockets. He was silent for a painfully long time, then asked sternly, emphasizing each word, "What am I to do with you now?"

"Forgive me," came from Yevsey in a whisper.

"Klimkov?" mused the black-bearded man. "Seems to me I heard the name somewhere."

"Forgive me," repeated Yevsey.

"Do you feel very guilty?"

"Yes, I do."

"That's good. What do you feel guilty of?"

Klimkov was silent. The black-bearded man sat so comfortably and calmly in his chair that it seemed he would never let Yevsey leave the room.

"You don't know. Think!" he suggested.

Klimkov drew more air into his lungs, and began to tell about Rayissa and how she had strangled the old man.

"Lukich?" the man with the blue spectacles said, yawning indifferently. "Ah, that's why your name is familiar to me."

He walked over to Yevsey, lifted his chin with his finger, and looked into his face for a few seconds. Then he rang a bell.

A heavy tread was heard, and a large pockmarked man with huge wrists appeared at the door. He spread out his red fingers and moved them in a terrifying way as he looked at Yevsey.

"Take him."

"To the corner room?"

"Yes."

"Go!" said Semyonov.

Klimkov wanted to drop on his knees. He was already bending his legs, when the fellow seized him under the arm, and pulled him away, and down a stone staircase.

"What's the matter, sinner? Are you scared?" he asked, pushing Yevsey through a small door. "No face, no skin, and yet a rebel!"

His words completely crushed Yevsey. When he heard the heavy clang of the iron door behind him, he squatted on the floor, clasped his hands about his knees and bent his head. A heavy silence descended upon him and he felt he was going to die. Suddenly he jumped up from the floor, and began to run about the room softly, like a mouse, waving his arms. His groping hands felt the bed covered with a rough blanket; he ran to the door, touched it, discovered a little square window in the opposite wall, and rushed toward it. It was below the level of the ground in a hole covered with an iron grating; the snow sifted through it, and slid down the dirty panes. Klimkov turned noiselessly back toward the door and leaned his forehead against it.

"Forgive me," he pleaded. "Let me out."

Then he dropped to the floor again, and lost consciousness, drowned in a sea of despair.

The days and the nights dragged by slowly like black and grey stripes, destroying Yevsey with their corroding monotony. They passed in a dumb stillness that was filled with ominous forebodings and there was nothing to indicate that their slow, painful course would ever end. Yevsey's soul was paralyzed numb. He was unable to think; and when he paced his cage he tried to make his steps inaudible.

On the tenth day he was once again confronted with the man in the blue glasses and the man who had brought him to the Secret Police office.

"Not very pleasant where you are, eh, Klimkov?" the dark man asked, smacking his thick red lower lip. His high voice made an odd gurgling sound as if he were laughing inside himself. The electric light was reflected in the blue glass of his spectacles, its powerful rays penetrated Yevsey's empty heart and filled him with a slavish readiness to do everything that was required of him to put an end to these sinister days which plunged him into darkness and threatened him with madness.

"Let me go," he said in a low voice.

"Yes, I am going to, and I'll do more for you as well. I am going to take you into my service. Now it is going to be you who will put people into the place from which you have just come—into the same place and into other cozy little rooms." He laughed, smacking his lips. "The late Lukich interceded for you; and in memory of his honest services I will give you a job. You will receive twenty-five rubles a month to begin with."

Yevsey bowed in silence.

"Piotr Petrovich here will look after you and be your guide. You must do everything he tells you. You understand? He will live with you."

"Yes!" the grey-eyed man's response came with unexpected loudness. "It'll be best that way for me . . ."

"That's settled then."

Turning again to Yevsey, the dark man began to speak in a softer voice, telling him something that seemed more soothing and promising. Yevsey tried to absorb his words and followed the ponderous movement of the red lip under the mustache without blinking.

"Remember, you will now be guarding the sacred person of the Czar from attempts upon his life and upon his sacred power. You understand?"

"I thank you humbly," came Yevsey's voice, barely audible.

Piotr Petrovich raised his head abruptly.

"I'll explain everything to him. It's time for me to go."

"You may go then. Well, Klimkov, off with you. Serve well, and you will be happy. But don't forget, all the same, that you were a party to the murder of the secondhand book dealer Raspopov. You confessed to it yourself, and I took your testimony down in writing. You follow me? Good-bye."

Filip Filippovich nodded and his beard, so stiff that it seemed to be cut out of wood, nodded too. Then he held out to Yevsey a plump, white hand with a number of gold rings on the short fingers.

Yevsey closed his eyes and gave a start.

"What a little coward you are, brother!" Filip Filippovich exclaimed in a thin voice, with a tinkling laugh. "You have nothing and nobody to fear now. You are the servant of the Czar, and should not be afraid. From now on you stand on solid ground. You understand?"

When Yevsey walked out into the street, he could barely get his breath. He staggered, and almost fell; Piotr, raising the collar of his overcoat, looked around, and hailed a cab.

"We will drive to my house," he said quietly.

Yevsey looked at him from the corners of his eyes, and almost cried out in surprise. Piotr's smooth-shaven face had suddenly grown a small light mustache.

"Well, why are you gaping at me like that?" he asked gruffly, obviously annoyed by Klimkov's reaction.

Yevsey dropped his head, trying in spite of himself not to look into the face of this new master of his destiny. Piotr kept counting on his fingers silently, bending them one after the other, knitting his brows and biting his lips. Occasionally he called out angrily to the driver, "Hurry! Get a move on."

Sleet and rain were falling and it was cold. It seemed to Yevsey that the cab kept rolling rapidly down a steep hill into a black dirty ravine.

They stopped at a large three-storied house. Of the three rows of dark, blind windows only a few gleamed with yellow light from within. Streams of water splashed and poured from the roof.

"Go up the steps," commanded Piotr. He no longer had a mustache.

They climbed the steps and walked through a long corridor past a number of white doors. Yevsey thought the place was a prison, but the thick smell of fried onion and blacking did not accord with his conception of a prison and this reassured him. Piotr hastily opened one of the white doors, turned on two electric lights, and carefully scrutinized the corners of the room.

"If anybody asks you who you are," he said drily and quickly, removing his hat and overcoat, "say you are my cousin. You have come from Czarskoe Selo to look for a job. Remember this—and make no mistakes."

Piotr looked preoccupied, his eyes were cheerless, his speech abrupt, his thin lips twisted and twitched all the time. He rang a bell and thrust his head out the door.

"The samovar," he called out.

Standing in a corner of the room, Yevsey threw a dismal look around it, vaguely expecting something, he didn't know what.

"Take off your coat, sit down. You will live in the next room," said the spy, hastily unfolding a card table. He pulled a notebook and a pack of cards out of his pocket and started dealing four hands.

"You understand, of course," he went on without looking at Klimkov, "you understand that ours is a secret business. We must keep under cover, or else they'll kill us as they killed Lukich."

"Was he killed?" asked Yevsey in a low voice.

"Yes," said Piotr unconcernedly. He wiped his forehead and examined his cards. "Deal one thousand, two hundred and fourteen —I have the ace, the seven of hearts, the queen of clubs." He made a note in his book, and without raising his head continued to talk in two kinds of voice, indistinctly, with a preoccupied air when he counted the cards; drily, clearly, and rapidly when he continued his instructions to Yevsey.

"Revolutionaries are enemies of the Czar and of God. Ten of diamonds, three, Jack of spades. They are bought by the Germans in order to destroy Russia. We Russians have begun to provide all we want ourselves, and the Germans . . . King, five and nine —the devil take it! There's the sixteenth coincidence!"

Piotr suddenly cheered up, his eyes flashed and a soft, satisfied expression gleamed on his face.

"What was I saying?" he asked Yevsey, looking up at him.

"You were talking about the Germans."

"The Germans are greedy, they are enemies of the Russian people, they want to conquer us. They want us to buy all our goods from them, and to give them our bread. The Germans have no bread—queen of diamonds—that's splendid!—two of hearts, ten of clubs, ten? . . ." Screwing up his eyes, he looked up at the ceiling, sighed, and shuffled the cards. "In general, all foreigners, envious as they are of the wealth and power of Russia—one thousand, two hundred and fifteenth deal—want to stir up a revolt in our country, dethrone the Czar, and—three aces—hmm!—and put their own officials in power everywhere, their own rulers over us so that they can plunder us and ruin us. You don't want this to happen, do you?"

"I don't," said Yevsey, who understood nothing, and was dully following the rapid movements of the man's fingers.

"Of course, nobody wants it," remarked Piotr pensively. He laid out the cards again and stroked his cheeks meditatively. "As a Russian, you can't want it, therefore you must fight the revolutionaries, the agents of the foreigners, and defend the liberty of Russia, the power and life of the Czar. That's all. You will see afterwards the way it must be done. There's only one thing: you can't afford to be caught napping. Learn to carry out all orders precisely. People like us have to have eyes in the back of our heads too. If you haven't, you may catch it both ways—ace of spades, seven of diamonds, ten of spades . . ."

There was a knock at the door.

"Open the door," commanded Piotr.

A red, curly-haired lad came in carrying a samovar on a tray.

"Ivan, this is my cousin. He is going to live here with me. Get the next room ready."

"Mr. Chizhov was here," said Ivan in a low voice.

"Drunk?"

"A little. He wanted to come in."

"Make tea, Yevsey," said the spy after the servant had left the room. "Get yourself a glass and drink some tea. What salary did you get in the police department?"

"Nine rubles."

"You have no money now?"

"No."

"You'll need some, and you must order a suit. You can't keep wearing the same one all the time. You must notice everybody, but nobody must notice you."

He began to mumble again, counting the cards. Yevsey, noiselessly serving the tea, tried in vain to straighten out the strange impressions of the day, but he felt ill. He was shivering and his hands shook, he wanted to lie down in a corner, close his eyes, stay there quite still for a long time. Words he had never known before kept repeating themselves disconnectedly in his head.

"What is it then you are guilty of?" Filip Filippovich kept asking in a thin voice.

"Dorimedont has been killed," he heard the spy's dry words, "the sixteenth coincidence!"

There was a powerful rap on the door. Piotr raised his head.

"Is it you, Sasha?"

"Well, open the door," an angry voice answered.

When Yevsey opened the door, a tall man with a black mustache loomed before him, swaying on long legs. The ends of his mustache reached to the bottom of his chin, and the hairs of it must have been hard, for each one stuck out by itself. He removed his hat, displaying a bald skull, flung the hat on the bed, and began to rub his face vigorously with both hands.

"Your hat's wet and you throw it on my bed?" remarked Piotr.

"The devil take your bed!" said the guest through his nose.

"Yevsey, hang up the overcoat."

The visitor sat down, stretching out his long legs and lighting a cigarette.

"Who's that—Yevsey?" he asked.

"My cousin."

"We're all akin in our natural skin. Have you any vodka?"

Piotr told Klimkov to ask for a bottle of vodka and some refreshments. Yevsey did as he was told and then sat down at the table, putting the samovar between his face and the visitor's so that he could not be seen by him.

"How's business, card sharper?" asked the man, nodding his head at the cards.

Piotr suddenly half raised himself in his chair, and said with some animation, "I have discovered the secret! I have, you know."

"So you've discovered it at last?" sneered the visitor. "You fool!" he drawled, shaking his head in derision.

Piotr seized his notebook and rapping his fingers on it continued in a heated whisper, "But wait, Sasha! I have had the sixteenth coincidence already. You see the significance of that? And I made only one thousand, two hundred, and fourteen deals. Now the cards keep repeating themselves oftener and oftener. I must make two thousand, seven hundred, and four deals. You understand? Fifty-two times fifty-two. Then I make all the deals over again thirteen times, according to the number of cards in each suit. Thirty-five thousand, one hundred, and fifty-two times. And repeat these deals four times according to the number of suits. That makes one hundred and forty thousand, six hundred and eight times."

"You perfect fool!" the visitor drawled again through his nose, shaking his head and curling his lips in a sneer.

"Why, Sasha, why? Explain!" Piotr cried softly. "Don't you see, then I'll know all the deals possible in a game. Think of it! I'll look at my cards"—he held the book nearer to his face and began to read quickly—"ace of spades, seven of diamonds, ten of clubs. So among the other players one has the king of hearts, five and ten of diamonds, the other, the ace, seven of hearts, queen of clubs, and the third has queen of diamonds, two of hearts, and ten of clubs."

His hands trembled, sweat glistened on his temples, his face became soft and gentle.

Peering from behind the samovar, Klimkov saw Sasha's two large dim eyes, the whites suffused with red veins, a big nose which seemed to be swollen, and a network of pimples spread on the yellow skin of his forehead from temple to temple like a band. He emanated a sharp, unpleasant smell and reminded Yevsey of something eerie.

Piotr pressed the book to his breast, and waved his hand in the air.

"I shall then be able to play without a single mistake," he whispered ecstatically. "Hundreds of thousands, millions, will smile at me, and there won't be any jugglery in it, just a simple matter of knowledge—that's all. Everything within the law."

He struck his chest so severe a blow with his fist that he began to cough. Then he dropped back in his chair, and began to laugh softly.

"Why aren't they bringing the vodka?" growled Sasha, throwing the stump of his cigarette on the floor.

"Yevsey, do go and tell . . . ," Piotr began hastily, but at that instant there was a knock at the door and the vodka was brought in. "You're drinking again?" Piotr asked, smiling.

Sasha stretched out his hand for the bottle.

"Not yet, but I will be in a second."

"It's bad for you with your sickness."

"Vodka is bad for healthy people, too. Vodka and imagination. You, for instance, will soon be an idiot."

"I won't. You needn't worry about me."

"You will. I know mathematics. And I see you are a blockhead."

"Everyone has his own mathematics," replied Piotr, disgruntled.

"Oh, be quiet!" said Sasha, slowly sipping the glass of vodka and smelling a piece of bread. He proceeded to fill a second glass for himself.

"Today," he began, bending his head and resting his hands on his knees, "I spoke to the general again. I made him an offer. I said, 'Only give me the means and I'll unearth the right people; I'll open a literary club and trap the pick of the bunch for you, the whole lot of them.' He blew out his cheeks, stuck out his belly and said—the idiot!—'I know better what has to be done and how it must be done.' He knows everything! But he doesn't know that his mistress danced naked before von Rutzen, or that his daughter had an abortion."

He drained the second glass of vodka and filled a third. "Rats, every one of them. They have no right to live! Moses once ordered that twenty-three thousand syphilitics should be killed. At that time there weren't many people in the world, mark you. And if I had the power I would destroy millions."

"Yourself first?" suggested Piotr, smiling.

Sasha sniffed without answering, as if he were in a dream.

"All those liberals, generals, revolutionaries, loose women—I'd make a great pyre of them and burn the lot. I would drench the earth with blood, manure it with ashes. And there would be a fine harvest. Well-fed peasants would elect well-fed rulers. Man is an animal, and needs rich pastures, fertile fields. I would destroy the cities. And everything superfluous, everything that hinders one from living simply as the sheep do and the roosters. I would get rid of it all, to hell with it!"

The cloying, pungent phrases glued themselves to Yevsey's heart, and sickened him. It was hard and dangerous to listen to them.

"What if they suddenly summon me and ask what he said? Maybe he's talking like that to trap me. Then they'll seize me." He trembled and moved uneasily in his chair. "May I go?" he asked Piotr in a low voice.

"Where?"

"I want to sleep."

"Yes, you may go."

"You may go—to hell!" was Sasha's farewell to Yevsey.

Chapter 9

KLIMKOV UNDRESSED noiselessly without lighting a lamp. He groped for the bed in the dark, and rolled himself up tightly in the cold, damp sheet. He wanted to see nothing, to hear nothing, he wanted to squeeze himself into a small unnoticeable lump. Sasha's sneering words clung in his memory. His smell stuck in Yevsey's nostrils, he saw the red band on the yellow skin of his forehead. In fact he could hear the angry exclamations through the door, coming from outside.

"I am a peasant myself, I know what needs to be done."

Without wishing to do so, Yevsey found himself listening, anxiously racking his brain, trying to remember who it was this wicked man reminded him of and not wanting to remember.

It was dark and cold. Dull, trembling reflections of light came and went behind the window panes. A thin scraping sound came from somewhere. The wind-swept rain beat with great heavy drops against the windows.

"To a monastery, that's where I'd like to go!" Klimkov mused mournfully. And suddenly he remembered God, whose name he had seldom heard during his life in the town. He had hardly ever thought of him the whole time. There had been no place in his heart, always so full of fear and of a sense of injury, for hope in the mercy of Heaven. But now it unexpectedly appeared and suffused his breast with warmth, extinguishing his heavy, dull despair. He jumped from the bed, and knelt on the floor; pressing his hands hard to his breast, he turned his face to the dark corner of the room and closed his eyes; he waited speechless, listening to the beating of his heart. But he was too tired, it was too cold; the cold penetrated his skin with thousands of sharp needles. He shivered and returned to bed.

When he awoke he saw that in the corner to which he had directed his mute prayer there was no ikon, but instead two pictures on the wall, one representing a hunter with a green feather in his hat kissing a plump girl, the other a fair-haired woman with a naked bosom, holding a flower in her hand.

He sighed as he looked without any interest about his room. When he had washed and dressed he sat down at the window. The pavement, the street itself, the houses, everything was dirty. The horses plodded slowly by, shaking their heads; drenched drivers sat on the box seats that shook as if they had come unscrewed. As always, people were hurrying somewhere. Today, splashed with mud, wet through, they seemed less dangerous than usual.

Yevsey was hungry, but did not know whether he had the right to ask for tea and bread; he remained motionless, like a stone, until he heard a knock on the wall. Then he walked into Piotr's room, and stopped at the door.

"Have you had tea yet?" asked the spy, who was lying in bed. "Ask for it."

Piotr stuck his bare feet out of the bed, and wriggled his toes, studying them for a minute.

"We'll drink our tea, and then you'll come with me," he said, yawning. "I'll show you a man, you will follow him. Where he goes —you go—you understand? Note the time he enters a house and how long he stays there. Find out whom he visited there. If he leaves the house, or meets another man on the way, you must note the appearance of that man. Then—well, you won't be able to understand everything to begin with." Piotr looked at Klimkov, and whistled softly; then turning aside he continued lazily, "Last night Sasha was talking a lot of nonsense when he was here—you must not consider repeating any of it. He's a sick man, and he drinks, but he's a power to be reckoned with. You can't hurt *him*, but *he'll* eat *you* alive. Remember that. Let me tell you, brother, he was a student once himself, and he knows all their business inside out. He even went to jail for political offense. Now he gets a hundred rubles a month!" Piotr's flabby face, crumpled with sleep, gathered in a frown. He dressed and went on in a bored, grumbling voice: "Our work is no laughing matter. If you could just catch people by their throats at one go—well, then, of course, —but before you can do that you have to tramp about a hundred versts after each one, and sometimes more."

The evening before, in spite of the agitations of the day, Klimkov had found Piotr interesting and stimulating. Now, noticing that he spoke without ease, moved reluctantly, and that everything dropped from his hands, Yevsey felt bolder in his presence.

"Must we walk the streets the whole day long?" he plucked up the courage to ask.

"Sometimes you have a nightly outing, too, in the cold, at about thirty degrees. It must have been a very evil demon that invented our profession."

"And when will they all be caught?" Yevsey asked again.

"Who?"

"These enemies . . ."

"Say revolutionaries or political offenders. You and I won't ever catch them all. They all seem to be born twins."

At tea Piotr opened his notebook, looked at it, and suddenly became excited. He jumped from his chair, laid out the cards at great speed, and began to calculate, "One thousand, two hundred and sixteenth deal. I have the three of spades, seven of hearts, ace of diamonds."

Before leaving the house he put on a black overcoat and an astrakhan cap, pushed a briefcase under his arm and began to look like a regular government official.

"Don't walk close to me in the street," he said sternly, "and don't speak to me. I have to call at a certain house; you go into the yardman's lodge, tell him you have to wait there for Timofeyev. I won't be long . . ."

Afraid to lose Piotr in the crowd Yevsey walked behind without taking his eyes off him. But all of a sudden Piotr vanished. Klimkov was genuinely disconcerted. He rushed forward, then stopped, pressing himself against a lamppost. Opposite him rose a large house with bars across the windows of the first floor and darkness behind the window panes. Through the narrow entrance he saw a bleak gloomy yard paved with large stones. Klimkov was afraid to go in. He looked around, uneasily shifting from one foot to the other.

A man with a little reddish beard suddenly appeared walking quickly out of the yard. He wore a short coat and a cap pulled down on his forehead. He winked a grey eye at Yevsey, and said in a low voice, "Why didn't you go to the yardman?"

"I lost you," Yevsey admitted.

"Lost me? You'd better be careful! Could get into trouble for that. Listen. Three doors away from here is the local Government Board building. A man will soon leave that house. His name is Dmitry Ilyich Kurnocov. Remember it. Come, and I will show him to you."

Several minutes later Klimkov, like a small dog, was hastily walking along the pavement behind a man in a worn overcoat and a crumpled black hat. The man was tall and corpulent; he walked quickly, swinging a stick and rapping it vigorously on the pavement. Black, curly hair with a sprinkling of grey tumbled from under his hat on to his ears and the back of his neck.

Yevsey was suddenly gripped by a feeling of pity for human beings—a feeling that was rare for him. A sweat of fear was pouring down his face as he darted across the street with mincing steps, ran ahead, recrossed the street, and met the man face to face coming toward him. Before him flashed a dark-bearded face, with thick brows, an absent-minded smile and blue eyes. The man's lips moved. He was either humming a tune or talking to himself.

Klimkov stopped and wiped the perspiration from his face with his hands. Then he followed the man with back bent and eyes cast to the ground, raising them only now and then to keep his victim in sight.

"Not young," he thought. "A poor man apparently. It all comes from poverty . . . Also from fear . . ."

He remembered Old Pipe and shivered.

"He'll beat me to death," he thought to himself. And he felt sorry for Old Pipe.

He became aware of the insistent noise of the street; the cold, liquid mud squirted and splashed and Klimkov was overcome by a sense of boredom and loneliness. He remembered Rayissa and longed to leave the streets behind him.

The man he was tracking stopped at the steps of a house, pushed the bell, raised his hat, fanned his face with it, and flung it back on his head. Yevsey stationed himself five steps away at the curb. He looked pityingly into the man's face, and felt a sudden desire to talk to him. The man noticed this, frowned, and turned away. Embarrassed, Yevsey dropped his head, sat on the stone and suddenly thought, "If only he had been rude to me . . . But to do it, just like that . . ."

"From the Security Department?" he heard a low, hissing voice. The question was asked by a tall, reddish-haired peasant in a dirty apron carrying a broom.

"Yes," answered Yevsey, and the very same instant thought, "I shouldn't have told him."

"Another new one?" remarked the janitor. "You are all after Kurnocov?"

"Yes."

"I see . . . Tell your bosses that this morning a guest came to him from the railway station with trunks, three trunks. He hasn't registered yet with the police. He has twenty-four hours' time. Quite a nice-looking, neat little fellow with a small mustache." The janitor fell silent, ran the broom over the pavement a few times, and splattered Yevsey's shoes and trousers with mud. Presently he stopped to remark, "You are too obvious here. They aren't fools either, they know your sort. You'd better stand at the gates."

Obediently Yevsey moved toward the gates. Suddenly he noticed Yakov Zarubin on the other side of the street wearing a new overcoat and gloves and carrying a stick. A black bowler hat was tilted on his head, and as he walked along the pavement he smiled coyly like a street girl conscious of her own beauty.

"Good morning," he said, looking around. "I came to replace you. Go to Somov's public house on Lebed Street, ask for Nikolai Pavlov there."

"Are you in the Security Department, too?" asked Yevsey.

"I got there ten days before you. Why?"

Yevsey looked at him, at his beaming, swarthy little face.

"Was it you who informed against me?"

"And didn't you inform against Old Pipe?"

After thinking awhile Yevsey answered glumly, "I did it after you had betrayed me. You were the only one I told."

"And you were the only one Old Pipe told. Ugh!" Yakov laughed, and gave Yevsey a poke in the shoulder. "Hurry up, you boiled hen!" He walked beside Yevsey, swinging his stick. "This is a good job; it suits me perfectly. You can live like a lord, take a stroll around and make sure you know what's going on. You see this suit? The girls will like me all the better . . ."

Soon he took leave of Yevsey and retraced his steps, walking quickly. Klimkov, deep in thought, watched him go resentfully. He considered Yakov empty-headed; he placed him in a class lower than himself, and it was annoying to see him so satisfied and so smartly dressed.

"He informed against me. If I told them about Old Pipe it was out of fear. But why did he do it?" And as a warning to Yakov, he added to himself, "Wait, we will see in the end who's the better man."

When he asked at the public house for Nikolai Pavlov, he was shown to a staircase. He climbed it and stopped, when he heard Piotr's voice on the other side of a door.

"There are fifty-two cards in a pack. In this town, in my district there are thousands of people, and I know a few hundred of them. I know who lives with whom, and where each of them works. But people change, while cards remain the same forever."

Besides Sasha there was a third man in the room. Tall and well-built, he stood at the window reading a paper, and did not move when Yevsey walked in.

"What a stupid mug!" were the words with which Sasha met Yevsey, staring at him maliciously. "It must be made to look different. Do you hear, Maklakov?"

The man reading the paper turned his head, and examined Yevsey with large bright eyes.

"Yes," he said.

Piotr, excited, his hair disheveled, and cleaning his teeth with a goose quill, asked Yevsey to report what he had seen. The remains of dinner were on the table; the smell of grease and sour cabbage titillated Yevsey's nostrils, and made him hungry. He stood before Piotr, and in a dispassionate voice repeated the information the janitor had given him. At the first words of the account Maklakov put his hands and the paper behind his back, and inclining his head, listened attentively, twirling his fair mustache, which like the hair on his head was a strange fair color, almost silver tinged with yellow. The clean, serious face with the knit brows and the calm eyes, the confident movements of his powerful body clad in a close-fitting, well-cut, sober suit, the strong bass voice—all this distinguished Maklakov advantageously from Piotr and Sasha.

"Did the janitor himself carry in the trunks?" he asked Yevsey.

"He didn't say."

"That means he did not. He would have told you whether they were heavy or light. They carried them in themselves." And he added, "It was probably literature. The current number."

"Well, we must have a search made at once!" said Sasha gruffly, and uttered an ugly oath, shaking his fist.

"I must find the printing press. Get me the type, boys, and I'll fix up a printing press myself. I'll find the imbeciles. We'll give them all that's necessary. Then we'll arrest them, and we'll have lots of money."

"Not a bad scheme!" exclaimed Piotr.

Maklakov looked at Yevsey, and asked, "Have you eaten?"

"No."

"There's your dinner," said Piotr with a nod toward the table. "Be quick about it."

"Why should he eat scraps?" asked Maklakov calmly; he walked to the door, opened it, and called out, "One dinner, please."

"You try," Sasha snuffled to Piotr, "to persuade that idiot Afanasov to give us the printing press they seized last year."

Maklakov looked at them, and silently twirled his mustache. A round, pock-marked, humble-looking man came into the room with the waiter. Dinner was served. He smiled at everyone benevolently, shook Yevsey's hand and said, "My name's Solovyov. Have you heard the news, friends? This evening there will be a banquet of the revolutionaries at Chistov's hall. Three of our men will go there as waiters, you yourself among others, Piotr."

"I'm to go again, am I?" shouted Piotr, and his face became covered with red blotches; he looked angry and older. "The third time in two months that I have had to play the waiter. This is too much. I simply will not do it!"

"You should not talk about it to me."

"Solovyov! Why do they always choose me to be a servant?"

"You look like one," said Sasha with a laugh.

"There will be three of you," Solovyov repeated with a sigh. "What do you say to having some beer?"

Piotr opened the door and shouted:

"Half a dozen beers!"

And he walked to the window, his hands clasped, his joints cracking.

"There, you see, Maklakov?" said Sasha. "No one among us really wants to work seriously with any enthusiasm. But the revolutionaries push ahead all right—banquets, meetings, a shower of literature, open propaganda in the factories!"

Maklakov kept silent, and did not look at Sasha. The short fat Solovyov took up the conversation, smiling amiably.

"I caught a girl with books at the railway station today. I had noticed her already this summer at a holiday resort. 'Well,' thought I, 'enjoy yourself, my dear.' Then today, as I was walking in the station with nobody to follow, I was looking around, and there I saw her marching along carrying a suitcase. I went up to her, and respectfully proposed that she have a couple of words with me. I noticed she started and paled, and hid the case behind her back. 'Ah,' thought I, 'my stupid little one, you're in trouble.' So I took her straightway to the police station, they opened her luggage, and there was the latest issue of *Emancipation* and a whole lot more of their treacherous rubbish. I took the girl to the Security Department. What else was I to do? If you can't get pike, you must eat sprats . . . In the carriage she kept her little face turned away from me. I could see her cheeks were burning and there were tears in her eyes. But she held her tongue. I asked her, 'Are you comfortable, miss?' She didn't answer."

Solovyov laughed softly, a trembling network of wrinkles covered his pock-marked face.

"Who is she?" asked Maklakov.

"Dr. Melikhov's daughter."

"Ah—ah—" drawled Sasha. "I know him."

"A serious person. He has the orders of Vladimir and Anna," remarked Solovyov.

"I know him," repeated Sasha. "A charlatan like all the others. He tried to cure me . . ."

"God alone would be able to cure you now!" Solovyov said gently. "Your health's going rapidly downhill."

"To hell with you!" shouted Sasha.

Maklakov, looking out of the window without turning round, asked, "Did the girl cry?"

"No. But she wasn't happy, either. I don't like getting girls, you know, as I have a daughter myself. . . ."

"What are you waiting for, Maklakov?" Sasha asked angrily.

"I'll wait till he finishes his dinner . . . There's plenty of time . . ."

"Say, can't you eat faster?" Sasha shouted at Klimkov.

As he ate, Yevsey listened and watched carefully and saw with satisfaction that none of them except Sasha was more terrifying, more malicious than the others.

He was overcome with a desire to ingratiate himself, to make himself useful to them. He put down his knife and fork and wiped his mouth with a dirty napkin.

"I'm ready," he said.

The door was flung open and a loose-limbed untidy youth half fell into the room, and hissed, "Ssh! Ssh!"

He thrust his head into the corridor, listened, then carefully closed the door. "Doesn't it lock?" he asked. "Where is the key?" He looked around, and drew a deep breath. "Thank God!" he exclaimed.

"You half-wit," sneered Sasha. "Well, what is it this time? Were they after you again?"

The young man rushed up to him. Panting, waving his arms and wiping the sweat from his face, he began to mutter in a low voice, "They were, of course. They wanted to kill me with a hammer. Two of them followed me from the prison. I was there during visiting hours. As I walked out, they were standing at the gate, two of them, and one of them had a hammer in his pocket."

"Maybe it was a revolver," suggested Solovyov, stretching his neck.

"It was a hammer."

"Did you see it?" inquired Sasha sarcastically.

"Ah, don't you think I know? They decided to kill me with a hammer, without any noise. Wham!"

He adjusted his necktie, buttoned his coat, searched for something in his pockets, and smoothed his wet curly head. His hands twitched nervously about his body; they seemed ready to break off at any moment. His grey bony face was covered with sweat, his dark eyes were dilated and rolled from side to side. Suddenly they became fixed. With unfeigned horror they rested upon Yevsey's face, and the youth backed to the door.

"Who's that? Who's that?" he demanded hoarsely.

Maklakov went up to him, and took his hand.

"Calm yourself, Yelizar. He's one of us, a new one."

"Do you know him?"

"You fool!" came Sasha's exasperated voice. "You ought to see a doctor."

"Have you ever been pushed under a trolley bus? Not yet? Then wait before you call me names."

"You see, Maklakov," began Sasha, but the youth continued in great agitation, "Have you ever been beaten at night by unknown people? Ah! Do you understand? People you don't know! There are hundreds of thousands of such people, unknown to me in the town, hundreds of thousands. They are everywhere, and I am alone."

Solovyov began to talk in his soft, reassuring voice, but his words were drowned out by a fresh outburst from this terrified young man, who carried within himself a whirlwind of fear. Klimkov began to grow dizzy, overwhelmed and alarmed by the whispered flow of words, blinded by the movements of the broken body, and the darting of the cowardly hands. He felt that any minute something huge and black would tear its way through the door, would fill the room and crush everybody.

"It's time to go," said Maklakov, touching his shoulder.

When they were sitting in the cab, Yevsey remarked sullenly in an undertone, "I am not fit for this work."

"Why?" asked Maklakov.

"I'm a frightened man. I'm a coward."

"That'll pass."

"Nothing ever passes," Yevsey retorted quickly.

"Everything does," rejoined Maklakov calmly.

It was cold and dark, and sleet was falling. The reflections of the lights lay upon the mud in golden patches; people and horses trampled upon them and extinguished them. Yevsey, his brain empty, looked ahead, and felt that Maklakov was watching his face.

"You'll get used to it," Maklakov went on, "but if you have another job, leave at once. Have you got one?"

"No."

"Have you been a long time in Security?"

"Since yesterday."

"Ah, that's how it is . . ."

"Where are you taking me now?" Yevsey asked softly.

Without replying Maklakov asked, "Have you any relatives?"

"No, I have no one."

The spy stirred but did not say a word. His eyes were half-closed, he breathed through his nose and the hair of his whiskers quivered. The deep chimes of a church bell floated in the air, warm and soft. The pensive copper song crept mournfully over the roofs of the houses without rising from under the heavy cloud that covered the town with a solid dark canopy.

"Tomorrow is Sunday," Maklakov said slowly. "Do you go to church?"

"No," replied Yevsey.

"Why not?"

"I don't know . . . Just like that . . . It's crowded in there."

"I do go. I love the morning service. The choir sings and the sun peers through the windows . . . It's fine . . ."

Maklakov's simple words emboldened Yevsey to talk about himself.

"Yes, it's nice to sing," he began. "When I was a small boy, I sang in our village church. You sing—and you don't know where you are . . . As though you don't exist . . ."

"We're there," said Maklakov.

Yevsey sighed, glancing sadly at the sprawling building of the station—it suddenly loomed in front of their eyes and barred the way.

They went to the platform where a large crowd had already gathered, and there stopped and leaned against the wall. Maklakov lowered his eyelids, and seemed to be starting to doze. Here and there came the jingling of the gendarmes' spurs; a slender woman with dark eyes and a sunburned face was laughing; her voice was young and resonant.

"Remember the woman who is laughing and the old man beside her," Maklakov said in a distinct whisper. "Her name is Sarah Lurie, a midwife. She lives in the Sadovaya, No. 7. She's been in prison, also in exile, and she is a very clever woman. The old man is also a former exile, a journalist."

Suddenly Maklakov seemed to take fright at a glimpse of a familiar face. He pulled his hat well down over his face with a quick movement of his hand, and continued in a still lower voice. "The tall man in the black coat and the battered hat, a red-haired man, do you see him?"

Yevsey nodded his head.

"That's the writer Mironov. He's been in prison four times already, in different towns. Do you read books?"

"No," said Yevsey.

"You're wrong there. He writes in an exciting way . . ."

A black iron worm with a horn on its head and three fiery eyes, its huge metal body rumbling, uttered a shriek, and glided swiftly into the station. It stopped, and hissed spitefully, filling the air with its thick white breath. The hot steamy smell beat against Yevsey's face. Black human shadows began to bustle and dart around before his eyes.

It was the first time Yevsey had seen this mass of iron at such close range. It seemed alive, charged with emotion. It drew his attention powerfully, and at the same time aroused in him a hostile, painful premonition. The fiery eyes, round, blinding, dazzled and threatened him, imprinting themselves in his memory, the large red wheels turned, the steel lever glittered, rising and falling like a gigantic knife. Maklakov uttered a subdued exclamation.

"What is it?" asked Yevsey.

"Nothing," answered the spy, annoyed. His cheeks were flushed, he was biting his lips. By the look on his face Yevsey guessed that he was watching the writer, who was walking along without haste, twirling his mustache, accompanied by an elderly, thick-set man, with an unbuttoned coat and a light summer hat on a large head. The latter was laughing aloud, and exclaiming as he raised his red-bearded face, "I drove on and on . . ."

The writer lifted his hat, and bowed to somebody. His hair was cut short, his forehead was lofty. He had high cheekbones, a broad nose, and narrow eyes. Klimkov found his face coarse and unpleasant. His large red mustache added something military and harsh to it.

"Come," said Maklakov. "They will probably drive away together. We must be very careful. The one who just arrived is a man with great experience."

In the street they took a cab.

"Follow that carriage," Maklakov said to the driver. He was silent for a long time, sitting with bent back and swaying body. "Last summer," he finally muttered, "I was in his house making a search."

"At the writer's house?" asked Yevsey.

"Yes. Drive on farther," Maklakov ordered quickly, noticing that the cab in front had stopped.

A minute later he jumped from the cab, and thrust some money into the driver's hand.

"Wait," he said to Yevsey, and disappeared in the damp darkness. Yevsey heard his voice: "Excuse me, is this Yakovlev's house?"

Someone answered in a hollow voice, "This is Pertzev's house."

"And which is Yakovlev's?"

"I don't know."

"Sorry . . ."

Yevsey leaned against the fence, counting Maklakov's leisurely steps.

"It's a simple thing, just to follow people," he thought.

The spy returned and seemed upset by something.

"We can do nothing here," he said. "Tomorrow morning you will put on a different suit, and watch this house."

They walked down the street. Maklakov's quick talk throbbed in Klimkov's ears like the rumble of a drum.

"Remember the faces, the dress, and the walk of the people who enter this house. There are no two people alike. Each has something peculiar to himself. You must learn at once to seize upon this peculiar something in a person—in his eyes, in his voice, in the way he holds his hands when he walks, in the manner in which he lifts his hat in greeting. Our work above all demands a good memory."

Yevsey felt that the spy was talking to him with concealed hostility and this upset him.

"Your face is too noticeable, especially your eyes. This won't do. You mustn't go about without a disguise, without something to occupy you. Your general appearance is perhaps that of a street hawker. You ought to have a tray to carry pins, and needles, and tape, hairpins, ribbon, all sorts of haberdashery. I will see that you get it. Then you can call at back doors and get acquainted with the servants." Maklakov fell silent, removed his beard, put it in his pocket, set his hat straight, and settled down to a more leisurely walk. "Servants are always ready to spring something unpleasant upon their masters. It's easy to wheedle something out of them, especially the women—cooks, nurses, chambermaids. They like to gossip. I must say I'm chilled to the bone," he said, ending his instructions on a different note. "Let's go to a public house."

"I have no money."

"That's all right."

In the public house he asked in the stern voice of one used to prompt attention, "A glass of brandy, a large one, and two beers. Will you have some brandy?"

"No, I don't drink," answered Yevsey, embarrassed.

"That's a good thing."

The spy looked searchingly into Klimkov's face, smoothed his mustache, closed his eyes for a minute, and stretched his whole body, so that his bones cracked. When he had drunk the brandy he continued in an undertone, "It's good, too, that you're not talkative. Tell me what you think about all the time."

Yevsey lowered his head, and answered after a pause, "About myself, about everything . . ."

"But what in particular?"

Maklakov's eyes gleamed softly and Yevsey answered frankly, "I think perhaps it would be better for me to retire to a monastery."

"Why? Do you believe in God?"

After a moment's thought Yevsey said as if apologizing, "I do. Only I am not thinking about God, but about myself. What am I to God?"

"Well, let's drink anyway."

Klimkov bravely gulped down a glass of beer. It was cold and bitter and sent a shiver through his whole body. He licked his lips, and suddenly asked, "Do they beat you often?"

"Me? Who?" the spy exclaimed, both amazed and offended.

"Not you, but all spies in general."

"You must say 'agents,' not 'spies,'" Maklakov corrected him, smiling. "Yes, they do beat people, but I, personally, have never been beaten."

He became lost in reflection. His shoulders drooped, he seemed to shrink and a shadow crept over his white face.

"Ours is a dog's life. People look upon us in an ugly enough light," he whispered, then his face broke into a smile, and he bent toward Yevsey. "Only once in five years have I seen myself treated as another human being . . . It was in Mironov's house. I came to him with gendarmes, in the uniform of a superintendent. I was not well at the time, I had a fever, and was scarcely able to stand on my feet. He received us civilly, with a smile, slightly embarrassed. Such a large man he is, with long hands and a mustache like a cat's. He walked with us from room to room, addressed us all with the respectful 'you,' apologized if he happened to push against us. We all felt awkward in his presence—the colonel, the inspector, and the rest of us small fry. Everybody knew the man; his pictures had appeared in the newspapers, he's even known abroad. And here we were paying him a night call. One almost felt ashamed. I noticed him look at me. Then he walked up closer to me, and said, 'You ought to sit down. You know, you look as if you were ill. Please sit down.' His words upset me very much. I sat down and thought to myself, 'Get away from me.' But he went on, 'Will you take a powder?' Everybody was silent, no one looked at me or at him." Maklakov laughed softly. "He gave me some quinine in a capsule, and I chewed it. There I was, with an insufferable bitterness in my mouth and a turmoil in my soul. I felt I would collapse if I attempted to stand. Here the colonel intervened, and ordered me to be taken to the police station; the search was just about completed anyway. The inspector said, 'I'm sorry, but I am afraid I must arrest you.' 'Well, what of it?' he said. 'Arrest me! Everyone does what he can.' He said it so simply with a smile on his face."

Yevsey liked the story. It touched his heart like a soft caress and reawakened in him the desire to be useful to Maklakov.

"He's a good man," he thought approvingly of the spy.

The spy sighed. He called for another glass of brandy, and sipped it slowly. Suddenly he began to look drawn and dropped his head on the table.

Yevsey wanted to speak, words darted about in disorder in his brain, but failed to arrange themselves in any sort of intelligible, clear language. Finally, after many attempts, Yevsey found what he wanted to ask.

"Is he, too, in the service of our enemies?"

"Who?" asked the spy, scarcely raising his head.

"The writer."

"What enemies? What do you mean?" The spy's face was mocking and his lips curled in derision. Yevsey felt embarrassed, and Maklakov without awaiting his answer rose and tossed a silver coin on the table.

"Put it on the bill," he said to someone.

He put on his hat, and walked to the door without another word to Klimkov. Yevsey followed on tiptoe, not daring to put on his hat.

"Be on the spot at nine o'clock tomorrow. You will be relieved at twelve," said Maklakov, already in the street.

He thrust his hands in his coat pockets and disappeared.

"He didn't even say 'good-bye,'" thought Yevsey offended, as he walked along the deserted street.

He felt ill. Darkness surrounded him on all sides. It was cold. The clinging bitter taste of the beer sank from his mouth into his chest, and his heart beat unevenly. Vague thoughts stirred in his head like heavy flakes of autumn snow.

"There, I've served a day. If only somebody had liked me a little . . ."

Chapter 10

IN THE NIGHT Yevsey dreamed that his cousin Yashka was sitting on his chest, had seized him by the throat, and was strangling him. He awoke and heard Piotr's angry, dry voice in the next room, "I spit upon the empire and on all this humbug!"

A woman laughed, and someone's thin voice resounded, "Hush, hush, don't bawl."

"I have no time to distinguish who is right, and who is wrong. I am not a fool, I am young, and I want to live. This scoundrel reads me lectures about autocracy when I have been running around for four hours dressed up as a waiter, serving every sort of rogue. My feet are sore, my back aches from bowing. If autocracy is of such importance to you, then you have to pay for it. But I'm not going to sell my pride to autocracy for a mere penny. My God, I won't!"

Several hours later Yevsey was sitting on the curbstone opposite Pertzev's house. He paced back and forth past the house for a long time, counted the windows, measured its length with his steps, studied in all its details the grey front that seemed to have spread from old age; finally he grew tired and sat down on the stone. But he had not much time to rest. The writer came out of the door with an overcoat flung over his shoulders, no overshoes, his hat on one side. He crossed the street and came straight up to Yevsey.

"He's going to hit me," thought Yevsey, looking at the stern face and the frowning reddish brows. He tried to rise to his feet and go, but was unable to move, chained to the spot by fear.

"What are you sitting there for?" he heard an angry voice.

"For no particular reason . . ."

"Get away from here."

"I can't."

"Here's a letter. Go. Give it to the man who sent you."

"I can't . . ."

"Why not?"

The large blue eyes commanded. Yevsey had not the power to disobey the glance. Turning his face aside, he mumbled, "I— I—I have no permission—to take anything from you—or to exchange words with you."

The author smiled a wry smile and pushed the envelope into Yevsey's hand.

Klimkov took the grey envelope and walked away, holding it in his right hand on a level with his breast, as if it were something murderous, threatening unfathomable misfortune. His fingers ached as if from the cold.

"What will happen to me now?" the terrifying thought rang insistently in his brain.

Suddenly he noticed the envelope was not sealed. This amazed him. He stopped, looked around, and quickly pulled out the letter.

"Relieve me of this fool. Mironov," he read.

He heaved a sigh of relief.

"I must give this to Maklakov. He is sure to scold me though . . ."

His fear had disappeared, but he felt sad as he realized how unfit he was for the work and that he had again failed to please the spy whom he liked so much.

He found Maklakov at dinner in the company of a little squint-eyed man dressed in black.

"Let me introduce you. Klimkov—Krasavin."

Yevsey put his hand in his pocket to get out the letter and said in an embarrassed tone:

"This is the way it happened—"

Maklakov held up his hand. "You'll tell me later. Sit down and eat."

His face was weary, his eyes dim, his light straight hair untidy.

"He must have been drunk last night," thought Yevsey.

"No, Timofey Vasilyevich," the squint-eyed man went on coldly and solemnly. "You are wrong. There's something pleasant in every type of work if your heart is in it."

Maklakov glanced at him, and drank a large glass of vodka in one gulp.

"They are men, just as we are, but that doesn't signify anything. One says one thing, the other says another and I, in all that, do as I like."

The squint-eyed man noticed that Yevsey was watching the uncontrolled movement of his eyes, and put on a pair of spectacles with tortoise-shell rims. His movements were soft and alert, like a black cat's. His teeth were small and sharp, his nose straight and thin. When he spoke his little pink ears stirred. His crooked fingers kept rapidly rolling the bread into little pellets, which he placed on the edge of his plate.

"An assistant?" he asked, nodding his head toward Yevsey.

"Yes."

"How are things going, young man?"

"I only started yesterday . . ."

Krasavin nodded his head. Twisting his thin dark mustache, he began to speak smoothly. "Of course, Timofey Vasilyevich, you can't step on the tail of destiny. According to God's law, children grow old, old people die. Only all this doesn't concern you and me. We've got our appointed task. We have been told to catch the people who try to sabotage law and order, that's all. It's a hard business, a complicated one. Perhaps we could call it a kind of hunt."

Maklakov rose from the table, and walked to a corner, where he beckoned Yevsey.

"Well, what was it?"

Yevsey handed him the note. The spy read it, looked into Klimkov's face in astonishment, and then read it again.

"Where did this come from?" he asked in a low voice.

Yevsey answered in an embarrassed whisper, "He gave it to me himself. He came out into the street . . ."

Expecting a rebuke, or even a blow, he bent his neck, but when he heard a low laugh he cautiously raised his head, and saw the spy looking at the envelope with a broad smile on his face and a merry gleam in his eyes.

"What a queer one you are!" said Maklakov. "Now you'd better keep quiet about this."

"Am I to congratulate you on a successful piece of work?" asked Krasavin.

"Yes, indeed," said Maklakov. "But the Japs licked us after all, Gavrilo," he exclaimed merrily, rubbing his hands.

"I cannot, I admit, accept your delight at this event," said Krasavin, moving his ears. "Although it was a lesson, as many say, still so much Russian blood was shed and our lack of strength was made so apparent . . ."

"And who is to blame?"

"The Jap. What does he want? Every country ought to live within its own boundaries."

An earnest discussion followed, to which Yevsey, reassured by Maklakov's attitude, paid no attention. He looked into the spy's face, and thought it would be well to live with him instead of with Piotr, who grumbled against his lot and the authorities, and could well be arrested for it as they had arrested Old Pipe.

Krasavin left. Maklakov took out the letter, read it once again, and burst out laughing, looking at Yevsey.

"Now don't say a word about this to anybody. Do you understand? He came out himself, you say?"

"Yes. He came out and said, 'Get away from here.'" Yevsey smiled guiltily.

Narrowing his eyes, the spy looked through the window, and said slowly, "Yes, you ought to take to the hawker's trade. I told you so. Today you are free. I have nothing more for you to do. Good-bye. I'll try and arrange something else for you very soon."

Maklakov held out his hand. Yevsey touched it gratefully, and walked away feeling for once quite happy.

Chapter 11

AFTER A FEW weeks Klimkov began to feel more at ease. Every morning, warmly and comfortably dressed, with a box of haberdashery slung across his chest, he set off to receive instructions either at one of the pubs where the spies gathered, or at a police station, or at the lodgings of one of his colleagues. The directions given him were simple and clear.

"Go to such and such a house. Get to know the servants. Find out how the masters live."

On his first visit to the servants' quarters, he would try to bribe them by the cheapness of his goods and by little presents. Then he would carefully question them about those particular details his bosses were interested in. When he felt that the information gathered was insufficient, he was inclined to make up the deficiency from his own head, inventing it according to the plan drafted for him by the old, fat, and very sensitive Solovyov.

"Men that interest us," Solovyov once had said in a smug, sugary voice, "all have the same habits. They believe in God, they go to church, they dress poorly, but they are civil in their manners. They read many books, sit up late at night, often have large gatherings of guests, but drink little wine and don't play cards. They talk about foreign countries, about systems of government, about socialism and freedom for the people. They also talk about the great masses of the poor, declaring it necessary to stir them up to revolt against our Czar, to overthrow the entire government and take possession of the highest offices, and by means of socialism again introduce serfdom, under which they will have complete liberty." The spy's warm voice broke off. He coughed and heaved a heartfelt sigh. "Liberty—everybody likes and desires liberty. But if you give me liberty, who knows that I won't become the worst villain in the world? This is the problem. It is impossible to give complete freedom even to a child. The Holy Fathers, God's saints, even they were subject to temptations of the flesh, even they fell from grace. People's lives are held together, not by liberty but by fear. Man must be governed by laws. But the revolutionaries reject law. They are divided among themselves. Some want to make quick work of the ministers and the faithful subjects of the Czar with the help of bombs and things like that. The others are willing to wait a little; first they'll have a general riot, they say, then they'll massacre everybody at once." Solovyov raised his eyes pensively to the ceiling and and paused for a second. "It is difficult for us to make head or tail of their politics. Maybe they do, in fact, understand something, but as far as we are concerned it is all treacherous nonsense. We fulfill the will of the Czar, the anointed sovereign of God. It is he who is responsible for us before God, so it is our duty to do what he bids us. And in order to gain the confidence of the revolutionaries you must complain, 'Life is very hard for the poor'; you must say, 'The police ill-treat us, and there's no law of any sort.' Although they are people of villainous intent, yet they are a credulous lot, and you can always catch them with that bait. Be cunning with their servants, for they aren't at all stupid, either. If you have to, reduce the price of your goods rather than lose them as customers. But beware of arousing suspicion. They could well begin to think, 'What is it all about? He sells very cheap, and asks prying questions.' The best thing for you to do is to strike up friendships. Take a dainty, hot, full-breasted little thing, and you'll reap all sorts of benefits from her. She will sew shirts for you, and invite you to spend the night with her, and you can then ferret out all you want to know. You know the kind—a tiny, soft little mouse of a girl. A woman can open many a door to you."

This round, pock-marked man, with hairy arms and thick lips, was inclined to talk about women. He would lower his soft voice to a whisper, his neck would begin to sweat, his feet would shuffle uneasily, and his eyes, which lacked both eyebrows and eyelashes, would fill with warm, oily moisture. Yevsey, with his keen sense of smell, was quick to observe that Solovyov always smelt of hot, greasy, decaying meat.

When Yevsey had been working for the police, spies were considered to be people who knew everything, held everything in the palms of their hands, and had friends and helpers everywhere. Though they could have seized all the dangerous people at once, they avoided doing this simply because they had no wish to deprive themselves of future employment. On entering the Security Department they all swore an oath to show no mercy, either to father, mother, or brother, or to discuss together the sacred task which they vowed they would serve all their lives.

Yevsey had expected to find stern-looking individuals; he had pictured them as speaking little, using words unintelligible to ordinary people, possessing the miraculous powers of a sorcerer, able to read a man's thoughts and knowing all the mysteries of life.

Now, however, from his careful observation of them he could see quite clearly that they were not unusual at all and no more dangerous than other people. In fact they seemed to live in a greater spirit of friendliness than people usually did. They spoke frankly of their mistakes and their failures, they often laughed at themselves, and without exception, all were equally fervent in abusing their superiors, though admittedly with varying degrees of wrath.

One was conscious of a close bond uniting them, and of their solicitude for one another. When it happened that someone was late for a meeting or failed to appear at all, there was a general sense of uneasiness about the absent member, and Yevsey, Zarubin, or some one of the numerous group of "assistants" would be dispatched to look for him at some other meeting place.

One striking feature was the lack of greed about money among the majority of the spies and the readiness to share it with comrades who had gambled it away or squandered it in some debauchery. They all loved games of chance, took a childish interest in card tricks, and envied the dexterity of the cardsharp.

With acute envy they informed one another of the debauchery of their superiors, described in detail the anatomies of the loose women they happened to know, and hotly discussed the various methods of their sexual relationships. Most of them were unmarried, almost all were young, and for each of them a woman was something like alcohol—she soothed and lulled one to sleep, brought relief from the anxieties of their dog's life. Almost all kept pornographic photographs in their pockets, which from time to time they examined to the accompaniment of various obscene remarks which roused in Yevsey a sharp, intoxicating curiosity, mixed sometimes with incredulity and nausea. He soon learned that some of them were homosexuals, that many were infected with unmentionable diseases and that all of them drank a great deal, mixing vodka with beer, and beer with brandy, in an effort to get drunk as quickly as possible.

Only a few of them applied the eagerness of the hunter to their work, boasted of their skill, and imagined themselves as heroes. The majority did their work in a bored, routine, uninspired way.

When they discussed the men whom they tracked like beasts of prey there was rarely any hint of the fierce hatred that seemed to well up in Sasha like a hot spring. One person who stood out was Melnikov, a heavy, hairy man with a thick, bellowing voice, who walked with an oddly bent neck and spoke little. His dark eyes were always alert, expectant, and it seemed to Yevsey as if he must be always thinking of something terrifying. Krasavin and Solovyov were also unlike the others, the first because of his cold vindictiveness, the other because of the sensual pleasure with which he spoke about beatings, bloodshed and women.

Among the young spies, the most prominent was Yakov Zarubin, constantly busy and constantly engaging the others in conversation and plying them with questions about the revolutionaries. He would knot his brows in anger and jot down notes in a little book. He was obsequious with all the important spies, though it was evident that no one liked him and his notebook was regarded with suspicion.

Most of them talked of the revolutionaries with the indifference one is inclined to feel toward a particularly boring individual; sometimes ironically as one would talk about an amusing eccentric; sometimes, too, with the annoyance with which one speaks of a child who deserves to be punished for his bad behavior. Yevsey began to imagine that all revolutionaries were empty-headed people, not at all serious, who did not know what they wanted, but merely brought disturbance and disorder into life.

Once Yevsey asked Piotr, "You said one day that the revolutionaries were in the pay of the Germans, and now I hear the others say quite different things about them."

"What do you mean by 'different'?" Piotr demanded with annoyance.

"That they are poor and stupid, and now nobody mentions the Germans any more."

"Go to the devil! What difference does it make to you? Do what you are told. Your suit is diamonds, so you lead with diamonds."

Klimkov tried to keep as far away as possible from Sasha. The ominous face of the sick man frightened him, and he was repelled by the smell of iodine and by the sniffling cantankerous voice.

"The villains!" cried Sasha, swearing at the officials. "They have millions at their disposal; they toss us a few pennies and squander hundreds of thousands on women and on all sorts of elevated individuals who, they want us to believe, work for the cause in the upper reaches of society. But it's not there, it's not the gentry that make revolutions—they ought to know that, the idiots,—revolution grows underneath, in the soil, among the people. Give me five million and in one month I'll lift the revolution up into the streets; I'll bring it out of the dark corners into the light of day."

Sasha was continually planning horrible tactics for the mass extermination of undesirable persons. His face would turn leaden, his red eyes grow strangely dim, and foam spurt from his mouth.

There was an element of distaste in people's attitude toward him but everybody feared him and tried to conceal their distaste for his disease. Maklakov alone calmly avoided any contact with him and did not even give him his hand in greeting or farewell. Sasha, in his turn, who ridiculed everybody and called all his comrades fools, plainly put Maklakov in a category by himself. He was always serious when talking to him and in fact talked more readily to him than to any of the others. He did not swear at him even behind his back.

Once when Maklakov had walked out as usual without saying good-bye to him, he said, "The gentleman is squeamish about me. He has the right to be, the devil take him! His ancestors lived in lofty rooms, they breathed pure air, ate healthy food, wore clean undergarments. He does, too, for that matter. And I'm a peasant, born and brought up like an animal, in filth, among lice, on coarse black bread. His blood is better than mine, yes, indeed, both his blood and his brain. And the brain is the soul." After a pause he added gloomily, but without any sarcasm; "Only fools talk about the equality of man! Yes, fools and liars, aristocrats and scoundrels. The aristocrat preaches equality because he is an impotent scoundrel and can't do anything himself. 'You are just as good a man as I am. Then do something to enable me to live better.' This is the theory of equality."

Sasha received sullen support from Melnikov, whose particular job was spying on the working people.

"Yes," Melnikov would say, "they are deceivers, all of them!", and nod his dark shaggy head in confirmation, firmly clenching his hairy fists.

"They ought to be destroyed as the peasants kill horse thieves," shrieked Sasha.

"To kill may be going a bit too far, but sometimes it would be a great pleasure to give one of these gentlemen a box on the ear," said the spy Chashin, a celebrated billiard player, curly-haired, lean, sharp-nosed. "Take a disgraceful case like this one, for example. About a week ago I was playing in Kononov's hotel with a gentleman. I saw his face was familiar, but then all hens have feathers! He stared at me, too. 'Go on, look at me,' I thought, 'there's no harm in that.' I fixed him for three rubles and half a dozen beers, and while we were drinking he suddenly rose to his feet and said, 'I recognize you. You are a spy. When I was in the university,' he said, 'thanks to you I spent four months in prison. You are a scoundrel,' he said. At first I was frightened, but soon I felt my temper rise. 'You got into prison not because of me but because of your politics,' I said, 'and your politics are no concern of mine. But what about me having to run after you day and night for almost a year, in all sorts of weather and then having to go into the hospital for thirteen days.' That's the truth. Fancy jumping on me like that, the pig! He had filled out his cheeks as fat as a priest, was wearing a gold watch, and had a diamond pin stuck in his tie."

Akim Grokhotov, a good-looking man with the mobile face of an actor, remarked, "I know men like that, too. When they are young, they walk on their heads; but when the serious years approach, they prance at home peacefully around their wives and for a livelihood are even ready to enter our Security Department. It's a law of nature."

"There are some among them who have no talent for anything but revolutions. And these are the most dangerous," said Melnikov.

"Yes, yes," came as a shot from Krasavin, avidly rolling his squinting eyes.

Once, having lost a great deal at cards, Piotr was heard asking in a weary, exasperated tone:

"When will this dog's life of ours ever come to an end?"

Solovyov looked at him, and chewed his thick lips.

"We are not called upon to judge such matters. Our business is simple. All we have to do is to take note of a dangerous person that the bosses have pointed out to us, or to find him for ourselves, gather information, make observations, write reports to the authorities, and then let them do as they please. For all we care they may flay people alive. Politics do not concern us. Once there was an agent in our department, Grisha Sokovnin, who also began to brood over such matters, and ended his life with the help of consumption in a prison hospital."

Conversations among the spies varied very little: one day, for example, Viekov, a hairdresser, always dressed in the latest garish fashion, but nonetheless a modest, quiet person, announced, "Three men were arrested yesterday."

"Great news!" someone responded indifferently.

But Viekov was determined to tell his comrades all he knew. A spark of gentle stubbornness flared up in his small eyes as he continued in an almost provocative tone, "The revolutionaries, it seems, are hatching plots again on Nikitskaya Street—there are great goings on there."

"What fools! All the janitors there are old hands."

"A janitor can be bribed, however," said Viekov cautiously.

"So can you. Every man can be bribed—it's a simple matter of price."

"Did you hear, boys, Siekachev won seven hundred rubles yesterday."

"But then he's a cheat at cards."

"Yes, of course. But he's a young wizard, not just a sharper."

Viekov looked around, smiled shyly, then silently and carefully smoothed out his suit.

"A new proclamation has appeared," he announced another time.

"There are scores of them. The devil knows which of them is new."

"There's a great deal of evil in them."

"Did you read them?"

"No. Filip Filippovich told me. And he's enraged about it."

"The authorities are always angry. Such is the law of nature," remarked Grokhotov with a sigh.

"Who reads those proclamations?"

"Oh, they're read all right—very much so."

"Well, what of it? I have read them, too, yet I didn't turn black. I remained what I was, red-haired. It's not a matter of proclamations, it's a matter of bombs."

"A proclamation doesn't explode."

The spies, however, did not like to talk of bombs, and each time they were mentioned, they all made a strenuous effort to change the subject.

"Forty thousand worth of gold articles were stolen in Kazan."

"Did they catch the thieves?" someone asked anxiously and excitedly.

"They're bound to be caught," prophesied another sadly.

"Well, before that happens they'll have a good run for their money."

A mist of envy enveloped them all, and they sank into dreams of revelries, big gambling stakes, and costly women.

Melnikov was more interested than the others in the course of the war and he often asked Maklakov, who read the newspapers carefully, "Are they still beating us?"

"They are."

"But why is it?" Melnikov exclaimed in perplexity, rolling his eyes. "Aren't there people enough, or what is it?"

"Not enough sense," Maklakov retorted drily.

"The workers are dissatisfied. They don't understand. They say the generals have been bribed."

"That's certainly true," Krasavin broke in. "None of them are Russians"—he swore obscenely—"what's our blood to them?"

"Blood is cheap," said Solovyov, with a strange smile.

As a rule the spies spoke of the war reluctantly, as if uneasy in one another's presence and afraid of going too far. On the day of a defeat they all drank more vodka than usual, and once drunk quarreled over trifles.

If Sasha was present at these meetings he would explode and swear at them, "You imbeciles!" he would say. "You understand nothing, you degenerates!"

In answer some would smile apologetically, while others maintained a sullen silence.

"For forty rubles a month you can't be expected to understand too much," one of them would mutter.

"You ought to be wiped off the face of the earth," Sasha would shriek back at him.

Seeing that nobody liked Sasha, Yevsey also took a dislike to him.

Many of the spies suffered from the mental strain caused by the constant dread of being attacked and killed. Fear drove some of them, as it had Yelizar Titov, into an insane asylum.

"I was playing in the club yesterday," said Piotr, embarrassed, "when I felt something pressing on the nape of my neck and a cold shiver running up and down my back. I looked around, and there in the corner stood a tall man staring at me as if he were measuring me inch by inch. I could not go on playing. I rose from the table and saw him move in his corner. I ran down the back stairs into the yard, and out into the street. I hailed a cab, sat in it sideways, and looked back. Suddenly the man appeared from somewhere in front of me, and crossed the street under the horse's very nose. Maybe it wasn't the same man at all. But when it's like that you can't think. I opened my mouth and yelled. How I yelled! He stopped, and I jumped out of the cab, and ran off as hard as I could go with the cabman after me. My God, how I ran!"

"Yes, it certainly can happen," said Grokhotov, smiling. "I once hid myself for a similar reason in a yard. But it was even worse there, so I climbed up to the roof, and sat there behind the chimney until daybreak. Man must beware of man. Such is the law of nature."

Once Krasavin came in pale and sweating, his eyes still for once.

"They are following me," he announced desperately in a low voice, pressing his hand to his head.

"Who?"

"They . . . They do . . ."

Solovyov attempted to calm him.

"Lots of people walk the streets, Gavrilo."

"I could tell by the way they were walking that they were after me."

And for more than a fortnight Yevsey did not see Krasavin at all.

The spies treated Klimkov good-naturedly, and their occasional laughter at his expense did not offend him. When he was upset over his mistakes, they comforted him, "You'll get used to the work. It'll pass!"

He was puzzled as to when the spies did in fact do their work. They seemed to spend the greater part of their time in pubs sending such insignificant fellows as himself out for observation.

He knew that behind all the spies whom he knew there were still others, desperate, fearless men, who mingled with the revolutionaries and were known by the name of *agents provocateurs*. There were only a few of them, but these few did most of the work, and directed it entirely. The authorities prized them very highly, while the street spies, envious of them, were unanimous in their dislike of them because they were aloof.

Once in the street Grokhotov pointed out one of these men to Yevsey, "Look, Klimkov!"

A tall, well-built man was walking along the pavement. His fair hair was combed back and cascaded down under his hat to his shoulders. His face was large and aristocratic, his mustache luxuriant. His well-cut clothes suggested that he was important, well-fed; a gentleman.

"You see what a fellow that is?" said Grokhotov with pride.

"He's fine, isn't he? He's one of our crack guard, a real expert. He denounced twelve bomb makers; helped them make the bombs himself. They wanted to blow up a minister. He taught them how to use them, and then denounced them. Clever, wasn't it?"

"Yes," said Yevsey, dazzled by the man's splendid appearance, so unlike the fussy street spies.

"That's the kind they are, the real ones," said Grokhotov. "Why, he could well pass as a minister himself; he has the face and figure for it. And we—what are we? Poor beggars belonging to a hungry master."

Yevsey sighed—the glorious looking spy had aroused his envy.

Ready to serve anyone or anything for a friendly look or a kind word, Klimkov ran around the town obediently, followed, questioned, and informed, and if he succeeded in pleasing, was sincerely happy. He worked hard, grew infinitely tired and had no time to think.

The serious-minded Maklakov seemed better and purer to Yevsey than any person he had ever met. He always wanted to be asking him about something, and telling him about himself—the young spy's face itself induced a feeling of confidence!

Once Yevsey asked him, "Timofey Vasilyevich, how much are the revolutionaries paid a month?"

A light shadow passed over Maklakov's bright eyes.

"What nonsense you talk," he answered in a low but angry voice.

Chapter 12

THE DAYS PASSED quickly in a constant bustle, each day just like the one before. At times Yevsey felt they would continue just like this far into the future—noisy, filled with the now familiar conversations and the now habitual running around.

But in the middle of the winter everything suddenly quivered and shook as from an earthquake. People began to open their eyes wide in anxiety, gesticulated, disputed furiously, swore, stampeded in bewilderment on one spot, as though staggering, half-blinded by a terrible blow.

It began in this way. One evening on reaching the Security Department to hand in an urgent report of his investigations, Klimkov found the atmosphere there somehow different and incomprehensible. The officials, the agents, the clerks, and the detectives appeared to have put on new faces, had become unlike their usual selves. They looked half-astonished, half-rejoicing, spoke at one moment in very low and mysterious tones, at another, loudly and angrily. There was a senseless running from room to room, listening to one another's words, a suspicious screwing-up of anxious eyes, shaking of heads and sighing; there would be a sudden lull in the talk, and an equally sudden outburst of argument. A whirlwind of fear and perplexity seemed to be sweeping the room in ever widening circles. It drove people about like dust, first blowing them into a pile, then scattering them to all sides, playing with them, knowing them to be powerless. Klimkov stood in a corner and watched the turmoil with vacant eyes, and listened with strained attention.

He saw Melnikov, his powerful neck bent and his head thrust forward, seize people by the shoulders with his hairy hands and demand in his low hollow voice, "Was it really the people?"

"More than a hundred thousand, they say."

"Hundreds killed! And the wounded . . . !" shouted Solovyov.

From somewhere came Sasha's repulsive ear-splitting voice.

"The priest ought to have been seized before anyone else. The idiots!"

Krasavin walked around with his arms folded behind his back, biting his lips and squinting in every direction.

Quiet little Viekov came and stood beside Yevsey, fiddling nervously with the buttons of his waistcoat.

"So it's come to this," he said. "My God! Bloodshed!"

"What has happened exactly?" Yevsey asked, in a low voice.

Viekov looked around warily, took Klimkov by the sleeve, and whispered:

"Yesterday the people in St. Petersburg marched with a priest and church banners to see the Czar. You understand? But they were not admitted. The soldiers were called out and blood was shed."

A handsome, respectable-looking gentleman, Leontyev, ran past them, glanced at Viekov through his pince-nez, and asked, "Where is Filip Filippovich?"

Viekov gave a start and ran after him.

Yevsey closed his eyes to search in the darkness for the meaning of what he had heard. It was easy to visualize a mass of people walking through the streets in a church procession, but he could not understand why the soldiers had fired at them and he did not believe it. He could not avoid sharing in the general agitation and he felt disturbed and ill at ease. He wanted to take part in the bustle, but unable to make up his mind to approach the spies he knew, he merely retreated still further into his corner.

Men dashed past him with what seemed to him also a desire to find some safe place where they might stop to collect their thoughts.

Maklakov, his hands thrust into his pockets, looked stealthily at the crowd. Melnikov came up to him.

"Was it on account of the war?"

"I don't know."

"What were they asking for?"

"The constitution," replied Maklakov.

The sullen spy shook his head.

"I don't believe it."

Melnikov turned heavily, like a bear, and walked away grumbling.

"No one understands anything. They're just making a noise . . ."

Yevsey went up to Maklakov, who glanced at him.

"What is it?"

"I have a report."

Maklakov waved him aside.

"Who wants to bother about reports today!"

"Timofey Vasilyevich, what does 'constitution' mean?"

"A different order of life," answered the spy quietly.

Solovyov, perspiring and red, came running up to them.

"Have you heard if they are going to send us to St. Petersburg? I think they probably will. What a thing to happen! This is a revolt, a genuine revolt. Blood has really been flowing. What does it all mean? Where will it lead?"

Something seemed to be revolving in Yevsey's brain. Over and over again he seemed to hear Maklakov's grimly spoken words, "A different order of life."

They gripped at his heart, and he longed to understand them. But around him everything was confused and senseless and the room was filled with Melnikov's angry, irritating voice.

"It is important to know what kind of people they were. The worker is one thing, the man in the street is another. One must distinguish between the two."

And Krasavin spoke distinctly, "If the ordinary people also begin to revolt against the Czar, then there are no ordinary people any more, only rebels."

"Yes, but wait, suppose there's some deception here."

"Listen, you old devil," whispered Zarubin, sliding up to Yevsey. "I've lit upon something good. Come with me, and I'll let you into the secret."

Klimkov followed him in silence for a while and then stopped.

"Where are we going?"

"To a public house. You see, there's a girl there, called Margarita. She has a friend, a little milliner and at the milliner's lodgings they read books on Saturdays—students and people like that. I'll catch them all in one go!"

"I don't want to go," said Yevsey.

"Oh, you! Ugh! You're impossible!"

A long ribbon of strange impressions was quietly winding itself round Yevsey's heart and hindered him from understanding what had happened. He walked home unobserved, carrying with him the premonition of impending misfortune, a misfortune that that seemed always to have been lying in wait somewhere for him but was now beckoning to him again, and filling his heart with a new dread. He tried to walk in the shadows close to the houses, and recalled the agitated faces and excited voices, the incoherent talk of death and blood, and the graves that dozens of bodies had been flung into like refuse on a rubbish heap.

At home he stood by the window for a long time staring at the yellow light of the streetlamp. The passers-by walked for a moment in the circle of its light, then plunged into the darkness again. So in Yevsey's brain a feeble light glimmered and across its timid glow cautious grey thoughts, helplessly holding on to one another like a procession of blind people, began slowly, clumsily to creep.

The days passed as in a delirium, filled with terrible rumors of massacre and destruction. To Yevsey these days seemed to crawl slowly over the earth like eyeless black monsters swollen with the blood they had devoured. They crawled with their huge jaws wide open, poisoning the air with a stifling, salty smell. People ran and fell, shouted and wept, mingling their tears with their blood. And the blind monsters destroyed them, crushing the old and the young, the women and the children. They were pushed ever nearer to their doom by the ruler of their lives, by fear—fear as powerful as the current of a great stream.

Though the thing had happened at some distance, in a strange city, Yevsey knew that fear was everywhere. He felt it surrounding him on all sides.

No one understood what had happened in St. Petersburg, no one could explain anything. It stood before the people like a huge riddle and terrified them. The spies stayed in their meeting places from morning until night, reading the newspapers; they crowded in the office, where they argued, and pressed close to one another, drinking vodka and impatiently awaiting something.

"Can anybody tell me the truth?" Melnikov kept asking.

One evening a few days after the event they all met in the Security Department and Sasha delivered a sharp speech.

"Stop this nonsensical talk," he said. "It's all a plot of the Japanese. The Japanese gave Father Gapon 18,000,000 rubles to stir up the people. You understand this, don't you? The people were made drunk on the way to the palace; the revolutionaries ordered a few wineshops to be broken into. Do you follow me?" His red eyes roved about the company as if seeking those of his listeners who disagreed with him. "They thought that the Czar, loving the people as he does, would come out to them. And this was to be the moment to assassinate him. Is this quite clear?"

"Yes, it's clear," shouted Yakov Zarubin, and began to jot something down in his notebook.

"Idiot!" shouted Sasha in a surly voice. "I wasn't asking you. Melnikov, do you understand?"

Melnikov was sitting in a corner, clutching his head with both hands and swaying to and fro as if he had toothache. Without changing his position he answered, "It's all a fraud!" and his voice seemed to strike the floor with a thud, as if something soft and yet substantial had been dropped. "It's a lie, the whole of it!"

"Yes, a lie," repeated Sasha, and began again to speak quickly and coherently. Sometimes he would touch his forehead, then look at his fingers and wipe them on his knee. Yevsey had the sensation that even his very words reeked with his own particular putrid smell. He understood everything the spy said, but felt that his speech did not erase, in fact, could not erase, from his mind the terrible picture of the feast of death.

Everybody was silent; they shook their heads from time to time and refrained from looking at one another. The room was still and dismal. Sasha's words seemed to float a long time in the air over their heads, and touched nobody.

"If it was known that the people had been deceived, then why were they killed?" the unexpected question suddenly burst from Melnikov.

"Fool!" screamed Sasha. "Suppose you had been told that I was your wife's lover, and you got drunk and came at me with a knife, what should I do? Say 'Strike!' even though they told you a lie and I am not guilty?"

Melnikov started to his feet, drew himself up, and roared, "Stop barking, you dog!"

A tremor ran through Yevsey at his words, and frail and nerveless little Viekov, who sat beside him, whispered in fright, "Oh, God! Hold him!"

Sasha bared his teeth, thrust one hand into his pocket and drew back. All the spies—the room was crowded—sat silent and motionless, watching Sasha's hand. Melnikov waved his hat and walked slowly to the door.

"I'm not afraid of your pistol."

He slammed the door behind him. Viekov got up to lock it, and said as he returned to his place, "What a dangerous man!"

"So," continued Sasha, pulling a revolver from his pocket and examining it. "Tomorrow morning each of you is going to get down to business, do you hear? And you must bear in mind that now you will all have more to do than you had before. Some of us will be going to St. Petersburg. That's the first thing. The second thing is that this is the time when you'll have to keep your eyes and ears particularly wide open, because people are going to babble all sorts of nonsense about all this. The revolutionaries will not be so cautious now, you understand?"

The handsome Grokhotov drew a loud breath and said, "If it's true about the Japs . . . and such large sums of money . . . it explains everything, of course."

"Without some explanation it doesn't make sense," said someone.

"Everybody is interested in this revolt."

The voices sounded apathetic and strained.

"Well, now you know what you are about, and how you should reply to the rabble," said Sasha angrily. "And if some donkey should begin to bray, take him by the neck, whistle for a policeman, and off with him to the police station. They'll know how to deal with people like that. Here, Viekov, or somebody, ring the bell and order some soda water!"

Yakov Zarubin rushed to the bell.

Sasha glanced at him, and baring his teeth, said, "You puppy, don't be angry with me for shutting you up . . ."

"I'm not angry . . ."

"Ye-e-s," Grokhotov drawled pensively. "Still they are a power, you can't deny it. To raise a hundred thousand people is no easy matter, after all . . ."

"Stupidity is as light as air, it's easy to raise," Sasha interrupted him. "They had the money to do it. Just you give me a sum of money like that, and I'll show you how to make history." Sasha uttered an ugly oath, rose from the sofa, stretched out the thin yellow hand which held the revolver, screwed up his eyes, and aiming at the ceiling, cried through his teeth in a yearning, sobbing voice, "My God, I would show you!"

This talk seemed to Yevsey to be as effective as a few drops of rain fighting the flames of a fire. It did not extinguish the mounting fear, and could not halt the quiet growth of a premonition of disaster.

It was about this time that a new attitude toward the people unconsciously developed in Yevsey's mind. He learned that on the one hand one section of the people might gather in the streets in the thousands in order to go to the rich and powerful Czar and ask him for help, while another section might kill these tens of thousands for doing so. He recalled everything Old Pipe had said about the poverty of the people and the wealth of the Czar, and was convinced that both sides acted in the way they did from fear. Some of them were perpetually frightened by the poverty they lived in, the others lived in fear of becoming poor.

Nevertheless people astonished him by their desperate bravery, and aroused in him feelings he had never known before.

Now, when he was walking the streets as usual with the little tray across his chest, he would carefully step aside to make way for the passers-by, taking either to the middle of the street, or pressing himself against the walls of the houses; he began, however, to look into people's faces more attentively, with a feeling akin to respect. The faces of human beings seemed suddenly to have changed, to have acquired more variety and significance; the people seemed to talk with one another more readily and more simply, and to walk more briskly, and with a firmer tread.

Chapter 13

YEVSEY OFTEN WENT to a house occupied by a doctor and a journalist upon whom he was assigned to spy. The doctor employed a wet nurse named Masha, a plump, round woman with merry sky-blue eyes, full-breasted, luscious and healthy. Yevsey took a fancy to the warm-hearted young creature. Always neatly dressed in a white or blue tunic with a string of beads around her bare neck, she had a quick way of speaking, but now and then drawled in a kind of singsong voice. It seemed to Yevsey that she smelled of hot rye bread and he liked to hear her talk about her village.

He saw her five days after Sasha had explained the cause of the uprising. He found her sitting on the bed in the cook's room. Her face was swollen, and her lower lip stuck out in a comic fashion.

"Good morning," she said sullenly. "We don't want anything. You can go away. We don't want anything."

"Have the masters upset you?" Yevsey asked. Though he felt that this was not the case, he considered it his professional duty to ask this question. Then he sighed affectedly and added, "You work for them your whole life long . . ."

The cook, a thin, ill-tempered woman, suddenly cried out, "Her brother-in-law was killed, and her sister whipped so hard that she had to be taken to the hospital."

"In St. Petersburg?" Yevsey inquired softly.

"Yes, of course."

"What for?"

"Who knows why they killed them all, the fiends!"

Masha took a great breath, and groaned plaintively. "Oh, God!

He was a bookbinder, a peaceful fellow, he didn't drink at all. He made about forty rubles a month. They beat Tania, and she's going to have a child soon. They put a bullet through his friend's leg; maimed and killed them all, the brutes! May they live in torment!"

Disheveled and pitiful, she shrieked in desperate rage, then flung herself on the bed and buried her head in the pillow, moaning and trembling convulsively.

"Her uncle sent her a letter from there," said the cook, dashing from the table to the stove and back again. "You ought to hear what he has to say! The whole street is reading the letter. Nobody can make head or tail of it all. The people marched with the holy ikons, and they had the priests with them—everything in Christian fashion. They went to the Czar to tell him, 'Father, our Emperor, don't let's have so many officials. Life isn't worth living with so many of them; we have all these taxes to pay for them but they are never satisfied and there's no limit to their greediness, they are drinking our very blood!' Everything was honest and open, they had been preparing it for a whole month, the police had been informed, and no one stopped them. So, they started out and marched along, when suddenly out of the blue the soldiers began firing on them. They surrounded them on all sides and shot at them, and hacked them and trampled them down under their horses' hooves! Children and all! They kept up the massacre for two days. Can you imagine it?"

Her sharp, unpleasant voice sank into a whisper, above which could be heard the spluttering of the butter on the stove, the angry gurgle of the water boiling in the kettle, the dull roaring of the fire, and Masha's groans. Feeling he had to say something in reply to the cook's questions, and wanting to console Masha, Yevsey coughed cautiously, and said without looking at anybody, "They say it was the Japs who were behind the whole business."

"S-s-s-o?" the cook almost yelled in derision. "The Japs, why, of course, it was the Japs! We know these Japs, they all come from home. Our master explained to us who they are. You just talk to my brother about the Japs, he, too, knows their real names. Blackguards, they are, not Japs!"

From what Melnikov had said Yevsey knew that the cook's brother Matvey Zimin worked as a joiner in a furniture factory and read prohibited books. Now, all of a sudden, he was seized with the desire to tell her that the police knew about Zimin's political unreliability. But at that minute Masha jumped down from the bed, and screamed as she tidied her hair; "They can't find any decent explanation, so they have to invent the Japs!"

"The blackguards!" drawled the cook. "Yesterday in the marketplace someone was also preaching about the Japs. One old man was listening, and you should just have heard what he had to say about the generals, and the ministers, and even the Czar himself. He really let himself go! No, you can't fool the people!"

Klimkov looked down at the floor and was silent. The desire to tell the cook that watch was being kept upon her brother had now vanished. He could not help thinking that each one of the dead had had relatives now left just as bewildered as these two, and asking one another "Why did it happen? What was it all for?" They wept, and hatred welled up in their hearts, hatred of the murderers and of those who endeavored to justify the crime. He sighed and said, "A horrible deed has been done." He thought to himself, "But I have to defend the officials too . . ."

Masha pushed the door into the kitchen with her foot, leaving. Yevsey remained alone with the cook, who threw a sidelong glance at the door and mumbled, "The woman is in despair. Even her milk has turned. This is the third day she hasn't been able to nurse. Look here, hawker, Thursday week is her birthday, and I'll be celebrating my namesday then, too—suppose you come here as a guest, and make her a little present, say, of a good string of beads. You've got to comfort a person some way or another."

"Thank you. I'll come."

Klimkov walked away slowly, weighing in his mind all that the women had said to him. The cook's talk was too noisy, too sure, so that one realized at once that what she expressed were not her own sentiments but those of others. As for Masha, her grief did not touch him. Nonetheless, he felt that such was unusual and courageous beyond the usual run. Yevsey had his own explanation of the uprising; it was simply fear that had pushed the people one against the other, and those who were armed and crazed with fear had wiped out those who were unarmed and crazed with despair. But somehow this explanation failed to bring him peace of mind. He realized from what he had seen and heard that people were apparently beginning to free themselves from the grip of fear, were obstinately seeking out the guilty, and when they found them, they issued their verdict. Everywhere thousands of secret leaflets were appearing, describing the bloody days in St. Petersburg, cursing the Czar, and urging the people not to trust their rulers. Yevsey read a few of these leaflets. Though their language was unintelligible to him, he sensed something dangerous in them, something that irresistibly made its way into his heart and filled him with fresh alarm. He resolved not to read them any more.

Strict orders were given to find the printing office from which the leaflets poured out, and to catch the persons who distributed them. Sasha swore, and even on one occasion slapped Viekov's face for some vague offense. Filip Filippovich invited the agents to come to him in the evenings, to discuss matters with them. He usually sat in the middle of the room behind his desk, resting his hands on it, his long fingers gently toying with pencils, pens, and papers. Various gems sparkled in different colors on his fingers. From under his black beard gleamed a large yellow medal. He moved his short neck slowly, and the blue, fathomless glasses of his spectacles rested in turn upon the faces of all the people present, who meekly and silently sat against the wall. He scarcely ever rose from his armchair. Nothing moved but his fingers and his neck. His heavy face, bloated and white, looked like a face in a portrait; his beard seemed to be artificial. When silent, he was impressive, but the instant he spoke in his thin, shrill voice, which screeched like an iron saw being filed, everything about him, the black frockcoat and the medal, the gems, and the beard, began to look as if they belonged to somebody else. Sometimes Yevsey fancied that sitting in front of him was a cleverly contrived puppet and hidden inside it a shriveled-up manikin, resembling a little devil. If someone were to shout at the puppet, he imagined, the little devil would get frightened, jump out with a squeak and leap through the window.

But he was afraid of Filip Filippovich, and in order not to at-

tract to himself the steady gaze behind the blue spectacles, he sat
as far as possible from him, trying hard not to move.

"Gentlemen," the thin voice trembled in the air, tickling Yevsey's heart like a cold steel probe. "You must remember my words.
Every one of you should put your entire mind, your entire soul,
into the struggle with the secret and treacherous enemy. In the
struggle for the life of our mother Russia, all means are permis-
sible. The revolutionaries are not squeamish as to the means they
employ; they do not stop at murder. Remember how many of your
comrades have perished at their hands. I do not tell you to kill.
No, of course not. To kill a man requires no cleverness. Any fool
can kill. The law is on your side. You go against the lawless. It
would be criminal to spare them. They mustn't be spared, they
must be destroyed like poisonous weeds. You must find out for
yourselves what is the best way to stifle the rising revolution. The
Czar and the country demand this of you." After a pause during
which he examined his rings, he went on, "You have too little
energy, too little love for your calling. For instance, you have let
slip the old revolutionary Saydakov. I happen to know that he
lived in our town for three and a half months. Second, up to now
you have failed to find the printing office."

"Without *agents provocateurs* it is hard," someone ventured
in an offended tone.

"Don't interrupt, if you please. I myself know what is hard and
what is easy. Up to now you have not been able to gather serious
evidence against a whole lot of people known for their seditious
tendencies; you cannot give enough grounds for their arrest."

"Arrest them without grounds," said Piotr with a laugh.

"Why be facetious? I am speaking seriously. If we were to arrest
them without grounds, we should simply have to let them go again.
That's all. And you personally, Piotr Petrovich, I would like to
remind you that you promised me something a long time ago.
Do you remember? You, too, Krasavin. You said you had succeeded in getting to know a man who might lead you to the
terrorists. Well, and what has come of it?"

"The man was a crook. But wait a bit longer. I know what I
have to do," Krasavin answered calmly.

"I have no doubt of it whatsoever, but I beg all of you to understand that we must work more energetically; we must get things moving faster."

Sometimes he would speak for an hour at a time, without apparently taking breath, calmly and in the same level tone. The only words that he uttered any differently were the words "You must." They seemed to seize Yevsey by the throat and make him choke. Again and again they came back till the "must" seemed to fill the room each time the blue rays of his glassy stare scoured his audience.

After meetings like these the spies would turn to one another, "Um, yes, himself a converted Jew, and just look at him!"

"They say he got a raise of six hundred rubles last New Year."

From time to time handsome, richly dressed Leontyev addressed the spies in place of Filip Filippovich. He did not remain seated, but paced up and down the room with his hands in his pockets, politely stepping out of everybody's way. His smooth face, perpetually drawn in a frown, had a cold and fastidious expression, his thin lips moved reluctantly, and one could hardly see his eyes.

Sometimes another man named Yasnogursky came from St. Petersburg. He was a small, broad-shouldered, bald man with a decoration on his breast. He had a huge mouth, a flabby face, hard eyes like two little stones, and long hands. When he spoke he smacked his lips loudly, pouring out streams of strong oaths. One sentence of his particularly impressed itself on Yevsey's memory. "They say to the people, 'You can organize another life, an easier life for yourselves.' But they lie, my children. The Emperor, our Czar and our Holy Church organize life, and the people can alter nothing, nothing."

All the speakers said the same thing; the police must serve more zealously, must work more keenly because the revolutionaries were growing more and more powerful. Sometimes they spoke about the czars, how good and wise they were, how people from foreign lands feared and hated them because they had always liberated other nations from a foreign yoke . . . : the Bulgarians and Serbians from the rule of the Turkish sultan; the Khivans, Bokhars, and Turkomans from the Persian Shah; the Manchurians from the Chinese emperor. The Germans, the English, and the Japanese looked upon this with disfavor. They would have liked to seize for themselves the nations Russia had liberated. But they knew the Czar would not allow this, and so they hated him and wished him all evil, and were trying to stir up the revolution in Russia.

Yevsey listened to these speeches, waiting for the moment when the Russian people themselves would be mentioned and it would be explained why all men were terrifying and cruel, why they loved to torture one another, and lived such restless, uncomfortable lives. He wanted to hear what the cause was for such dire poverty, such universal fear, and the angry groans that rose on every side. But of such things no one spoke.

After one of the meetings Viekov said to Yevsey as the two were walking down the street, "So it means that they are coming into power. Did you hear? It's impossible to understand how it can come about. There are secret people who live underground, and then suddenly they cause confusion and shatter one's whole life. It's very hard to comprehend where they get their power."

Melnikov was even more morose and taciturn than ever now; he had grown thin and was always disheveled. One day he struck his knee with his fist, and roared, "I wish to know the truth. How can one get at the truth?"

"What's the matter?" asked Maklakov crossly.

"What's the matter? This is the matter: as I understand it, one group of officials, our group, has lost its power. Now another group is taking over power over the people; it's as simple as that."

"And the result is—just rubbish!" said Maklakov, laughing.

Melnikov looked at him, and sighed, "Don't lie, Timofey Vasilyevich. You lie, you know. You are a wise man, but you lie."

The talks about the revolutionaries sank into Klimkov's mind, creating in it a thin layer of new soil for the growth of frail ideas. These thoughts disturbed him, and gently drew him into unknown territory.

Chapter 14

ON HIS WAY to take part in Masha's birthday celebration, the thought occurred to Yevsey, "I am going to meet the carpenter today. He's a revolutionary."

Yevsey was the first guest to arrive. He gave Masha a string of blue beads, and Anfissa a pink comb. They were both delighted with the gifts, and treated him to tea and cherry liqueur. Arching her full white neck, Masha peered into his face with a gentle smile and her eyes warmly caressed his heart. Anfissa poured out the tea and asked, "Well, our generous little merchant, when are we going to celebrate your wedding?"

Yevsey, trying not to show his embarrassment, said frankly, "I'll never be able to make up my mind to get married. It's too difficult."

"Difficult? Oh, the timid man! Marya, do you hear? He says it's difficult to get married."

Masha smiled in answer to the cook's loud laugh, looking at Klimkov from the corner of her eye.

"Maybe difficult has another meaning for him."

"Yes, it has," said Yevsey, raising his head. "You see what I think is that it would be difficult to find a person with whom one could live soul to soul, without fearing each other . . . I mean to find a person whom one could trust."

Masha sat down beside him. He glanced sideways at her neck, at her breast and sighed.

"Suppose I were to tell them where I work?" he wondered. Frightened by the idea, he made an effort to suppress it.

"If a man does not understand life," he went on hastily, raising his voice, "it's better for him to remain alone."

"It's also hard to be alone," said Masha, pouring out another glass of liqueur for him. "Drink this up."

Yevsey longed to talk to them openly, without restraint. He saw that they listened to him willingly; and this together with the two glasses of liqueur excited him. But the journalist's housemaid, Liza, came in at that moment, also excited, and immediately held Anfissa's and Masha's attention. With a cast in one eye, lively, her hair well groomed and smartly dressed, she seemed a pretty and unashamed young woman.

"My so-and-so's have invited guests for dinner, and did not want to let me go," she said, sitting down. "'No, no,' I said, 'I don't mind what you do, but . . .'"

"Many guests?" Klimkov asked automatically, remembering his duty.

"Oh, yes! But what sort of guests! There's not one of them would ever slip a coin into your hand. Even on New Year's Day all I got from them all was a tip of two rubles and thirty kopeks."

"They're probably not rich, are they?" asked Yevsey.

"Rich? Oh, no! All their galoshes have holes in them."

"Who are they? Where do they work?"

"In different places. Some write for the newspapers, some are just students. Oh, what a handsome boy one of the students is! Black eyebrows, curly hair, and a little mustache, white even teeth —and lively as a cricket. He came from Siberia not long ago; he's always talking about hunting."

Yevsey looked at Liza, and bent his head. He wanted to say "Stop!" to her. Instead he asked in a low voice, "An exile, I suppose?"

"Who can tell? My master and mistress were exiles, too, so the policeman told me."

"Yes, and nowadays who hasn't been an exile?" exclaimed the cook. "I used to live in an engineer's house; his name was Popov and he was rich, had his own house and horses and was getting ready to marry. Suddenly the police came one night, and pounced on him. And he was sent off to Siberia."

"I can't criticize my masters at all," Liza interrupted, "not a bit of it. They are decent people. They don't scold. They're not grasping, like other people are. And they know everything and can talk about everything."

Yevsey looked helplessly at Masha's rosy cheeks, and thought, "I'd better go and find out about her masters another time . . . But I'd so much rather stay . . . If only she would stop talking, the little fool!"

"Our masters can understand everything, too," Masha announced with pride.

"When that thing happened, that riot in St. Petersburg," Liza began in great excitement, "they stayed up the whole night talking."

"Yes, our master and mistress went to your house then," the wet nurse remarked.

"Yes, the house was full of people. They talked, wrote complaints, and one of them even began to weep. I swear he did!"

"There's plenty to weep about," sighed the cook.

"This man clutched his head, and sobbed. 'Unfortunate Russia!' he kept saying. They gave him water, and even I was sorry for him and started to cry myself."

Masha began to look around wildly.

"My God, when I think of my sister!" She rose and went into the cook's room. The women watched her go with sympathetic glances. Klimkov sighed with relief and again automatically asked Liza, with an air of boredom, "To whom did they make these complaints?"

"That I don't know," answered Liza.

"Marya went off to cry," said the cook.

The door opened, and the cook's brother came in coughing.

"It's bitterly cold," he said, pulling a red scarf off his neck.

"Here, have a drink, then!"

"Thank you, I certainly will," he said. "Your good health and best wishes!"

He was lean and moved about easily, without haste. There was a grave note in his voice that somehow did not fit in with his light beard and his pointed skull. His face was small, thin, and modest, his eyes large and hazel.

"A revolutionary," Yevsey reminded himself, silently pressing the carpenter's hand. "It's time for me to be going," he announced.

"Where to?" cried Anfissa, seizing his hand. "Say, merchant, surely you don't have to break up the party just yet? Look, what a present he's given me!"

Zimin looked at Yevsey, and said thoughtfully, "Yesterday our factory got another order. A drawing room, a study, a bedroom. All the orders come from the military nowadays. With the money they've stolen they all want to live in the latest style."

"There you are!" Yevsey registered mentally, with some annoyance. "He begins the minute he comes in! Oh, Lord!"

Without thinking what his question might lead to, he asked the carpenter, "Are there any revolutionaries in your factory?"

As if touched on the raw, Zimin quickly turned to him, and looked into his eyes. The cook frowned, and said in a low, grumbling voice, "They say that they're all over the place nowadays."

"Is it because they're clever or stupid?" asked Liza.

Unable to withstand the carpenter's hard, searching look, Klimkov slowly bowed his head.

"Why should that interest you?" Zimin inquired, politely but sternly.

"I have no particular interest," Yevsey answered listlessly.

"Then why do you ask?"

"For no particular reason," said Yevsey; and in a few seconds added, "Just for something to say."

The carpenter smiled.

It seemed to Yevsey that three pairs of eyes were fixed on him suspiciously, severely. He felt ill at ease, and something bitter was nipping his throat. Masha came out of the cook's room, smiling guiltily. When she saw the others' faces, the smile faded.

"What's the matter?"

"It's the wine," flashed through Yevsey's mind. He rose to his feet, staggered, and said, "I asked because I wanted long ago to tell your sister—about you."

Zimin also rose. His face gathered in wrinkles, and turned yellow.

"Tell her what about me?" he asked with calm dignity.

Masha's quiet whisper reached Yevsey's ears. "What's going on between them?"

"I know," said Yevsey. He had the sensation that he had levitated from the floor and was floating about in space as light as a feather. He could see everything, and observe everything with marvelous clarity. "I know you're being followed by an agent of the Security Department."

The cook swung in her chair, crying out in astonishment and fright, "Matvey? What does that mean?"

"Wait," said Zimin, stretching his hand reassuringly before her face. "This is a serious matter." To Yevsey, he said in a firm, stern tone, "Look here, young man, you should be going home. And I, too, must go. Put on your overcoat."

Yevsey smiled. He still felt empty and light and it was not an unpleasant sensation. He hardly remembered how he walked away, but he did not forget that they all remained silent, and no one said good-bye to him.

In the street Zimin nudged his shoulder, and said in a clear low voice, "I must ask you not to visit my sister any more."

"Why? Have I offended you?" asked Yevsey.

"Who are you?"

"A pedlar."

"How is it you know that I am being followed?"

"A friend told me."

"A spy?"

"Yes."

"And you are a spy, too?"

"No," said Yevsey. But looking into Zimin's lean, pale face, he remembered the calm and dull sound of his voice, and without any effort corrected himself. "Yes, I am."

They walked a few steps in silence.

"Well, go away!" said Zimin, suddenly stopping in his tracks. His voice sounded subdued, he shook his head strangely. "Go away, I'm telling you!"

Yevsey leaned with his back against the hedge and gazed at the man, his eyes blinking. Zimin, too, looked at Yevsey, and waved his right hand.

"But don't you see," said Yevsey, bewildered. "I only told you the truth, that you are being followed . . ."

"Well?"

"And you are angry?"

Zimin bent toward him, and poured a stream of hissing sounds upon Klimkov.

"Yes, damn your miserable soul! I know without your help that they are following me. So what? Is your business going badly? Did you think you'd bribe me and betray people behind my back? You loathsome creature! Or was it just to salve your own conscience? Well, you can go to the devil, then, and I am telling you, go now, or else I'll tear you limb from limb!" Yevsey braced himself, and walked away.

"Vermin!" he heard behind him in a contemptuous whisper.

Klimkov turned around, and for the first time in his life swore at a man, with the whole power of his voice, "Vermin yourself!" he shouted. "You son of a bitch!"

Zimin did not reply. His steps were inaudible. Somewhere Yevsey heard the snow crunching under the runners of a sleigh and the grinding of iron on stone.

"He went back there," thought Klimkov, walking slowly along the pavement. "He'll tell them. Masha'll be angry with me . . ." He spat, then started humming a song. Then he stopped again beside a lamppost, feeling he had to find some consolation somewhere.

"Here I am, walking along, and I can sing if I want to. If a policeman hears me and asks, 'What are you bawling there for?' I'll show him my ticket from the Security Department. 'Oh, my apologies!' he'll say. But if the carpenter should sing, he'll be hustled off to the police station at once. 'You can't disturb the peace like that!' Klimkov smiled, and peered into the darkness. "Yes, brother, not much chance for you to sing."

This failed to reassure him. There was sadness in his heart, and a thick bitter taste clung to his mouth, causing tears to well up in his eyes. He went on with the song, but this time using all the power of his lungs, shutting his eyes tight. It made no difference. Dry, prickly tears trickled through his eyelids and chilled the skin on his cheeks.

"Driver!" he called out in a low voice, still trying to put on a bold front. But when he had sat down in the sleigh he felt the tension inside him suddenly loosen. His head drooped, and swaying from side to side he mumbled, "A fine way to treat a man—very fine way—thank you! Oh, you good people, you wise people."

He found this indulgence in self-pity quite pleasurable. It filled his heart with an intoxicating sweetness that he had often experienced in his childhood. It made him look like a martyr to other people, and of more significance to himself.

Chapter 15

NEXT MORNING Yevsey lay in bed frowning up at the ceiling, deliberating despondently on what had happened the day before. "No, it's not other people I ought to be watching at all," he thought, "I ought to be watching myself." The idea seemed strange to him. "Why? Am I then my own enemy?"

He began to dress lazily, forcing himself to think about the duties of the day—he was assigned to a factory suburb.

The sun was shining, gurgling water flowed down the roofs and washed away the dirty snow. People were going about quickly and merrily. The kindly chimes of the Lenten bells floated slowly in the warm air, the wide ribbon of soft sounds soared and flew away from the town into the pale blue distance.

"If only I could go away somewhere in the country, into the fields!" thought Yevsey, as he entered the narrow streets of the factory suburb.

All around him rose the red grimy walls; the sky overhead was dirty with smoke, the air was steeped in the smell of warm oil. It was all unlovely, and the eyes quickly wearied at the endless row of smoke-blackened factories where the men worked.

Klimkov walked into a public house, sat down at a small table next to the window, ordered some tea and began to listen to the general conversation. There were not many people there, but all were workers, who lazily exchanged a few words as they ate and drank. Somewhere from a corner came a bold young voice, "When you think about it, where does wealth come from?"

Yevsey turned away, annoyed. He frequently heard people talking about wealth, and it always aroused in him a sense of bored perplexity. He felt that such talk was dictated only by envy and greed. He knew also that officially these matters were considered particularly dangerous.

"You work for nothing, and what you buy you pay a lot for. Isn't it so? All wealth is simply accumulated from the money which we ought to be getting. For example . . ."

"How greedy they all are, how grasping," thought Yevsey. "How greedily Masha grabbed my beads, last night . . . they're worth nothing, all of them . . . And her brother didn't hit me simply because he was scared I'd call the police . . . Threw me out of the house but kept my presents . . . The swine . . ."

Delighting in the satisfying bitterness that comes from criticizing others, he no longer heard or saw anything. Suddenly a hearty voice rang out beside him, "Why, it's Yevsey Klimkov!"

He raised his head hastily, and saw standing before him a curly-headed youth he did not recognize.

"You don't recognize me? Don't you remember Yakov? We're cousins."

He laughed and sat down at the table. His laughter enveloped Klimkov in a warm cloud of reminiscences—of the church, the quiet ravine, the fire, and the blacksmith's talks. Smiling silently in embarrassment, he timorously shook his cousin's hand.

"I didn't recognize you."

"No wonder!" exclaimed Yakov. "In town one's memory grows weaker, so many new things crowd in your brain, leaving no room for old ones. But I did—at once! You haven't changed at all . . . How have you been getting on?"

Klimkov answered cautiously. He did not quite understand why he felt that this meeting could be dangerous for him. But Yakov spoke for both. He gave a rapid account of the village, as if it were necessary for him to get through with it as quickly as possible. In two minutes he had told Yevsey that his father had become blind, that his mother was ailing, and that he had been living in the town for three years working in a factory.

"There you've got the whole story."

Yakov was thickly, almost affectedly, begrimed with soot; he spoke loudly, and though his clothes were torn, there was an air of prosperity about him. Klimkov looked at him with curious pleasure; he recalled without malice how often this strong boy had beaten him and at the same time he asked himself anxiously, "Is he perhaps also a revolutionary?"

"Well, how are you getting along?" repeated Yakov.

"And how about you?"

"Work is hard, and life is simple. In fact there's so much work— there's no time to live at all. Your whole day, your whole life goes to your employer, you keep only minutes for yourself. There's never any time to read a book. I'd often like to go to a theater, but then when would I sleep? Do you ever read books?"

"I? No."

"Of course, you have no time either. I do find time to read a bit, though. You can get such wonderful books here! You start one and you're carried away, as if you were in your lover's arms. It's true! How do you manage with girls? Are you lucky?"

"Not too bad," said Yevsey.

"They're wonderful to me! The girls here, too—oh, yes, they're fine! Do you go to the theater?"

"Yes, now and then."

"I love it. I lap it all up, as if I were going to die tomorrow. I love listening to music, for instance . . . The zoological gardens —now there's a wonderful place for you, too."

The flush of excitement broke through the black layer of dirt on Yakov's cheeks. His eyes burned. He smacked his lips, as if he were enjoying something refreshing and nourishing.

Envy stirred in Yevsey, envy of this healthy body with its keen appetites. He stubbornly reminded himself how Yakov had pummeled his sides with his powerful fists. But Yakov's radiant talk went on and on; the ringing exultant words and exclamations fluttered around Yevsey like swallows. He could not help smiling, but it seemed to him that he was being split in two, torn between the desire to listen and an awkward, almost guilty feeling. He turned his head, and suddenly caught a glimpse of Grokhotov through the window. Torn trousers, dirty jackets, and shirts hung across the spy's left shoulder and arm. He gave Yevsey a barely perceptible wink as he shouted in a sour voice, "Old clothes, buy and sell old clothes!"

"It's time for me to be going," said Yevsey, jumping to his feet.

"You are free on Sundays, aren't you? Come to see me. No, perhaps I'd better come to you. Where do you live?"

Yevsey was silent. He did not want to tell him where he lodged.

"What's the matter? Are you living with a girl? Never mind. You'll introduce me to her, that's all. What are you ashamed of? Have I guessed right?"

"You see, I don't live alone."

"I understand."

"But I don't live with a girl. I live with an old man."

Yakov guffawed.

"You're a funny one, the way you talk! Well, we don't want an old man, of course. And I live with two friends, so it's not convenient to call on me either. Let's agree on a place where we can meet."

They decided on a meeting place, and left the eating house. Departing, Yakov gave his cousin an affectionate and vigorous handshake and Yevsey left him hurriedly as if he feared his cousin might return to take away the gesture. On his way he reflected dismally, "This is the toughest district of all; they say it's a hotbed of revolutionaries; Yakov is going to be in my way."

A feeling of angry irritation came over his soul like a grey shadow.

"Old clothes for sale!" sang Grokhotov behind him, then whispered, "What about buying one of my shirts?"

Yevsey turned round, took one of the tattered garments from Grokhotov and examined it silently, while the spy, as he praised his wares aloud, managed to get in a whisper. "You know, you're really on the track of something here. That curly haired fellow, I've had my eye on him. He's a socialist all right. You hold on to him, and you'll catch plenty of them that way." Then he snatched the rag from Yevsey's hand, and shouted as if cut to the quick. "Five kopeks for a garment like this? You mock me, friend, and I don't like it. We'd better part company, you and I." And shouting as he went Grokhotov strode down the street.

"There, now it's I who'll be followed," thought Yevsey, looking at Grokhotov's back.

When a spy with little experience made contact with one of the workers, he was obliged to report the fact immediately to his leader, and the latter either gave him as an assistant a spy with more experience, or he himself would join the workers; after which it would be said of him enviously, "He's 'noosed in' with the double agents."

The role of double agent was considered dangerous, but the authorities gave rewards for the betrayal of a complete group of people and therefore all the spies not only gladly "noosed themselves in," but sometimes even tripped one another up to snatch away the lucky opportunity, thus often ruining the whole business. More than once it happened that a spy had already wheedled himself into a group of workers when suddenly in some mysterious manner they learned of his profession and would beat him up if he didn't manage to get away in time. This was called "snapping the noose."

It was hard for Klimkov to believe that Yakov was a socialist, though at the same time he wanted to believe it. The envy his cousin had aroused in him was transformed again into an irritation against him for standing in his way. Once again Yevsey remembered the blows his cousin had rained upon him long ago.

In the evening, he informed Piotr of his meeting.

"Well, and what are you doing about it?" asked Piotr angrily. "Do you have to wait to be told what the next step is? What the devil is the use of teaching you people?" And Piotr hurried off, restless, drawn, with dark circles under his eyes.

"He's lost again at cards," thought Yevsey despondently.

The next day Sasha came to hear of Yevsey's stroke of luck. He questioned him in detail, thought for a while, then smiled his ugly smile and began giving Klimkov instructions.

"Let a little time go by, and then you can tell them discreetly that you've been made a clerk in a printing office, see? Very likely they'll ask you if you can get them some type. Tell them you can, but you have to talk offhandedly, so that they can see it doesn't matter to you whether you get it or not. Don't ask questions, act a little foolish, which should come natural to you. But let me tell you if you botch this little job, things will go hard for you . . . After every meeting report to me what you have heard."

In front of Sasha, Yevsey felt like a puppy on a lead. He looked
at the spy's pimply yellow face, and could think of nothing; he
simply waited for the moment when Sasha would release him
from the cloud of repulsive smells that made him want to vomit.

He went to meet Yakov feeling as empty as a funnel. But when
he saw his cousin with a cigarette between his lips and his hat
cocked on one side, he gave him a friendly smile.

"How's business?" shouted Yakov merrily.

"I've found a job," replied Yevsey and then the next instant he
thought, "I'm rushing my fences."

"What sort of job?"

"Clerk in a printing office."

Yakov gave a loud whistle.

"In a printing office? Indeed!" He grew thoughtful for a moment. Then, with sudden animation, "Well, are you coming out
with me this evening? We'll have good company, two girls, one a
milliner, the other works in a thread factory. There'll be a lock-
smith there, too, a young chap, he sings and plays the guitar. And
two others, as well, all fine people."

Yakov spoke quickly, and his eyes smiled happily at everything
he saw. He stopped in front of the shop windows and examined
their contents with the gaze of a man to whom all things are
equally attractive and interesting.

"Look, what a dress, eh? Think of our Olga wrapped in something like that, why, she'd trip on it! Books—I've read this one,
the little yellow one, *The Original Man*, it's interesting! You
should read it, you'd see how man has developed . . . Books open
up all the tricks of life. I don't like fat books; you forget the beginning when you've read to the middle and the middle when
you've read to the end. It's better when they write briefly!"

He pointed at a gun shop, and cried ecstatically, "Look at those
revolvers! Just like toys."

Surrendering to Yakov's mood, Yevsey let his gaze wander over
the articles in the window, and then he smiled in astonishment
as if he were seeing for the first time the beautiful, alluring multitude of bright materials, the gaily colored books, the dazzling
mixture of colors and metals. He liked the sound of Yakov's young

voice, the rapid talk steeped in the joy of living. It penetrated so easily the dark void of Klimkov's soul and allowed him to forget about himself.

"You're a jolly fellow," he said approvingly.

"I am. I learned to dance from the Cossacks. We've got about a score of Cossacks at the factory. Did you hear our men were on the point of striking? Yes, they were; it was in all the newspapers."

"Why are they going to strike?" asked Yevsey, provoked by the simplicity with which Yakov spoke of a strike.

"What do you mean by 'Why?' We workers don't get a fair deal! What else can we do about it?"

"And you'd do the same?"

"What? Rebel? Of course! What else? We're friends, all of us!"

"And what about the Cossacks?"

"The Cossacks? They're all right. At the beginning they thought they would lord it over us, but they came round in the end. 'Comrades, give us some leaflets, too,' they said."

Yakov suddenly broke off and looked into Yevsey's face, frowning. For a minute he walked in silence.

The mention of the leaflets reminded Yevsey of his duty. He wrinkled up his forehead as if in pain and wanting to push something away from himself and from his cousin, he said in a low voice, "I've read those leaflets."

"Well?" asked Yakov, slowing down.

"I don't understand them . . . What are they for?"

"You read them again."

"I don't want to."

"You're not interested, in fact?"

"No."

For a while they walked in silence. Yakov whistled meditatively, glancing from time to time at his cousin.

"No, these leaflets are something very precious, and all the slaves of labor ought to read them," Yakov began in a deep, low voice. "We are prisoners, brother, chained to toil for the rest of our lives. We are slaves of capitalism, that's what we are. Isn't it true? But these leaflets are a breath of freedom, they liberate our minds, they break the chains like rust breaks iron."

Klimkov walked more rapidly. He did not want to hear Yakov's smooth talk. The desire even darted through his mind to say, "You must not talk like that to me! Please!"

But Yakov himself stopped short.

"Here we are at the zoo!"

They drank a bottle of beer in the refreshment room, and listened to the military band.

"It's splendid, isn't it?" said Yakov, nudging Yevsey's side with his elbow. When the playing ceased, Yakov sighed. "That was *Faust* they were playing. An opera. I saw it three times in the theater. Oh, it's beautiful! The story is stupid, but the music, oh, so good! Come, let's have a look at the monkeys."

On the way to the monkey house he gave Yevsey an entertaining account of the story of Faust and the devil Mephistopheles. He even attempted to sing an aria or two, but this was beyond him and he burst out laughing.

The music, Yakov's account of the opera, the laughter and chatter of the crowds in their holiday clothes, and the dazzling spring sky—all this intoxicated Klimkov.

"How bold he is!" he thought in amazement, as he looked at Yakov. "And he knows what it's all about. Yet he's the same age as I am."

It seemed to Yevsey that his cousin was forcing open a row of little doors for him one by one and from behind each one of them came ever sweeter noise and light. He stared about him, absorbing the new impressions, and then for a second his eyes would open wide in anxiety. He thought he had seen the familiar face of one of the spies darting about in the crowd.

The two young men stood in front of the monkey cage. With a good-natured smile, Yakov said, "Just look at them! Aren't they exactly like human beings? Don't you think so? The eyes, the faces, how intelligent they are altogether, aren't they?" He suddenly broke off to listen to something. "Wait a minute, there they are!" He disappeared and in a minute returned leading a girl and a young man in a sleeveless jacket up to Yevsey. Yakov cried out happily, "You told me you wouldn't be coming here, you traitors! This is my cousin Yevsey Klimkov. I told you about him. This is Olga—Olga Konstantinovna, and this is Aleksey Stepanovich Makarov."

Klimkov bowed clumsily and silently pressed the hands of his new friends.

"There, he's going to 'noose me in,'" he thought. "I ought to get out now."

But he did not want to go at all, although he found himself anxiously searching the crowd for a glimpse of one of the spies. He saw none, however.

"He's not easy to get to know," said Yakov to the girl. "He's not like me, sinner that I am."

"You mustn't feel uneasy with us. We're simple people," said Olga.

She was a head taller than Yevsey, and her height was increased by her fair hair brushed up on top of her head. Her grey-blue eyes smiled serenely in a pale oval face.

The face of the man in the sleeveless jacket was kind, his eyes were friendly, his movements slow. As he walked he swayed his apparently powerful body with a sort of unconcern.

"Are we going to wander about here forever, like unrepentant sinners?" he asked in a soft, deep voice.

"Let's find somewhere to sit down."

Olga bent her head to look into Klimkov's face.

"Have you ever been here before?"

"No. This is the first time."

He walked at her side trying for some reason to lift his feet higher; this made walking more awkward. They sat down at a table and asked for beer. Yakov cracked jokes, while Makarov whistled softly and studied the passers-by through his screwed-up eyes.

"Have you any friends?" asked Olga.

"No, not one."

"That's what struck me straightway about you. I could see you were a lonely person. Lonely people walk in a special way," she said, smiling. "How old are you?"

"I'll be nineteen very soon."

"Look, there goes a spy!" Makarov exclaimed softly.

Yevsey jumped to his feet, but sat down again immediately. He looked at Olga to see if she had noticed his involuntary movement of alarm. It was impossible to tell, however. She was silently and attentively examining Melnikov's dark figure. The spy made his way with a great deal of effort between the tables, neck bent and eyes fastened on the ground. His arms hung by his sides as if they were dislocated.

"He walks like Judas toward the aspen tree," said Yakov in a low voice.

"He looks drunk to me," observed Makarov.

"No, he's always like that," was on the tip of Yevsey's tongue. He fidgeted in his chair.

Melnikov thrust himself into the crowd like a dark pebble and was soon lost in its gaily colored stream.

"Did you notice how he walked?" Olga asked Klimkov.

Yevsey raised his head, and looked at her attentively, with expectation.

"He must be a scoundrel, but miserable and lonely. I think that loneliness can drive a weak man to anything."

"Yes," said Klimkov in a whisper, with sudden awareness. He looked into the girl's face gratefully, and repeated in a louder tone. "Yes."

"I knew him about four years ago," Makarov said. His face seemed suddenly to have grown longer and leaner. His bones became visible, his eyes opened up, they grew darker and looked firmly into the distance. "He denounced one student who had given us books to read and a worker, Tikhonov. The student was exiled; Tikhonov went to prison for about a year and later died of typhus."

"Are you afraid of spies?" Olga suddenly asked Klimkov.

"Why?" Yevsey returned dully.

"You gave a start when you saw him."

Rubbing his throat vigorously, Yevsey answered without looking at her, "That was just because I know him, too."

"Aha!" Makarov drawled, smiling.

"You're a dark horse, you are!" exclaimed Yakov.

Klimkov did not understand their exclamations, or their kind looks, but he kept silent, terrified that in spite of himself he might say something that would destroy the precarious but sweet fool's paradise he was basking in.

The fresh spring evening came on softly, benignly, subduing sounds and colors. The sun was setting in a red sky and the brass band was playing a soft, pensive tune.

"Well," said Makarov, "are we going to stay here, or are we going home?"

They decided to go home. On the way Olga asked Klimkov, "Have you ever been in prison?"

"Yes," he answered, but after a moment added, "not for long."

They took the tramway, and then Yevsey found himself in a little room with blue wallpaper. It was close and stifling, and merriness alternated with gloom. Makarov played the guitar and sang songs which Yevsey had never heard before. Yakov boldly discussed everything in the world, laughing at the rich and swearing at the masters. Then he danced, shrieking and whistling and filling the whole room with the stamping of his foot. The guitar accentuated the rhythm and Makarov encouraged Yakov with cheers and shouts.

"Keep going, Yasha! The gay frighten sorrow away!"

Olga looked on serenely, and often asked Klimkov, smiling at him, "He's good, isn't he?"

Drunk with a quiet joy previously unknown to him, Klimkov smiled in response. He forgot himself, and only occasionally felt something tugging at his heart for a few seconds. Before his consciousness was able to transform this feeling into clear thought, it disappeared, without a trace.

It was not until he had reached his home that he remembered his obligation to deliver these happy souls into the hands of the police. The thought sent a wave of cold anguish to his heart. He stopped in the middle of the room, his brain numb! Breathing became difficult, and he passed a dry tongue over his lips. He quickly took off his clothes and sat down at the window in his underclothes. After several minutes of sitting there, half-paralyzed, he thought, "I will tell them, I will tell her, Olga . . ."

But at that very minute he recalled the angry and contemptuous cry of the carpenter Zimin, "Vermin!" Klimkov shook his head and abandoned the idea. "I'll write to her. I'll just say, 'Beware!'—and I'll tell her about myself."

The thought cheered him. The next minute, however, he reasoned, "They'll find my letter when they make the search, they'll recognize my handwriting and then I'm finished."

He sat at the window till almost daybreak. It seemed to him that his entire body had shriveled up, deflated like a burst balloon. He was sick at heart with misery; the outside world pressed upon him and was filled with faces lying in wait for him. Sasha's sinister face leered somewhere among them, like a red ball. Klimkov doubled up, trying to hide within himself and then, at last he rose, tiptoed to the bed, and noiselessly hid himself under the blanket.

Chapter 16

LIFE, LIKE A HORSE that has stood idle too long, began to be strangely capricious, refusing to submit to the will of those who held the reins just as senselessly, cruelly, and blindly as before.

Every evening the men of the Security Department spoke more and more alarmingly of new signs of general unrest among the people, of the secret league of peasants who had resolved to seize the land from the landowners, of the gatherings of workers who had begun openly to criticize the government, and of the power of the revolutionaries which was clearly growing from day to day. Filip Filippovich continued relentlessly to stir up the spies of the Department with his rasping, irritating voice, reproaching them for their lack of zeal. And Yasnogursky, despondently smacking his lips, cast his eyes to heaven in tragic appeal, pressing his hands to his heart, "My children! Remember that service on behalf of the Czar is never wasted."

But when Krasavin inquired gloomily, "What are we supposed to do?" he merely waved his hands. His deep black mouth gaped strangely, unable to find a reply.

"Catch them!" he finally shouted.

Yevsey heard the dapper Leontyev cough drily, and say to Sasha, "It seems our old methods of fighting sedition no longer work in these days of universal madness."

"Ye-e-e-s, you can't put out fire with spittle," hissed Sasha, a smile distorting his ugly face.

They were all nervous; the room was in an uproar with complaints and shouting. Sasha dragged his long legs and cried in bitter scorn, afraid of nothing, "So that's it, is it! The revolutionaries are getting the better of you, are they?"

The spies roamed about the streets day and night, and every evening brought back long reports of their observations. They said to one another gloomily, "Is this what we have to do now?"

No one, apparently, knew how to stop the growth of a nationwide uprising.

"They won't use gloves when they handle us," said Piotr, cracking his knuckles.

"They'll take us off the permanent staff if we remain alive at all," Solovyov added dismally. "If they would even give us a pension. But they won't."

"It'll be a noose around our necks, no pension," said Melnikov somberly.

The people who but a short time ago had been so awe-inspiring in Yevsey's eyes, who had appeared to him to be so powerful, now fluttered about the streets like last year's dried leaves.

He observed with amazement that there were other people, simple and trusting, who marched boldly ahead, cheerfully overcoming all the obstacles in their way. He compared them with the spies who crept along the streets and into houses wearily, stealthily, spying on these people in order to throw them into prison some night, and he saw quite clearly that the spies did not believe in what they were doing.

He liked Olga, her deep, active compassion for people; he liked the noisy, somewhat boastful chatterbox Yakov, the easygoing Aleksey, who would give away his last shirt to anyone who asked him. He met more and more new people, convinced of the victory of their dreams and unthinkingly surrendered to their faith.

Observing the quick crumbling of that power which he had hitherto submissively served, Yevsey began searching for some way to avoid the necessity of betraying his friends.

"If I go to see them," he reasoned, "it will be impossible for me not to denounce them. To hand them over to another agent is still worse. I must tell them. Now that they are becoming more powerful, it will be better for me to be on their side."

So, yielding to the attraction these new people had for him, he visited Yakov more frequently and spent more and more time with Olga. After each visit he quietly reported to Sasha every detail of what they said and what they intended to do. He enjoyed talking about them, in fact, he repeated their talks with secret satisfaction.

"Oh, you idiot," sniffed Sasha, angrily and sarcastically staring at Klimkov with his dim eyes. "You must lead them on yourself. For instance, did you hint that you could supply the type? . . . Well, did you, you fool?"

"No, I haven't yet."

"Well, what are you waiting for? Suggest it to them tomorrow, you half-wit!"

It was easy for Klimkov to do what Sasha told him. Both Olga and Yakov had already asked him if he could get type for them. Each time he had avoided giving them a definite answer.

The next evening he went to Olga, feeling the dark feeling of emptiness in his heart that was always there in moments of nervous tension. The resolution to carry out the mission was the work of another person's will; he did not have to think about it. This resolution spread, grew within him, and crowded out all fear, all awkwardness, all sympathy.

But when he saw the tall figure of Olga standing before him in the small dimly lit room and behind her her large shadow on the wall which slowly moved to meet him, Klimkov lost courage, grew confused, and stood in the doorway without a word.

"What's the matter with you? Are you sick?" Olga said, pressing his hand.

She turned up the light in the lamp and, pouring out the tea, went on, "You look very ill . . ."

Klimkov decided to get the business over at once.

"Look here. You said you needed type."

"I did. I know you'll give it to us."

She said these words simply, but they were like a blow to Yevsey. He threw himself back in the chair, very surprised.

"What makes you think so?" he asked in a hollow voice.

"When I asked you you didn't say yes or no. So naturally I concluded you would give it to us."

Yevsey did not understand. He tried not to meet her eyes. "But why?" he queried again.

"It must be because I consider you a serious man. I trust you."

"You mustn't trust anyone," said Yevsey.

"What nonsense, of course you must be trusting."

"And suppose you are mistaken?"

She shrugged her shoulders.

"Not to trust a man, to take him for a cheat and a liar before knowing him, how can one do such a thing?"

"I can supply the type," said Yevsey with a sigh. The task was accomplished. He sat silently for several minutes, his head bowed, his hands pressed tightly between his knees, while he listened to Olga.

Olga leaned her elbows on the table, and whispered to him when and where the promised type was required. Now that he had fulfilled his duty a stifling nausea slowly rose from the depths of his soul; the ghastly feeling that created a deep rift within him, awakened again, filling him with misery.

"Have you noticed," the girl said in a soft voice, "how little time it takes for people to know one another? We all seek friends and find them. People have become more trusting, more bold."

Even her words seemed to smile. Not daring to look Olga in the face, Klimkov watched her shadow on the wall and mentally drew upon it her blue eyes, the small mouth with the pale lips, her face, somewhat weary, soft, and kind.

"Shall I tell her now that it's all a trick to destroy her?" he asked himself.

And then he heard his own answer. "She'll throw me out. She'll curse me and throw me out."

"Do you know Zimin the carpenter?" he suddenly asked.

"No, why?"

Yevsey sighed heavily. "For no reason. He's a good man, too, a socialist."

"If she had known the carpenter," Klimkov thought slowly, "I would have told her to ask him about me. Then, perhaps—"

The chair seemed to be giving way beneath him; the nausea, he thought, was going to surge up into his throat and choke him. He coughed, threw a cursory glance around the little room, and once again she played havoc with his heart, so pure, so pale and vulnerable. The moon, as round as Yakov's face, stared in at the window, and the lamplight became irritatingly useless.

"I'll put out the light and go on my knees to the girl, embrace her and tell her everything. But would she push me away?"

The thought did not deter him. He raised himself heavily from his chair and put out his hand to the lamp. Then his hand dropped listlessly and his legs began to tremble. He swayed on his feet.

"What are you doing?" demanded Olga.

He tried to answer, but a soft gurgle came instead of words. He dropped to his knees, and seized her dress with trembling hands. She pressed her hot hand against his forehead and grasped his shoulder with the other, pushing her legs farther under the chair.

"No, no, get up!" she exclaimed sternly. "Oh, what a dreadful thing! I cannot bear it—please get up. My dear, I understand you so well, I'm sorry for you, but do get up, I don't want you to be begging . . ."

The warmth of her body roused a sensual desire in him, and he interpreted her pushing hands as an encouraging caress.

"She's no saint," darted through his mind, and he clasped the girl's knees with more determination.

"I tell you, get up!" she cried, no longer persuasively, but as a command.

He rose without having succeeded in saying anything. The girl had mixed up all his emotions and left him with something prickly in his heart.

"Try and understand—" he mumbled, spreading out his hands.

"Yes, yes, my God, I understand—my God! This always comes to block the way!" she exclaimed. Looking into his face she went on harshly, "I am sick of it. I can't be just a woman to you all . . . How pathetic you all are . . ."

She went to the window; the table was between them. A cold perplexity enveloped his heart; he was consumed with a slow, scorching wave of shame.

"Don't come to see me any more—please. It would be embarrassing for both of us."

Yevsey took his hat, flung his coat over his shoulders, and walked away with bowed head. Several minutes later he was sitting on a bench at the gate of a house, mumbling in an artificial attempt at violence, "She's a whore!" He ransacked his brain for every shameful name he could find and poured them out on the picture of Olga's slender figure in his desire to soil her whole body, to blacken her from head to toe. But oaths did not cling to her, and though Yevsey tried doggedly to rouse himself to anger, all he felt in fact was shame.

He gazed for a long time at the round solitary circle of the moon which seemed to cross the sky in bounds, as if leaping silently like a large bright rubber ball; and he could hear the soft sound of its movement like the beating of a heart. He did not care for this pale, melancholy disc which in the tragic moments of his life always seemed to eye him with cold insistence. It was late but the town was not asleep yet. Its murmur floated in the night air.

"The nights used to be quieter before," thought Klimkov. He rose and walked away without putting his arms into the sleeves of his coat; his hat was pushed back on his neck.

"Well, all right, just wait and see!" he thought. "I'll denounce them, and ask to be transferred to another town."

He turned over a few bundles of type to Makarov in three installments and found out where the printing press would be set up. This elicited public commendation from Sasha.

"Good boy! You will receive a reward."

Yevsey reacted indifferently to his praise. When Sasha left he was struck by the sharp, suddenly emaciated face of Maklakov. The spy, sitting on a sofa in a dark corner of the room, gazed from there at Yevsey's face, twirling his mustache. There was something in his eyes that touched Yevsey to the quick, and he turned aside.

"Klimkov, come here," the spy called out.

Klimkov went and sat beside him.

"Is it true that you are denouncing your brother?" asked Maklakov in a low voice.

"My cousin."

"You have no regrets?"

"No." Remembering words he had often heard from above,

Yevsey repeated them softly, "For us, as for soldiers, there is neither mother, nor father, nor brother, only enemies of the Czar and of our country."

"Well, of course," said Maklakov, smiling.

Klimkov understood from his voice and smile that the spy was mocking him. He felt offended.

"Maybe I am sorry. But if I have to serve honestly and faithfully . . ."

"Of course. I'm not arguing with you, odd one."

Then Maklakov slapped him on the knee, and suddenly said, "You poor wretched little man."

Yevsey rose. "Timofey Vasilyevich," he murmured in a trembling voice.

"Well, what is it?"

"Tell me . . ."

"Tell you what?"

"I don't know."

"Well, I don't either."

Klimkov mumbled, "I am sorry for my cousin! And there's a girl there, too. They are all so much better than we are; my God they are!"

Maklakov also rose to his feet, stretched himself, and moving to the door remarked coldly, "Go to the devil!"

Yevsey remained alone. A feeling of revenge against Olga arose in his heart and it became mingled with a hatred for everyone, feeding upon his very impotence to resist it. Yevsey surrounded himself with a thoughtful defense and began to serve with a zeal previously unknown to him.

Chapter 17

GRADUALLY THE NIGHT approached on which it had been decided to arrest Olga, Yakov, and all those involved in the affair of the printing press. Yevsey knew that the secret press was located in the garden of a small house occupied by a large red-bearded man named Kostya and his wife, a stout, pock-marked woman where Olga worked as a servant. Kostya's head was closely cropped; his wife had a grey face and vague, wandering eyes. They both seemed to Yevsey like people not quite in their right mind, as though they had spent a long time in a hospital.

"What weird people they are!" he remarked to Yakov when he pointed them out one evening at Makarov's lodgings. Yakov loved to boast of his acquaintances. He proudly shook his curly head, and explained with an air of importance, "It's from their hard life. They work in cellars at night where it is damp and the air is close. They get their rest in prison. A life like that would turn anybody inside out! But they have remained happy. When Kostya tells the story of his life—in which you would think there's nothing but tears—he makes you laugh your head off . . ."

Klimkov longed to get a last look at Olga. He learned the streets the prisoners would be driven through and went to meet them, trying to persuade himself that all this did not concern him. But he could not help thinking about the girl.

"She'll certainly be frightened. She'll cry."

He walked as always, keeping in the shadows. He tried once or twice to whistle unconcernedly, but he never succeeded in stopping the steady stream of recollections about Olga. He saw her calm face, her trusting eyes, listened to her somewhat broken voice, and remembered her words, "You shouldn't speak so badly about people, Klimkov. Have you nothing to accuse yourself of? What right have you to humiliate people?"

Listening to Olga, Yevsey had always felt that she was right. Even now, he had no cause to doubt it. But he was filled with the naked desire to see her frightened, pitiful, and crying.

In the distance the wheels of a carriage began to rumble, the horses' shoes clattered. Klimkov pressed himself against the gate of a house and waited. The carriage rolled by him. He looked at it unmoved, saw two dejected faces, the grey beard of the driver, and the large mustache of the sergeant at his side.

"And that's all there is to it," he thought, "and I didn't even get a chance to see her."

But another carriage came rolling from the end of the street, and flashed past him. Yevsey could hear the cut of the whip on the horse's body and its tired snorting. The sounds seemed to hang motionless in the air. He thought they would hang there forever.

Olga was sitting beside a young gendarme, her head wrapped in a shawl. The figure of the policeman appeared on the coach box beside the driver. The familiar face, white and kind, passed him. Yevsey understood rather than actually saw that Olga was perfectly calm, not in the least afraid. For some reason he felt suddenly happy, and he said to himself as if arguing with some unpleasant interlocutor, "She won't cry, not she!"

Closing his eyes, he stood there a while longer. Then he heard steps and the jingling of spurs, and understood that the arrested men were being led along the street. He tore himself away from the spot and, trying not to make too much noise, quickly ran down the street and turned the first corner. He got home exhausted and covered with sweat.

The evening of the next day, turning his blue eyes upon Yevsey, Filip Filippovich said in an even thinner voice than usual and with considerable ceremony, "I must congratulate you, Klimkov, upon your achievement. I hope it will be the first link in a long chain of successes."

Klimkov shifted from one foot to the other, and gently

stretched out his arms as if wishing to free himself from invisible chains.

There were a few spies in the room. They listened in silence to the screeching of a saw and looked at Yevsey who sensed their glances upon him and felt awkward and bored.

When Filip Filippovich had finished talking, Yevsey asked him softly if he might be transferred to another town.

"That's nonsense, brother," said Filip Filippovich drily. "Shame on you for being such a coward. What's the matter with you? This is your first success, and you want to run away? Only I decide when a transfer is necessary. You can go now."

The reward came from Sasha.

"Hey, toadstool," he called to him, "there, take this."

Touching Yevsey's hand with his moist yellow hand, he thrust a note into his fist and walked away.

Yakov Zarubin leaped up to Yevsey. "How much?"

"Twenty-five rubles," said Klimkov, clumsily unfolding the note.

"How many people were there?"

"Seven."

Zarubin raised his eyes to the ceiling, and mumbled, "Three times seven is twenty-one. Four into seven—three and a half per person."

He whistled softly and, looking around, announced, "Sasha got a hundred and fifty, and his expense account for the affair was sixty-three rubles. They cheat the whole lot of us, fools that we are. Well, what about it, Yevsey? What about a treat . . . ?"

"Come on then," said Klimkov gingerly, holding the money. He could not decide to put it in his pocket.

On the way Zarubin said in a practical tone, "After all, your people seem to have been small fry."

"Why?" asked Klimkov, offended. "They were not small fry at all."

"They gave you little enough for them, very little indeed. I know all the rules. You can't fool me, no, indeed you can't. Krasavin once caught a single revolutionary, and he got a hundred rubles here and then they sent him another hundred from Petersburg. Solovyov got seventy-five for a lady without a passport. You see? And Maklakov? Of course he catches lawyers, professors, and writers, and they have a special price. They're not dangerous, but it must be a hard job to catch them."

Zarubin spoke without drawing breath. Klimkov was content with his chatter—it kept him from thinking.

They walked into a brothel. Zarubin, in the loud voice of an old hand there, asked the tall, gaunt, one-eyed housekeeper, "Is Lydia well? And Kapa? Yevsey, you must get to know Kapa. She's a girl, I tell you, what a girl! She'll teach you what you wouldn't learn in a hundred years without her. We want some lemonade and brandy. First of all, Yevsey, we must have this brandy and lemonade. It works like champagne, you're up in the air in a second. . . ."

"It's all the same to me."

The house was apparently an expensive one. The windows were hung with sumptuous curtains. The furniture seemed remarkable to Yevsey, the prettily dressed girls haughty and inaccessible. All this confused him. He squeezed himself into a corner, making room to let the girls pass; they appeared not to notice him as they went by, their skirts swishing past his legs. A great number of halfnaked bodies floated lazily by; differently colored mascaraed eyes rolled and flashed in their orbits, all looking nonetheless the same.

"Students?" a red-haired girl asked of her companion, a stout brunette with a high naked bosom and a blue ribbon round her neck. The latter whispered something into the redhead's ear and the girl made a face at Yevsey. He turned away from her, and said to Zarubin with annoyance in his voice, "They know who we are."

"Yes, of course. That's why they take only half the entrance price and a discount of twenty-five percent from the bill."

Yevsey drank down two glasses of the sweet sparkling liquid. It made him no merrier, but he became more insensitive to his surroundings. Two girls, Lydia and Kapitolina, joined them at their table, the one tall and strong, the other huge and heavy. Lydia's head was absurdly small in proportion to her body; her forehead was narrow, her chin prominent, her mouth round with the small

teeth of a fish, and her eyes dark and sly. Kapitolina appeared to be composed of a number of balls of various sizes. Her protruding eyes were part of the pattern, and dim as though she were blind.

Black-haired little Zarubin was restless as a fly. He sniffed, turned his head from side to side, crossed and recrossed his legs, sent his thin dark hands flying over the table to seize everything and feel everything. Watching him, Yevsey suddenly began to feel a heavy, dull irritation mounting inside him.

"The dirty rat!" he thought. "It's my money and he's chosen a hideous girl for me and a pretty one for himself."

He realized that the irritation lay far deeper than that. He filled a large glass of brandy, swallowed it, then opened his scorched mouth and rolled his eyes.

"Well done!" shouted Yakov.

The girls laughed, and for a minute Yevsey was deaf and blind, as though fast asleep.

"This Lydia, Yevsey, is my true friend, a wise girl, oh, so very smart!" Zarubin pulled Yevsey's sleeve to rouse him. "When I have deserved the attention of my superiors I'll take her away from here, marry her, and establish her in my business. Yes, Lydia darling?"

"We'll wait and see," replied the girl, languidly, looking at him sideways with her cunning eyes.

"Why art thou so silent, my friend?" asked Kapitolina in a deep bass voice, slapping Yevsey's shoulder with her heavy hand.

"She addresses everybody with 'thou,'" Yakov remarked.

"It's all the same to me," said Yevsey, without looking at the girl, and moving away from her. "Only tell her that I don't fancy her, and she'd better go away."

Everyone remained silent for a few seconds.

"The devil with you!" said Kapitolina, thickly and calmly. Supporting herself with her hand on the table, she slowly lifted her heavy body from the chair. Yevsey was annoyed because the insult didn't seem to have upset her. He looked at her, and said, "A kind of elephant, that's what she is!"

"Oh, what manners!" cried Lydia.

"Yes, Yevsey. That's impolite, brother!" Zarubin agreed. "Kapitolina Nikolayevna is an excellent girl. All connoisseurs appreciate her."

"To me it's all the same," said Yevsey. "I want some beer."

"Hey, there, give us some beer!" shouted Zarubin. "Kapa dear, be so kind as to see that we get beer."

The stout girl turned and left silently, dragging her feet on the floor. Bending over to Yevsey, Zarubin began, insinuating great experience, "You see, Yevsey, of course this is an establishment of a particular kind, and all that, but the girls are still human beings like you and me. Why insult them unnecessarily?"

"Leave me alone!" said Klimkov.

He wanted everything around him to be quiet. He wanted the girls to stop floating in the air like melancholy drifts of spring clouds. He wanted the clean-shaven pianist with the dark blue face of a drowned man to stop rapping his fingers on the yellowed teeth of the piano which resembled the jaw of a huge monster, a monster that roared and shrieked with noisy laughter. He wanted everyone to sit down and be quiet and still. He wanted the curtains of the windows to stop flapping so strangely, as if someone's unseen and spiteful hand were pulling at them from the street. Above all, he wanted Olga, dressed in white, to appear at the door. He would then rise, walk around the room, and slap everybody in the face with all his might so that Olga could see how odious he found them all and realize that she was wrong and understood nothing.

The plaintive words of Zarubin obstinately penetrated his ears, "We came here to have a good time and there you go, immediately making trouble."

Yevsey, his whole body swaying, glanced dully at Yakov's face and suddenly said to himself with cold precision, "It's on account of that son of a bitch that I got into this mess. It's all because of him."

He lifted a full bottle of beer, filled a glass for himself, drank it down, and clasping the bottle in his hand, rose from his seat.

"The money is mine, not yours, you ape!"

"What of it? You and I are comrades!"

Zarubin's black head, cropped and prickly, was thrown back.

Yevsey saw the sharp gleaming little eyes, the swarthy face, the snarling teeth.

"You sit down," he said.

Klimkov flung the bottle and hit him in the face, aiming at his eyes. The crimson blood gleamed oily and moist, and a wild joy flooded Klimkov's heart at the sight of it. He swung his arm once again, pouring the beer over himself. Everybody began to gasp, scream, and howl. Somebody's nails were driven into Klimkov's face. He was seized by the arms and legs, lifted from the floor, and carried off. Somebody spat warm sticky saliva into his face, squeezed his throat, and tore at his hair.

He came to his senses in the police station, bedraggled, scratched and wet, his clothes torn to ribbons. It all came back to him instantly and for the first time he thought, without any alarm, "What will happen now?"

A police officer whom he knew advised him to wash his face and go home. "Are they going to try me?"

"I don't know," said the police officer. He sighed, and added enviously, "Hardly that. Your bones are respected, they are privileged . . . So are you . . . You're protected."

After several quiet days Yevsey was summoned to Filip Filippovich who shouted shrilly at him, "You idiot, you ought to be setting an example of good conduct, not making scandals! If I learn anything of the kind about you again, I'll put you under arrest for a month. Do you hear me?"

Klimkov was frightened. He shrank into himself and began to live in his shell, silently, unseen, trying to exhaust himself as much as possible in order to avoid thinking.

When he met Yakov Zarubin, he noticed a small red scar over his right eye; this new feature on the spy's mobile face was a pleasure to him. The consciousness that he had found the courage and the power to strike another human being elated him.

"Why did you do it to me?" asked Yakov.

"For no reason," said Yevsey. "I was drunk."

"Well, it was stupid of you! You devil! You know what a face can mean in our service. We can't afford to spoil it."

Zarubin demanded a good dinner as recompense from Yevsey.

Chapter 18

KLIMKOV DID NOT succeed, however, in hiding from the power of hostile thoughts. The news got around among the spies that some of the ministers themselves were known to have been bribed by the enemies of the Czar and Russia. They had hatched a plot to rob the Czar of his power and replace the existing good way of life by another one, borrowed from foreign governments and harmful to the Russian people. These ministers had issued a manifesto in which they announced that with the will and consent of the Czar, freedom would soon be given to the people to assemble in crowds wherever they pleased, to speak about whatever interested them, and to write and publish anything they wanted in their newspapers. They would even be granted the liberty not to believe in God.

Filip Filippovich would consult secretly for hours with Krasavin, Sasha, Solovyov, and other experienced agents. Afterwards they all seemed gloomy and preoccupied and gave brief, unintelligible responses to their comrades' questions.

One day through the half-open door between the outer office and Filip Filippovich's study came the sound of Sasha's voice, shrill with excitement, "It's not about the constitution, it's not about politics that we ought to speak to them. We've got to convince them that the new order would destroy them—the meek ones among them would die of starvation, the bold ones would rot in jail. What sort of men have we got in our service, scum, degenerates, mentally sick, dumb animals?"

"What in the name of God are you saying?" Filip Filippovich cried out.

Then came Yasnogursky's mournful voice, "What is your plan, anyway? My good man, I must say I can't understand what you're driving at."

Piotr, Grokhotov, Yevsey, and two new spies were sitting in the office. One was a red-haired, hook-nosed man with large freckles on his face and gold spectacles; the other was clean-shaven, bald, and red-cheeked with a broad nose and a purple birthmark on his neck near his left ear. They listened avidly and in silence to every word that Sasha said, often stealing a glance at one another. Piotr rose a number of times and walked toward the door. Finally he coughed loudly as he reached the door and an unseen hand immediately closed it. The bald spy carefully felt his nose with his thick fingers and asked in a low voice, "Who was it he was calling degenerates?"

At first nobody responded, then Grokhotov sighed meekly and said, "He calls everybody that."

"He's a cunning devil!" exclaimed Piotr, smiling dreamily. "Rotten to the core, but just you watch him get stronger and stronger! That's what education will do for you!"

The bald-headed spy looked from one spy to the other with his half-blind eyes, and again inquired of them pensively, "He means us, doesn't he?"

"Politics is a clever business. And it has a strong stomach," said Grokhotov.

"If I had had an education, I might have turned up trumps, too," declared Piotr.

The red-haired spy lolled unconcernedly in his chair, his mouth constantly gaping in a yawn.

Sasha emerged from the study, purple and disheveled. He stopped at the door and looked at them.

"Eavesdropping, eh?" he asked sarcastically.

The spies came into the room one by one, sweating, grimy, exchanging weary and dismal remarks with one another. Maklakov came in frowning and ill-humored, his eyes sharp and insulting. Krasavin walked straight through into the study, his eyes half-closed, and banged the door behind him.

"The tables are going to be turned," Sasha said to Piotr. "We'll be the secret society and they'll remain utter fools. That's what's going to happen. Hey," he shouted, "no one is to leave the office. We're going to have a discussion!"

Suddenly everyone was quiet and motionless. Yasnogursky came out of the study smiling broadly; his large, fleshy ears stuck flat to the back of his neck and he gave the impression of a slippery cake of soap. He walked among the crowd of spies pressing their hands, kindly and humbly nodding his head. Suddenly he walked to a corner and began to speak in fine dramatic style, "Good servants of the Czar, it is with a broken heart that I address myself to you—to you, men without fear, men beyond reproach, true children of the Czar, your father and your mother, the true Orthodox Church."

"He's begun his litany!" somebody whispered near Yevsey, who thought he detected an ugly oath from Yasnogursky's direction.

"You know already of the enemy's new cunning, of the new and poisonous plot. You have read the proclamation of Minister Bulygin, which says that our Czar allegedly wishes to renounce the power entrusted to him by our Lord God over Russia and the Russian people. All this, dear comrades and brothers, is the insidious game of people who have delivered over their souls to the foreign capitalists. It is a new attempt to ruin our sacred Russia. What is it they want to achieve with the parliament they have promised? What do they want to gain by this constitution, this liberty?"

The spies moved closer together.

"In the name of the Father, the Son, and the Holy Ghost, let us examine in the light of truth the devious ways of these snakes in the grass. Let us look at them with our simple Russian mind and we shall see how they will crumble to dust before our very eyes. Just think a little. They want to deprive the Czar of his divine power, of his liberty to rule the country according to the dictates from above. They want to organize popular elections so that the people should send their representatives to the Czar to promulgate laws undermining his power. They hope that our people, befuddled and ignorant, will allow themselves to be bribed with wine and money and will bring men into the palace of the

Czar whose names shall be dictated by the traitors, liberals, and revolutionaries. And who will these men be? Jews, Poles, Armenians, Germans, and other foreigners, all enemies of Russia."

Klimkov could see Sasha standing behind Yasnogursky, smiling sardonically like a devil, and he bent his head to prevent the sick spy from noticing him.

"This gang of venal swindlers will surround the serene throne of our Czar and will close his wise eyes to the destiny of our country. They will deliver Russia into the hands of strangers and foreigners. The Jews will establish their rule in Russia, the Poles theirs, as will the Armenians and the Georgians, the Letts, and other paupers whom Russia took under the shelter of her powerful hand. They will establish their rules, and then we Russians will remain alone, and then, then—I mean to say . . ."

Sasha, standing beside Yasnogursky, began to whisper into his ear. The old man waved him aside in irritation, and continued louder than before. "Then the Germans and the English will rush upon us and will clutch us in their greedy paws. Russia is threatened with destruction, dear comrades, my very dear friends. We must beware!"

He shouted the last words of his speech and lapsed into a moment's silence. Then, raising his hands above his head, he resumed. "But our Czar has loyal friends. They guard his power and his glory like faithful watchdogs. They have organized a society for the struggle against the dastardly conspiracies of the revolutionaries, against the constitutions, and every other abomination so destructive to us, the true Russian people. Counts and princes honored for their services to the Czar and to Russia are joining this society as are governors faithful to the will of the Czar and to the traditions of our sacred past. Perhaps even the very highest . . ."

Once again Sasha interrupted Yasnogursky. The old man listened to him, flushed, waved his hands, and suddenly shouted, "Well, speak to them yourself then. What is going on? What right have you got? . . . I don't want to . . ."

He suddenly gave an odd little leap, and pushing the crowd of spies apart, walked out of the room. Sasha came forward and took his place; he stood there, tall and stooping, his head thrust forward. Throwing a cursory glance at his audience with his blood-shot eyes, and rubbing his hands, he asked sharply, "Well, did you understand something of that?"

"We did—we did," a few low voices were heard to answer here and there.

"I wonder!" exclaimed Sasha in derision. Then he began to speak, passionately, violently, yet with astonishing precision.

"Listen, and those among you who have brains, explain my words to the fools. The revolutionaries, the liberals, our Russian gentry in general have got the upper hand. Do you understand? The government has resolved to yield to their demands; it wants to give them a constitution. And what do you think a constitution will mean to you? Let me tell you. It will mean starvation and death because you are idlers and good-for-nothings, not fit for any work. It means prison for many because most of you have deserved it; for a few of you it means the hospital or perhaps the lunatic asylum—plenty of you are half-wits if not insane. The new way of life will make short work of the lot of you. The police department will be abolished, the Security Department will be shut down, you will be turned out into the street. Is this quite clear?"

They were all silent as if turned to stone.

"Then I would go away somewhere," Klimkov thought to himself.

"I think I have made it clear," said Sasha after a period of silence, and again glanced at his audience. The red scar on his forehead appeared to spread over his entire face, and his face was a leaden blue.

"This new order is not to your advantage. Therefore you must fight against it, isn't that so? For whom, in whose interest, are you going to fight? For your own selves, for your own interests, for your right to live as you have lived up to now. Is that clear? So what will you do?"

There was a dull, heavy stirring in the stifling room, as if a huge, sick heart were heaving and sighing. Some of the spies walked away silently and sullenly with drooping heads. Somebody was heard to grumble angrily, "They tell us this and they tell us that. Why don't they increase our salaries instead?"

"They're always trying to scare us, always."

About a dozen men gathered in the corner around Sasha. Yevsey slowly moved up to the group and heard the excited voice of Piotr. "That's the way to talk! Twice two are four, and all the cards are aces!"

"Well, it doesn't satisfy me," said Solovyov, his voice mellow and prying. "Think! What does it mean to think? Everyone may think in his own way. I want to be told what to *do*."

"You *have* been told!" injected Krasavin roughly and sharply.

"*I* don't understand," Maklakov declared calmly.

"You?" shouted Sasha. "You lie! You understand perfectly well!"

"No, I do not!"

"And I say you do, but you're a coward; you're of the gentry besides—I know you."

"That may be," said Maklakov. "But do you know exactly what you want?" He spoke in so cold a tone and so significantly that Yevsey trembled and wondered, "Will Sasha hit him?"

Sasha, however, merely repeated the question in a low rasping voice, "I? Do I know what I want?"

"Yes."

"I will tell you." Sasha raised his voice menacingly. "I am soon going to die. I fear nobody. I am a stranger to life. I live in hatred of the good people before whom you crouch on your knees in your thoughts. If you say you don't—you lie! You are a slave, a slave in your soul. You are a lackey even if you are of the gentry, and I am a peasant, a peasant whose eyes are now open. Even though I went to the university, nothing has corrupted me."

Yevsey pressed through to the front of the group and stood beside the two men, trying to see the faces of both.

"I know my enemy. It's you, the gentry. You are the masters, even when you're spies. You are repulsive, detestable, wherever you are; men and women, writers or spies. But I know how to fight your sort, you gentry. I know a way. I know what ought to be done with you, how to destroy you!"

"This interests me considerably more than your hysterics, I must say," said Maklakov, thrusting his hands in his pockets.

"So you find it interesting, do you? Very well then. Let me tell you."

Sasha obviously wanted to sit down. He was rocking on his feet like a pendulum, staring around and speaking without a pause, choking over the hot, dry words.

"Who is it who directs our lives? The gentry. Who was it who corrupted man, the good-natured animal, and made a dirty beast of him, a sick beast? It was you, the gentry. And for this very reason the whole of our lives here ought to be directed against you. Because you have done this we must open up all the ulcers of life and drown you in the stream of abomination, in the vomit of the people you have poisoned. May you rot in eternal damnation! The time of your execution and destruction has come. All those you have mutilated will rise against you and choke you, crush you—you understand? Yes, that's how it is going to be! In some towns they have already tried to find out how firmly the heads of the gentry are fixed upon their shoulders. You've heard that, haven't you?"

Sasha staggered back and leaned against the wall, stretching his arms forward and choking with hysterical laughter. Maklakov glanced at the men standing around him and asked loudly, also with a laugh, "Did you understand what he said?"

"Anyone can say whatever he pleases," replied Solovyov, but the next instant added hastily, "in one's own company. The most interesting thing would be to know for certain whether a secret society has been organized in Petersburg and for what purpose. And who has joined it."

"That's what we must find out," said Krasavin in a tone of great determination.

"As a matter of fact, brothers, it's true; the revolution is indeed moving to other quarters," exclaimed Piotr, gleefully and animatedly.

"If there really are a few princes in this society he was talking about," Solovyov meditated dreamily, "then perhaps our situation will improve."

"You have twenty thousand in the bank already, you old devil."

"And maybe thirty. Count again," Solovyov answered in an offended tone, moving away.

Sasha coughed dully and hoarsely; Maklakov stood scowling at him.

"What are you staring at me for?" shouted Sasha at Maklakov.

Maklakov turned and walked away without answering. Yevsey involuntarily followed him, gradually freeing himself from the sudden fascination Sasha had roused in him, and the effect of his speech vanished like dust under the rain.

"Did you understand any of that?" Maklakov asked Yevsey.

"I don't like it."

"No? Why?"

"He's always so bitter and there's enough bitterness without him."

"Yes," said Maklakov, nodding his head. "You're right there, there is enough bitterness."

"It's impossible to understand anything," Klimkov continued, looking around cautiously. "Everybody talks differently."

He said this and then suddenly glanced sideways at Maklakov, frightened by his own words.

The spy pensively brushed the dust from his hat with his handkerchief, apparently oblivious to the dangerous words.

"Good-bye," he said.

Yevsey wanted to accompany him, but the spy put on his hat and, twirling his mustache, walked out without so much as looking at him.

A strange imperceptible change came over the town as if it were in a dream. People seemed to have completely lost the sense of fear. Faces flat and humble only a short time ago, suddenly appeared with an expression of sharp, overwhelming preoccupation. They appeared like builders preparing to pull down an old house, busily considering the best way to start the demolition.

Almost every day the workers in the industrial suburbs openly organized meetings which were attended by revolutionaries well known to the police and to the Security Department. They openly condemned the present order and made it clear that the minister's manifesto convening the parliament was part of a scheme by the government to placate the people—stirred up now by their misfortune—and then simply to deceive them in the end,

as usual. They urged their listeners to believe nothing but their
own reason. And when a rebel orator once shouted, "The people
alone are the true and legal masters of life; to them belongs all
the world and all freedom," a triumphant roar went up in reply,
"True, brother!"

Deafened by the shouts, Yevsey turned around and saw Melnikov standing behind him. His eyes were aflame, he was dirty and
disheveled; he clapped his hands like a crow clapping its wings,
and bawled out, "Tr-r-r-ue!"

Klimkov tugged at his coat in amazement and whispered in a
low voice, "What are you thinking of? The speaker is a socialist.
He's under surveillance."

Melnikov blinked his eyes, and asked, "Is he?" Without waiting for a reply, he shouted again, "Bravo! It's the truth!" Then
turning angrily to Yevsey he said, "Leave me alone! It's all the
same to me who speaks the truth."

Listening to new speeches, Yevsey smiled timidly, looking
around helplessly for some person in the crowd with whom he
might speak openly; but when he found a face that inspired confidence, he sighed and thought, "I'll start talking to him but he'll
know in a minute that I'm a spy."

He often heard the revolutionaries speak of the necessity of
establishing another way of life upon earth and this brought back
his old childhood dreams. But faith grew feebly upon the un-
steady, clammy soil of his soul, choked as it was with foul impressions and poisoned by fear. It was like a child suffering from
rickets, bow-legged, with large eyes always gazing into the distance.

He believed in the words, but did not believe in the people.
A timid spectator, he walked along the bank of a river without
the desire to jump into its soul-refreshing waves. Nonetheless he
wanted someone who could make life peaceful and show him a
corner in it—to win.

The spies drifted aimlessly about the streets; they became
strangers to one another, maintaining a sullen silence; they peered
into each other's faces with suspicion, expecting danger everywhere.

"Has anything been heard about this Petersburg council of princes?" Krasavin asked almost every day.

One day Piotr joyfully announced, "Boys, Sasha has been summoned to Petersburg. He'll fix up something there, you'll see."

Viakhirev, the hook-nosed, red-haired spy, remarked lazily, "The Russian People's Union has been granted permission to organize fighting detachments to kill the revolutionaries. I'm going to join them; I'm a good shot."

"A pistol is a handy thing," someone said. "You shoot, and then you run away."

"How casually they talk about all this!" thought Yevsey, remembering other words, remembering Olga and Makarov, but pushed it all out of his mind, annoyed. Sasha came back from Petersburg apparently improved in health; green sparks flashed in his dim eyes, his voice was lower and his whole body seemed to have straightened out, become more robust.

"What are we going to do?" Piotr asked him.

"You'll soon learn about it!" replied Sasha, baring his teeth.

Chapter 19

AUTUMN CAME, still and dreary as always, but people did not seem to notice it. Always bold and noisy, they came out into the streets even more impudent and powerful; they strengthened Yevsey's faith in their victory, in the imminence of a calm, cosy life.

Then came the fantastic, terrible, magnificent days when all the people stopped working and the ordinary life that had oppressed everyone by its cruel, meaningless play suddenly stopped as though under the pressure of a powerful embrace. Workers refused bread, fire, and water to the town, their ruler. For a number of nights the town stood in darkness, hungry, thirsty, sullen, and affronted. During those dark, humiliating nights, the workmen walked through the streets singing, a childish joy shining in their eyes. They realized their power for the first time and were amazed at its significance; they became conscious of their grip on life and good-naturedly celebrated, watching the dark houses, the motionless, dead machines, the bewildered police, the closed jaws of the shops and public-houses, the frightened faces, the humble attitude of those who had never learned to work but had learned to eat a lot and who therefore considered themselves the elite in the town. During those days their power over life had been torn from their impotent hands, but their cruelty and cunning remained. Klimkov saw these people, once accustomed to command, silently submit to the will of the hungry, the poor, and the unwashed. He understood that the masters found life humiliating now; they tried to hide their humiliation and smiled approvingly upon the workmen, lying to them in their fear. It seemed to Yevsey that the past would not return; new masters had arisen, and if they were able to stop the course of life all of a sudden, then they would now also be able to organize it differently, more freely, and more easily for themselves, for others, perhaps even for him.

All the old cruel and malicious elements seemed to have fled the city. They seemed to have melted away under the cover of darkness. People grew perceptibly kinder, and though the town remained without light by night, yet the nights, too, were stirring, and as cheerful as the days.

Crowds of people gathered everywhere and spoke animatedly in free, bold speech; they talked of the approaching days of the triumph of truth. They believed in it ardently. Meanwhile the unbelievers were silent as they peered into the new faces, trying to memorize the new words.

Klimkov would often pick spies out in the crowd. Not wishing to be seen by them he would quickly walk away. He met Melnikov more frequently than the others. This man aroused his curiosity more than any of the others. A dense crowd always gathered around him, and his thick voice flowed from the center of the group like a dark stream.

"There, you see! The people wanted it, and everything turned out as it had to. If they want it they will take everything into their own hands. They're a power, the people are. Remember this— you people—don't let what you have gained slip from your grasp. Take care! More than anything, beware the cunning of the masters. Drive them away, and if they argue, destroy them! Get rid of them."

When Klimkov heard this, he thought, "People used to be thrown into prison by the score for such talk! And look what happens now. They speak that way themselves."

He wandered alone in the crowd from morning until late at night. Sometimes he had an irresistible yearning to speak; but as soon as he felt the desire coming upon him, he immediately walked off into the deserted side streets and dark corners.

"As soon as I open my mouth, they'll recognize me." The constant nagging thought never left him and he consoled himself, saying, "I'll have enough time to have my say . . ."

One night when he was wandering along the street he saw Maklakov hidden in a gateway, staring up at a lighted window on the opposite side of the street like a hungry dog waiting for a bone.

"He keeps at his work," thought Yevsey, and then asked Maklakov, "Would you like me to take your place for a bit, Timofey Vasilyevich?"

"Take my place, Yevsey?" exclaimed the spy in a subdued voice. Klimkov felt that something must be wrong for the spy's voice was quite different from his usual one. "No, you needn't bother, you can go," he said.

Usually so neat and tidy, Maklakov looked disheveled tonight. His hair, usually so smoothly and becomingly combed behind his ears, lay in disorder over his forehead and temples. He smelled of vodka.

"Good-bye," said Yevsey, raising his cap and walking away slowly. He had taken only a few steps, however, when he heard a low call behind him.

"Wait a moment!"

Yevsey turned back and then suddenly, without a sound, Maklakov was beside him.

"Let's walk together awhile," he said.

"He must be very drunk," thought Yevsey.

"Do you know who lives in that house?" asked Maklakov, looking back. "Mironov, the writer. Do you remember him?"

"I do."

"Yes, I should think you would. He made you look like a fool and he did it so simply."

"Yes," agreed Yevsey.

They walked slowly, making no noise. The narrow street was quiet, deserted, and cold.

"Let's go back," suggested Maklakov. He adjusted his hat, buttoned his overcoat, and announced pensively, "I'm going away, brother—to the Argentine. That's in America."

Klimkov sensed something hopeless and weary in his words, and he, too, began to feel sad and embarrassed.

"Why . . . so far?" he asked.

"I must."

Maklakov stopped again opposite the lighted window, and looked up at it in silence. Like a huge eye on the black crooked face of the house, it cast a peaceful beam of light into the darkness—a small island in black and heavy waters.

"That's Mironov's window up there," said Maklakov quietly. "He sits up writing all night."

Some people were approaching. They were singing softly and the words of their song, "It comes, the last decisive fight," hung like a challenge on the night air . . .

"We ought to cross to the other side," Yevsey suggested in a whisper.

"Are you afraid?" asked Maklakov, though he was the first to step from the pavement into the frozen mud of the street. "There's nothing to be afraid of. For all their songs of fighting they are peace-loving people. The wild beasts are not among *them,* no. Wouldn't it be good to sit down quietly in some warm place, in some public house maybe? But everything is closed. Everything has come to a standstill, my friend."

"Let's go home," Klimkov suggested.

"Home? Thank you, no," replied Maklakov.

Yevsey stood still, meekly yielding to the old sad recognition of something inevitable.

"Tell me! What sort of a spy are you, anyway?" Maklakov suddenly asked, nudging Yevsey with his elbow. "I've been watching you for a long time. Your face always looks as if you were suffering from an attack of nausea."

Yevsey was glad of the chance to talk about himself openly.

"I'll be going away, Timofey Vasilyevich," he mumbled quickly. "As soon as everything settles down I'll be going away. I'll gradually get a small business together, and I'll live quietly by myself."

"As soon as what settles down?"

"I mean the whole new order of things. When the people really take over for themselves."

"Eh, eh," drawled the spy, waving his hand and smiling. Somehow at his smile Yevsey's desire to talk about himself vanished.

An atmosphere of unutterable gloom descended on both of them.

"Look here," Maklakov exclaimed with unexpected roughness and impatience as they approached the writer's house once more. "I'm really going away; I'm leaving Russia forever. And I want to hand over some papers to him—to this writer. You see this parcel?"

He waved a white square parcel before Yevsey's face, and continued quickly. "I don't want to go to him myself. This is the second day I've been watching here, waiting for him to come out. But he's sick, and he won't leave the house. I would have given it to him in the street. I can't send it by post. His letters are opened and stolen in the Post Office and passed on to us, to the Security Department. And I can't go to him myself."

Pressing the parcel to his breast, the spy bent his head and looked into Yevsey's eyes.

"My whole life is in this parcel. I have written about myself, my life story, who I am and why. I want him to read it—he loves and understands people. I can't go myself . . . And I'm afraid to send it by post—it'll land in the Security Department . . ."

Gripping Yevsey's shoulder firmly, the spy shook him, and commanded, "You go and give it to him, into his own hands—go, tell him that"—Maklakov broke off, and then after a pause—"tell him that an agent of the Security Department sent him these papers and begs him most humbly—use these very words—'begs him most humbly' to read them. I'll wait for you here. Now go. But on no account tell him that I'm here. If he asks about me say I've gotten away, that I've gone to the Argentine. Repeat what I've told you."

"You've gone to the Argentine," said Yevsey.

"And don't forget to say 'begs him most humbly.' Go quickly."

Giving Klimkov a gentle shove in the back, he led him to the door of the house, walked away, and then stopped to observe what Yevsey did.

Disturbed and trembling slightly from the force of Maklakov's orders, Yevsey lost all consciousness of his own personality. He pushed the electric button, ready to crawl through the door in the desire to hide himself from the spy as quickly as possible. The door opened. A dark figure loomed in the lighted hallway and a voice asked testily, "What do you want?"

"The writer, Mr. Mironov—I want him personally. I have been told to deliver a parcel into his own hands. Please hurry!" said Yevsey, involuntarily imitating Maklakov's rapid and incoherent way of talking. Everything became confused in his brain, only the words of the spy lay there, white and cold as dead bones. And when he heard a strangely deep voice, "What can I do for you?" Yevsey answered automatically, like a timid child repeating a lesson, "An agent of the Security Department sends you these papers and he begs you most humbly to read them. He has gone away to Argentina." The strangely unfamiliar name embarrassed Yevsey, and he added in a lower voice, "which is in America."

"But where are the papers?"

The voice sounded kind. Yevsey raised his head and recognized the soldierly face with the reddish mustache. He pulled the package from his pocket, and handed it to him.

"Do sit down, please."

Klimkov sat down, his head bowed. The sound of the tearing of the wrapping made him jump. Without raising his head, he looked at the writer warily. Mironov stood before him, looking at the papers, his mustache quivering.

"You say he has gone away?"

"Yes."

"And you too are an agent?"

"Yes," said Yevsey in a low voice, and he thought, "Now he'll start abusing me."

"Your face seems familiar to me somehow."

Yevsey tried not to look at him. But he felt the writer was smiling.

"Yes, I suppose it is familiar," Yevsey said with a sigh.

"Have you, too, been tracking me?"

"Once. You saw me from the window. You came out into the street, and gave me a letter."

"Yes, of course. I remember now. My God, so that was you, was it? I seem to remember giving you a bit of my mind."

Yevsey rose from the chair, looked into the laughing face incredulously, and glanced around.

"That's all right," he said.

He felt unbearably awkward as he listened to the harsh yet

kindly voice. He was afraid that the writer would swear at him and throw him out after all.

"How strangely we meet this time, eh?"

"There's nothing else then?" asked Yevsey in confusion.

"That's all. But I think you are tired. Why not sit down and have a rest."

"I must be going."

"As you please. Well, thank you, and good-bye."

He extended a large hand with fingers covered in a reddish down. Yevsey touched it cautiously.

"Can I tell you my life story, too?" he blurted out suddenly. The minute he heard himself say these words, he thought, "This is the very person I ought to talk to. Timofey Vasilyevich respects him and he's a wise man, and a better man than all the rest of them . . ." Remembering Maklakov, Yevsey looked at the window and momentarily grew anxious, but then said to himself, "It doesn't matter. It's not the first time he's had to freeze in the cold."

"Well, why not? Tell me, if you feel you want to. Why don't you take off your overcoat? And perhaps you'll have a glass of tea. It's cold tonight."

Yevsey wanted to smile, but he restrained himself. A few minutes later, his eyes half closed, he monotonously began to recount his life in great detail, about the village, about Yakov, and about the blacksmith. He spoke in the same voice as when reporting his observations in the Security Department.

The writer was sitting on a broad, heavy stool by a large table. He had folded one leg under him and rested his elbow on the table; he leaned forward, twirling his mustache with a quick movement of his fingers. His round, closely cropped head was lit up by the light of two candles; his eyes were keen and serious but they were looking far ahead into the distance, beyond Klimkov.

"He is not listening to me," thought Yevsey, and raised his voice a little, his eyes furtively noting every detail of the room, and jealously watching the writer's face.

The room was dark and cheerless. Crowded bookshelves increased the thickness of the walls and apparently deadened the sounds of the street. Between the shelves there was the dull glim-

mer of window panes, sealed by the cold darkness of the night outside, and somewhere a white narrow stain that was the door. A
table in the center of the room, covered with a grey cloth, seemed
to melt into the gloom of everything around it.

Yevsey sat down on a chair covered with smooth hard leather
in a corner. For some reason when he leaned his head hard against
its high back, it kept sliding down. The flames of the candles disturbed him; the little yellow tongues seemed to be holding a never-
ending, silent conversation. They slowly inclined toward each
other, shivered, and straightened themselves out, struggling up
again toward the ceiling.

Behind the silhouette of the writer, over the safe, hung a large
portrait—the yellow face with a sharp little beard sternly glanced
down from it.

The writer began to play with his mustache more deliberately,
but his eyes still seemed to be looking somewhere far beyond the
confines of the room. All this distracted Yevsey, and it broke the
thread of his recollections. His eyes had ceased to see and it occurred to him to close them. Then darkness firmly enveloped him
and he sighed with relief. Suddenly he beheld himself divided
in two—the man who had lived and acted, and the man who was
able to stand aside and talk about the first as about a stranger.
His speech flowed on more easily, his voice grew stronger, and
the story of his life unraveled smoothly and easily like a ball of
grey thread. The telling of it freed the frail little soul from the
dirty and cumbersome rags of its experiences. Yevsey found it
pleasant to talk about himself. He listened to his own voice with
quiet astonishment. He spoke truthfully and saw clearly as he
spoke that he had not been guilty of anything; he had not lived
as he would have chosen. Somehow he had always been forced
to do the things he did not like. Filled with sincere self-pity, he
was very near to tears and yet could not at the same time avoid
a sense of self-satisfaction.

When the writer interrupted to ask him a question, Yevsey
barely took it in. Without opening his eyes, he said in a low, stern
voice, "Wait a minute, I must keep it in the right order."

He spoke tirelessly, but when he came to the moment of his
meeting with Maklakov, he suddenly stopped as before a pit. He

opened his eyes, and saw at the window the dull rays of the autumn sun, the cold grey depth of the sky. Heaving a deep sigh, he straightened himself. He felt washed within, unusually light, pleasantly empty. His heart was ready to submit to new orders, new domination.

The author rose noisily to his feet, tall and strong. He pressed his hands together, and made an ugly cracking noise with his fingers.

"And what do you intend to do now?" he asked, as he turned to the window without looking in Klimkov's direction.

Yevsey also rose, and repeated confidently what he had already told Maklakov.

"As soon as the new life is settled, I'll quietly go into some business—I'll go away to some other town—I've saved about one hundred and fifty rubles."

The author turned to him slowly.

"I see," he said. "You have no other desires whatsoever?"

Klimkov thought, and answered, "No, none."

"And you believe in the new way of life? You think it will be established?"

"Of course. Of course it will be. If all the people want it. Don't you think it will be established?"

"I'm not saying anything."

Mironov turned back to the window, keeping silent, and played with the ends of his mustache. Yevsey stood motionless, waiting and listening to the emptiness in his heart.

"Tell me," said the writer softly and slowly, "aren't you sorry for those people, that girl, your cousin, and his comrades?"

Klimkov bowed his head, and tugged nervously at his jacket.

"You have found out now that they were right, haven't you?"

"At first I was sorry for them. But now I'm not sorry any more."

"No? Why not?"

Klimkov did not answer at once. After a few moments he said, "Well, they are good people and they achieved what they wanted."

"And it never occurred to you that what you were doing was wrong?"

Yevsey sighed. "Well, I never liked it. I do what I'm told to do."

The author cautiously went up to him, and then turned aside.

Klimkov saw the door through which he had entered, saw it because the author's eyes were turned to it.

"I ought to go," he thought.

"Do you want to ask me anything?" said the writer.

"No, I am going now."

"Good-bye." His host moved to let him pass. Yevsey tiptoed out into the hall where he began to put on his overcoat. He heard the writer's low voice asking from the door of the room, "Listen, I'd like to know just why you told me all this about yourself?"

Crushing his cap in his hands, Yevsey thought for a second and then answered, "Timofey Vasilyevich, the one who sent me, has great respect for you."

The writer smiled.

"I see! Is that all?"

"Why really *did* I tell him?" Klimkov suddenly wondered. His eyes blinking, he stared into the writer's face.

"Good-bye, then," said the host, rubbing his hands. He moved away from his visitor.

Yevsey nodded to him politely.

He looked around when he came out of the house and immediately discerned the black figure of a man pacing up and down, head bent, along the hedge.

"He's waiting," Klimkov realized. He shrank back. "He'll be angry with me. He'll say I took too long," he thought.

The spy must have heard Yevsey's footsteps on the frozen earth in the stillness of the morning. He raised his head and walked quickly, almost running to meet Yevsey.

"Did you give it to him?"

"Yes, I did."

"Why were you so long? Did he speak to you?"

Maklakov was shivering. He seized the lapels of Yevsey's overcoat and then instantly released him, blowing on his fingers as if he had burned them and tramping his feet on the ground. Frozen and pathetic he could hardly inspire fear.

"I told him all about my life, too," Yevsey declared. He wanted Maklakov to know that.

"Well, and didn't he ask about me?"

"He asked if you had gone away."

"What did you say?"

"I said you had."

"Nothing else?"

"No, nothing."

"Well, let's go, then. I'm frozen." Maklakov darted forward, thrusting his hands in his overcoat pockets and hunching his back. "So you told him your life?"

"Yes, the whole of it, completely, down to this very day!" answered Yevsey, somehow enjoying saying it. It seemed to raise him to the same level as the spy whom he admired so much.

"What did he say to you then?"

Somewhat confused, Klimkov waited before he replied. "He didn't say anything."

Maklakov stopped, seized him by the sleeve, and asked in a stern though quiet tone, "Did you give him my papers?"

"You can search me, Timofey Vasilyevich," Yevsey cried sincerely.

"I won't," said Maklakov, after reflecting a minute. "Well, we must say good-bye now. Take my advice. I'm giving it to you because I pity you. Get out of this service and get out of it quickly. It's not for you, you know it yourself. Get away now. Now is the time to leave. You see the sort of times we're living in. The dead are coming to life, people trust one another, they can forgive much in a period like this; I think they can forgive everything. And above all, keep clear of Sasha. He has a sick, diseased mind. It was he who made you inform on your cousin, he—he ought to be put away like a filthy dog. Good-bye, brother!" He seized Yevsey's hand in his cold fingers and gripped it hard. "You really gave him my papers?" he asked once more. "You're quite sure of it, aren't you?"

"I swear to God I did."

"I believe you. Don't mention my name there for a few days, please."

"I'm not going there. I'll just call for my salary on the twentieth."

"You can tell them later on. Good-bye!"

He disappeared around the corner. Yevsey watched him go and

he suspiciously thought, "He's probably done something against the authorities, and got the wind up."

He felt almost bereaved at the thought that he would never again see Maklakov. But it was pleasant at the same time to recall how weak, frozen, and tormented the spy had looked, the spy who had always been so calm and sure of himself, who spoke boldly even with the heads of the Security Department as if he were their equal. Yet he seemed afraid of the politically unreliable writer. "And here am I, a little man," thought Yevsey as he strolled alone down the street, "a little man, afraid of everybody; yet the writer didn't frighten me. I drank tea with him while Maklakov shivered in the street." Content with himself for once, Klimkov smiled. "He hadn't much to say, the writer, had he?" Yevsey was suddenly seized with a mingled feeling of sadness and outrage. He slackened his pace, and wondered why he should feel this way.

"Why did I talk to him?" he kept thinking as he walked. "Instead, I should have told it all to Olga that time."

The town was waking up but Yevsey wanted to sleep, and he became aware of an uneasy feeling in his heart, as though in a small room from which all the furniture had been removed and stood there empty, with torn wallpaper, green stains from the dampness and an intricate design of cracks on the walls.

He wanted to sleep but did not want to get home, and so he walked slowly.

Chapter 20

IT WAS ABOUT midday when Viekov, wearing an overcoat and hat and looking very gloomy, came to waken Yevsey. He shook the back of the bed and said in a muffled monotone, "We've all got to go to the office. Klimkov, you've got to get up! Klimkov—listen to me! They've proclaimed the constitution. They are collecting all the agents from their lodgings. Do you hear me, Klimkov?"

His words fell like large drops of rain, full of grief; Viekov's face was drawn as if from a toothache, and his eyes blinked frequently as if he were about to cry.

"What is it?" asked Yevsey jumping from his bed.

Viekov pursed up his lips in a dismal grimace and said, "A manifesto. The Czar has proclaimed the constitution. Our department is a madhouse! Sasha is like a raving beast; it's unbelievable! He keeps shouting, 'Strike, slash!' My God, I wouldn't be capable of killing a man if you paid me five hundred rubles! Yet he proposes that we should do it for forty rubles a month. It's just crazy even to listen to him." He sighed and added, "And frightening, too . . . Now, get dressed—and quickly."

Pulling on his trousers, Klimkov asked musingly, "Who is it they want us to kill?"

"The revolutionaries. Although what revolutionaries can there be at all now, if according to the Czar's decree, the revolution has come to an end. They tell us we should gather the people in the streets, march with flags, and sing, 'God save the Czar!' Well, why not sing, if liberty has been granted? But then they say that at the same time we should be shouting 'Down with the constitution.' I can't make head or tail of it. Surely that's going against the manifesto and the will of the Czar!"

His voice sounded protesting, offended; his legs became curiously tangled, and he seemed somehow reduced to a jelly as if his bones had been removed from his body.

"I'm not going," said Klimkov.

"What do you mean?"

"What I say. First I'm going to walk about the streets a bit and see what they're going to do."

Viekov sighed. "Yes, of course. You're a single man. But when you have a family, that is when you have a woman who demands this, that, and the other thing, then you'll go even where you don't want to, oh, yes, you will! A man will walk any tightrope to provide for his family. When I see tricks on a tightrope, my head begins to turn, and I get a sinking feeling in my belly. But I say to myself, 'If you had to do it for your livelihood, then you, too, Ivan Viekov, would dance on a tightrope.' It's a law of nature . . ."

Viekov rushed about the room, knocking against the table and the chairs, mumbling and puffing out his cheeks so that his pink little face began to look like a soap bubble. His colorless eyes disappeared completely; the little red nose hid itself between the mounds of his cheeks. His despairing voice, his dejected figure, his hopeless words, all this tended to irritate Klimkov, and he said gruffly, "It will all be different soon. There's no need to keep complaining now."

"But our people don't *want* anything different to happen," exclaimed Viekov, gesticulating, and stopping in front of Yevsey. "Don't you understand this?"

Yevsey, his mind in a turmoil, turned in his chair, wishing to protest in some way, but he was unable to find the right words. He began to lace his shoes, sniffling as he did so.

"Sasha shouts, 'Beat them! Show them this freedom, so that they'd be terrified of it!' Viakhirev displays revolvers. 'I'll shoot,' he says, 'straight between the eyes.' Krasavin is gathering a gang of some sort and talks of nothing but knives, hacking people down, and all that sort of thing. Chashin is preparing to kill a student because he took his mistress from him. Another new fellow has appeared, he's one-eyed, and smiles all the time; all his front teeth are missing. He has a frightening face. It's all a kind of lunacy, all this."

Viekov lowered his voice to a whisper, and said mysteriously, "We've all got to protect ourselves in this life. That's understood —but preferably without having to murder in the process. Because if we start to kill, then it will soon be our turn to be killed."

Viekov shuddered, turned his head toward the window, and listened. Then he raised his hand and his face turned pale.

"What's the matter?" asked Yevsey.

A gathering noise beat against the window panes in soft uneven waves, as if to open them and pour into the room. Yevsey rose to his feet with a look of inquiry and alarm at Viekov, who was now standing at some distance from the window, apparently as a precaution against being seen from the street. Then, stretching out his hand, he opened the window and a great stream of sounds broke in, engulfed the spies, pushed against the door, opened it, and floated along the corridor, mighty, powerful, exultant.

"They're rejoicing!" Viekov said with a shudder.

"See what's going on," Yevsey advised, hurriedly pulling on his coat.

Viekov was already looking out and reporting every detail of what he saw, quickly turning his head from side to side. He spoke rapidly and abruptly.

"The people are marching—they have red flags—there's a great crowd of people—countless people—of all sorts of stations—an officer even—and Father Uspensky—without hats—I can see Melnikov with a flag—our Melnikov—come and look!"

Yevsey ran to the window, looked down, and saw a thick mass of people flowing along the street. Their faces shone like the stars of the Milky Way. Flags waved like great red birds over the heads of the throng. Klimkov was deafened by the increasing noise. In the first row he saw the tall, bearded figure of Melnikov; he was holding the short pole of the standard with both hands and waving it. Now and then the cloth of the flag swathed itself round his head like a red turban. Dark strands of hair fell from under his hat over his forehead and cheeks and mingled with his beard. The spy, his head shaggy as some wild beast, appeared to be shouting, for his mouth was wide open.

"Where are they going?" mumbled Klimkov, turning to his comrade.

"They are celebrating," said Viekov, resting his forehead against the window pane.

Both men were silent, eagerly watching the motley throng of people. Having well-trained ears, they could distinguish between the loud bursts of separate clamors in the deep sea of noise.

"What a power, eh?" said Viekov. "People have been living alone, each man in his own little world, and now suddenly they've all come together—it's like a miracle!"

"They're using their heads, . . . that means they'll get a better life . . ." Yevsey said with a smile. That was what he believed at that moment.

"And our Melnikov, did you see him?"

"He always stood up for the people," Yevsey explained knowingly and left the window, feeling a new, bold spirit overcome him.

"Now everything will go well. Nobody wants to be ordered about. Everyone wants to live according to his needs, quietly and peacefully, in a decent order of things!" he said gravely, examining his sharp face in the mirror. Wishing to strengthen the pleasant feeling of self-satisfaction, he wondered how he could raise himself in the eyes of his comrade. So he announced with an air of mystery, "Do you know that Maklakov has escaped to America?"

"Is that so?" the spy rejoined indifferently. "Well, he's a single man."

"Why did I tell him?" Yevsey reproached himself. Then with a feeling of slight alarm and uneasiness he asked Viekov, "Don't speak of this to anybody, please."

"About Maklakov? Very well. I must go back to the office now. Aren't you coming?"

"No, but we can go out together."

In the street Viekov remarked with dismal irritation, speaking in a subdued voice, "The people are stupid, after all. Instead of carrying flags and singing, now that they have begun to feel powerful they ought to ask the authorities immediately to do away with politics, transform everybody into ordinary people, both us and the revolutionaries, distribute awards to whom they are due, both on our side and on theirs, and to declare once and for all, 'Politics from now on are strictly prohibited.' Enough of those games of hide-and-seek."

Viekov suddenly disappeared around the corner without saying good-bye to Yevsey. Klimkov continued walking like someone who had all the time in the world and thought, "I have saved one hundred and fifty rubles, I like commerce and know something about it. Soon I'll get another twenty-five rubles . . ."

People were milling about in the street in great excitement, all talking at the top of their voices, their faces beaming with happiness; the gloomy autumn evening might have been a bright Easter Day. Songs started up, some close by and others at the end of the street; all the people were curtained by the twilight. Then shouting quelled the singing.

"Long live liberty!"

Laughter and the sound of kindly voices came from everywhere. All this seemed good to Klimkov. He stepped politely to one side as people passed him; he looked at them approvingly, with a smile of satisfaction and continued to see his future in warm, grey colors.

Two people suddenly appeared around the corner, laughing. One of them bumped into Yevsey and immediately pulled off his hat and exclaimed, "Oh, I beg your pardon."

"Not at all," answered Klimkov affably.

Grokhotov, clean shaven, looking as if he had been smeared with ointment, stood before Yevsey. He beamed all over, and his eyes gleamed and darted from side to side.

"Heavens, Yevsey, what an experience I've just been through! If it hadn't been for my talent, I don't know where I'd be now. Are you two acquainted? This is Panteleyev, one of us." Grokhotov was breathless and spoke excitedly in a rapid whisper, mopping the sweat off his face. "You see, I was walking along the avenue, when I came across a crowd of people circled around a speaker. Well, I went up and listened. He spoke so frankly, you know, without any restraint at all. So I thought I'd ask the man standing next to me who the clever fellow was. 'His face is familiar to me,' I said. 'Do you know his name?' 'His name is Zimin.' The words were scarcely out of his mouth when two fellows grabbed me under the arms. 'Look here,' they shouted, 'this is a spy!' And before I could say a word there I was in the middle of the crowd with all of them standing around me silently; their eyes seemed to dig into my very soul. I thought I was finished."

"Zimin?" asked Yevsey anxiously, looking over his shoulder and beginning to walk more briskly.

Grokhotov raised his eyes to the sky, crossed himself, and prattled on excitedly.

"Well, God gave me an idea. I recovered my presence of mind at once and shouted, 'My dear people, it's a terrible mistake. I'm no spy; I'm a well-known impersonator of celebrities and sounds. Won't you please give me a trial?' The men who had seized me shouted, 'No, he is lying; we know him!' But I had already made a face like the chief of police, and called out in his voice, 'Who gave you per-r-r-mission to hold this meeting?' And thank God, I heard them beginning to laugh. So then I began, I can tell you, to imitate everybody and everything I could think of—the governor, a saw, a piglet, a fly . . . They roared with laughter. Even the men holding me had to laugh—the swine!—and they let me go. They began to applaud, you can ask Panteleyev here, he'll tell you, he saw it all."

"It's true," said Panteleyev hoarsely. He was a stocky man with eyeglasses, wearing a sleeveless jacket.

"Yes, brother, they applauded," exclaimed Grokhotov in ecstasy, hitting himself on his narrow chest and coughing. "Now, of course, I have found myself at last; an artist, that's what I am. I may say I owe my life to my art. Yes, yes, I assure you it was a narrow squeak. A crowd of people aren't easily fooled today."

"People have become more trusting," remarked Panteleyev pensively and mysteriously. "Their hearts have greatly softened."

"That's true. Look what they're doing, eh?" Grokhotov exclaimed softly, and added in a whisper, "Everything has come to the surface. All over the place people we were paid to watch, all the old faces, they're all coming out into the open. What does it mean, I wonder . . ."

"The carpenter's name was Zimin?" Yevsey asked again.

"Matvey Zimin, implicated in the case of propaganda in the furniture factory of Knop," replied Panteleyev with stern emphasis.

"He should be in prison," said Yevsey, annoyed.

Grokhotov whistled merrily. "In prison? Don't you know they've let everybody out of prison?"

"Who has?"

"Why, the people have."

Yevsey walked a few steps in silence, then asked, "Why did they do that?"

"That's what I'd like to know, too. They oughtn't to have allowed it," said Panteleyev. His glasses moved on his broad nose. "What a position it puts us in. The authorities do not think about people like us at all."

"Did they release everybody?" asked Klimkov.

"Everybody." Panteleyev's hoarse voice was stern, his nostrils were dilated. "And there have been a number of unpleasant and even dangerous conflagrations already. Chashin, for instance, was hit in the eye and had to threaten his assailant with his revolver. He was standing quietly somewhere, when suddenly a woman comes up, and cries out to the crowd, 'This man's a spy!' Since Chashin is no impersonator of animals he had to defend himself with a gun. And not everyone has a gun."

"It has been decided to give one to everyone."

"That's no good either . . . a weapon teases the hand . . ."

"Good-bye," said Yevsey. "I'm going home."

He took to the narrow back streets. When he saw people coming his way, he crossed to the other side and tried to melt into the shadows. He could not rid himself of the premonition that sooner or later he would be bound to meet Yakov, Olga, or somebody else of their group.

"The town is large, there are many people in it," he comforted himself. Nevertheless each time he heard steps coming toward him his heart sank to his boots; his legs began to tremble and their strength ebbed away.

"They let them go," he thought with dismal annoyance. "They

didn't say anything, just let them go. And what about me? It isn't exactly a matter of indifference to me where they are."

It was already dark. A solitary lamp was burning in front of the gates of the police station. As Yevsey approached it he heard a muffled voice, "To the back courtyard."

Yevsey stopped and peered in alarm into the darkness. The gates were closed, but the black shadow of a man stood at the wicket in one of the heavy swinging doors, apparently waiting for him.

"Hurry up!" the man commanded in obvious displeasure.

Klimkov stooped, slid through the small wicket, and went along the dark corridor under the vaults of the building toward a feebly flickering light in the depths of the courtyard where he heard the scraping of feet on the stone, subdued voices, and a familiar, repulsive sniffling sound. Klimkov stopped, listened, turned softly, and walked back to the gate, hunching his shoulders so as to conceal his face in the collar of his overcoat. He had already reached the gate and was about to push it when it opened of itself and a man darted through, stumbling, clutching at Yevsey and cursing. "Who the devil is that?"

"Yevsey Klimkov."

"Aha! Well then, you can show me the way. Didn't you recognize me?"

"Yes," said Yevsey with a sigh. "You're Viakhirev."

Klimkov returned in silence to the courtyard, where his eyes could now distinguish a number of figures looming in the darkness like uneven hillocks, slowly shifting from place to place like large black fish in dark, cold water. The sickly tones of Solovyov's pompous voice resounded in his ears.

"That doesn't suit me. You can catch a girl for me, a little girl. I'll give her a good whipping for you."

"Always joking, the old devil . . . Hardly the right moment," murmured Viakhirev.

The voice of Sasha came from a corner like a clarinet, pouring out incessantly like water dripping from a roof on a rainy day, monotonous as the sound of psalms intoned in church.

"Every time you meet those fellows with red flags, beat them. First beat the men carrying the flags, the rest will take to flight."

"And if they don't?"

"You will have revolvers. Also if you see people you know already—people you've been paid to hunt and who have been released from the prisons today by the arbitrary desire of an unbridled rabble—these you kill outright!"

"That's reasonable," somebody said. "It's either we or they."

"Some have their liberty now, but what about the others?" cried Viakhirev sharply.

Yevsey walked to a corner where he leaned against a pile of wood and looked and listened in perplexity.

"A body, a little body, a tiny, wee calf, meat!" the senseless words of Solovyov spilled out like thick, oily stains.

Dark, heavy walls of unequal height surrounded the court. Overhead the clouds slowly floated by. Here and there on the walls gleamed the dull light from square windows; in one corner Sasha was standing upon a low porch, his overcoat buttoned to the neck, his collar raised, and a cap pushed well back on his head. Above him swung a small lantern whose feeble flame trembled and smoked, as if endeavoring to consume itself as quickly as possible. Behind Sasha was the dark outline of the door. A few shadowy figures sat on the steps of the porch at his feet. One of them, a tall, grey individual, stood in the doorway.

"You must get it into your heads that you have been given freedom for the struggle with the revolutionaries," said Sasha, folding his hands behind his back.

The air was filled with the scraping of feet on the stones, dry metallic raps, and from time to time, subdued preoccupied voices uttering exclamations and advice.

"Look out! Be careful!"

"We're not allowed to load!"

Figures unidentifiable in the dark, and all strangely alike—a quiet, black crowd scattered over the yard—they stood in compact groups and listened to Sasha's cloying voice, rocking and swinging on their feet as if swayed by powerful gusts of wind. Sasha's words filled Klimkov's breast with cold misery and an acute loathing of the man.

"You are given the right to attack the rebels in the open. It is your duty to defend the deceived Czar with all the means at your disposal. Generous rewards await you. Who has not yet received a revolver?"

Several muffled voices called out, "I haven't . . . , I . . ."

Several of the men moved toward the porch. Sasha stepped aside, the grey man squatted down on his heels.

"May I have two?" asked a lugubrious voice.

"What for?"

"For a comrade."

"Don't be a fool!"

Yevsey recognized voices of spies he knew; they sounded louder, braver, jollier.

Someone smacking his lips greedily, complained, "Not enough cartridges. We ought to get a whole boxful."

"I've got things moving in two places today," said Sasha.

"It'll be interesting tomorrow."

Words and sounds flashed like sparks before Yevsey's eyes and consumed his hopes of a different, quieter life. With his whole being he knew that in the darkness surrounding him, in these people about him, there lay a power hostile to him, that this power would snatch him and put him back on the old familiar road, would fill him again with terror. Hatred of Sasha began to seethe in his heart; it was the pliant hatred possessed by the weak, the implacable lust for vengeance of the slave who has once been tortured by the promise of freedom.

The men hurried from the yard in twos and threes, disappearing under the broad archway that yawned in the wall. The light above the head of the spy trembled, turned blue, and went out. Sasha seemed to jump from the porch into a pit from which he sniffed angrily, "Today seven men of the Security Department have not turned up. Many seem to think it's a holiday, perhaps? I won't tolerate stupidity. Nor laziness either. I want you to understand this. I am now going to introduce strict regulations. I am not Filip Filippovich. Who was it said that Melnikov is going about with a red flag? Who?"

"I saw him."

"With a flag?"

"Yes. Marching and crying 'Liberty!' "

Yevsey walked toward the gate, stepping as if on thin ice and terrified that he might disappear down a hole. Sasha's clinging voice overtook him, sending a painful shiver down the back of his neck.

"Well, that fool will be the first to strike. I know him." Sasha laughed a thin howling laugh. "I have a slogan for him, 'Strike on behalf of the people.' And who was it who said that Maklakov had left the service?"

"He knows everything, the ugly brute," Yevsey said to himself.

"I said it. I heard it from Viekov, and he got it from Klimkov."

"Viekov, Klimkov, Grokhotov—all parasites, degenerates, lazy good-for-nothings. Are any of them here?"

"Klimkov should be here," answered Viakhirev.

Sasha shouted, "Klimkov!"

Yevsey put his arm in front of him as if feeling his way and walked faster. His legs were near to collapsing. He heard Krasavin say, "It seems he's gone. You ought not to shout surnames like that."

"I'll thank you not to tell me what to do. I'll soon abolish surnames and all other similar stupidities."

"I'll abolish you!" murmured Yevsey to himself, clenching his teeth.

When he left the gate behind him, he was seized by the consciousness of his own impotence and mediocrity. It was a long time since he had experienced these feelings with such crushing clarity. He was frightened by their load and flattened by the weight of them; he tried to reassure himself.

"Maybe it will still be all right. Maybe he won't succeed."

But he did not really believe it.

Chapter 21

THE NEXT DAY Yevsey hesitated for a long time before leaving the house. He lay in bed staring at the ceiling. Sasha's leaden face with its dim eyes and the band of scarlet pimples on his forehead floated in the air above him. Today the face reminded him of his childhood, of the sinister disc of the moon in the mist over the marshes.

Empty, cold, and listless, he surrendered to the longing for the dreams of a new life, which Sasha had so cruelly smashed to pieces, and he felt himself capable of biting the spy and gouging out his eyes.

It occurred to him that some of his comrades might come to see him and he dressed quickly, left the house, and began to run through the streets. Soon he grew tired and stopped and waited for a tramcar. People passed by in a continuous stream. Today he thought he detected something new about them and he began to examine them closely. Soon he realized that what he had imagined was new about them was the familiar old fear he knew so well. People looked about them with distrust and suspicion, no longer with the soft expression their eyes had recently worn. Their voices sounded lower, and betrayed anger, resentment, sorrow. They exchanged only tales of horror.

Two men stopped beside him. One of them, a short, fat, clean-shaven man asked of the other, "How many were killed, did you say?"

"Five. And there were sixteen wounded."

"Did the Cossacks fire?"

"Yes. A boy was killed, a schoolboy."

Yevsey looked at them, and inquired with seeming indifference, "What for?"

The man with a long black beard shrugged his shoulders and dragged out a low, reluctant reply, "They say the Cossacks were drunk."

"It must be Sasha's work," thought Yevsey, convinced.

"And the mob attacked a student on the Spassky Bridge and threw him into the river," announced the clean-shaven man, drawing a deep breath.

"What mob?" Yevsey asked again, insistently.

"I don't know. Some kind of patriot."

The black-bearded man explained, "Ever since this morning there have been tramps waving tricolored flags and carrying portraits of the Czar marching around the streets and beating up respectable-looking people."

"Sasha!" Yevsey repeated to himself.

"They say it is organized by the police and the Security Department."

"Of course!" burst from Klimkov. But the next moment he bit his lip and, glancing out of the corner of his eye at the black-bearded man, decided to move away. Just at that moment, however, the tramcar arrived, and as the two men prepared to board it, he thought, "I must get on it, too, or else they'll guess I'm a spy. What else could they think of somebody who waited for a tramcar with them, and then didn't take it?"

The tramcar passengers seemed to Yevsey more composed than the people in the street.

"After all I suppose it's some sort of concealment, even if it's only behind glass," was his explanation of the difference, as he listened to the animated conversation around him.

A tall man with a bony face was complaining, spreading his hands in bewilderment:

"I, too, love and respect the Czar; I'm deeply grateful to him for the manifesto. I'm ready to shout 'Hurrah' as loud as you like and offer up prayers of gratitude. But why smash windows for patriotism and break people's heads?"

"Such barbarism, such savagery in our age!" said a fat woman.

"Oh, those people, how horribly cruel they are!"

From a corner came a firm, sure voice, "It's all the work of the police!"

There was a moment's silence.

From the corner the same voice came again, "They're preparing a Russian-style counterrevolution. You just take a close look at the men at the head of these patriotic demonstrations—they're police in disguise, agents of the Security Department."

Yevsey heard these words with joy and stole a furtive glance at the young face, dry and clean with a bony nose, a small mustache, and a tuft of fair hair on a determined chin. The young man was leaning back in his seat in a corner of the tramcar, his legs crossed. He gazed at his fellow passengers with wise blue eyes and spoke like a man in command of his words and thoughts and knew their power.

Dressed in a short, heavy jacket and high boots, he resembled a workman, but his white hands and the thin lines on his forehead betrayed him.

"He's disguised himself," thought Yevsey.

He began to follow the firm words of the fair young man with the greatest attention, watching his knowing, clear blue eyes and agreeing with him. But suddenly he shrank as if in answer to a warning. On the platform of the tramcar, beside the conductor, he saw through the window a figure with narrow, sloping shoulders and the back of a black head. The tramcar jolted, and the familiar figure swayed, trying to keep its balance.

"Zarubin!"

Dismayed, Klimkov turned his eyes back again to the blue-eyed young man who had removed his hat and was smoothing back his curly hair as he said, "So long as our government has the soldiers, the police, and the spies on its side, it will never give our people and our society their rights without fighting and bloodshed every inch of the way. We must remember that."

"This isn't true, my dear sir," cried the bony-faced man. "The Czar granted a full constitution, he did, yes, so how dare you . . . ?"

"But who is it that is arranging the street massacres? And who's shouting 'Down with the constitution?'" the young man asked coldly. "You had better take a look at the defenders of the old system. There they go!"

At that instant the tramcar came creaking and squeaking to a standstill, and when the grating noise of its movement had subsided, the passengers could hear loud, disturbing shouts, "God save the Czar!" "Hurr-ra-ah!"

A gang of youths came running around the corner in front of the tramcar and scattered noisily over the street, as if dropped from above. A crowd of people waving tricolored flags above their heads pushed after them in hurried disorder in a wedge. The air was filled with confused shouting.

"Hurrah! Stand still, boys!"

"Down with the constitution!"

"We don't want . . ."

"God save the Czar!"

People were pushing and jostling one another, gesticulating wildly, throwing their hats in the air. In front of them with his head bowed low like a bull walked Melnikov, holding aloft a heavy pole with the national flag. His eyes were fastened on the ground. He lifted his feet high and apparently pounded the street with great force, for at each step his body quivered and his head shook. His heavy bellow could be heard above the chaos of thin, confused shouts, "Down with deception!"

A crowd of ragged people, dark and grey, rolled down the street behind him, jumping and twisting their necks. They raised their heads and arms in the air, looked up at the windows of the houses, jumped on the pavement, knocking off the hats of passers-by, ran up to Melnikov again, shouted and whistled and punched one another, crowding into a heap. Still waving the flag, Melnikov clanged and tolled like an enormous church bell, "Halt!" Then lifting his head and waving the flag high in the air, the spy bellowed, "Sing!"

"Is he drunk?" Klimkov thought coldly.

From his broad mouth gushed a savage, mournful note, "God sa-a . . . !"

But at this same moment excited shouts exploded in the air and scattered disordered and rapacious, like a flock of hungry birds. They clawed at the voice of the spy, and greedily, hurriedly blotted it out.

"Hurrah for the Emperor! Hats off! True orthodox people! Down with treachery!"

It was quiet in the tramcar. Everyone stood with their hats off, silent, pale, observing the crowd that encircled them in an uneven, dirty ring. Only the disguised man did not remove his hat. Yevsey looked at his stern face, and thought, "He's showing off."

He peered through the glass at the street with a wry smile on his face. He distinctly sensed the insignificance of these restless jumping people, understood clearly that a dark terror within them was whipping them, pushing them this way and that and sweeping them from side to side. They were fighting this fear, lulling themselves with shouting in the desire to prove to themselves that they were afraid of nothing. They ran around the tramcar like a pack of hounds let loose, full of a wild joy, without having had time to free themselves from their accustomed fear. Apparently too timid to walk along the broad, bright street, unable to gather themselves into one body, they bustled about, roared, and glared around with alarm, as if they knew that any minute something unexpected was going to happen.

Near the tramcar stood a thin, sharp-bearded peasant in a torn, short fur coat. He kept his eyes closed and his face raised to the sky. His hungry mouth gaped, revealing his yellow teeth as he shouted in a thin voice, "D-o-o-wn! We don't want . . ."

Tears came to his eyes and ran down his cheeks in the excitement. His forehead glistened with sweat. Ceasing to shout, he bent his neck and looked suspiciously around him. Then he raised his shoulders, and closing his eyes again, yelled once more as if he were being beaten, "E-e-enough!"

"I might have done the same," thought Yevsey and felt sorry both for himself and for the peasant. He saw the familiar grim faces of the yardsmen; the large-whiskered ugly face of the church watchman Klimych, pious and sullen; the hungry eyes of the street urchins; the astonished expression of timorous peasants; and a handful of men who pushed everyone, ordered everyone about, and infected the other apathetic blind bodies with their will, with their own sick ferocity.

Yakov Zarubin was twisting and turning like an eel through the middle of the crowd. Now he ran up to Melnikov, pulled at his sleeve, and said something to him, nodding his head in the direction of the tramway.

Klimkov quickly glanced around at the man in the hat. He was already on his feet and walking toward the door, his head raised, his forehead wrinkled in a frown. Yevsey followed him, but Melnikov jumped up on the platform and blocked the doorway with his huge body.

"Hats off!" he bawled.

The man turned on his heel and walked to the other exit. There stood Zarubin, who shouted in a loud voice, "Look, friends, he won't take off his hat! I know him! He makes bombs! Take care, boys!"

A revolver flashed in Zarubin's hand. He swung it as if it were a stone and brandished it in front of him. People from the street clambered on to the platform and struggled with the passengers who were trying to get to the exits. A woman screamed, "Take off your hat! What's wrong with you, man!"

Everybody roared and shouted, crushing one another. All eyes were fixed in a wide stare upon the man in the hat.

"I shall fire! Get away from me!" the man shouted, advancing upon Zarubin. The spy retreated, but pushed in the back, fell on his knees to the floor, where he supported himself with one hand and stretched out the other defensively. A sudden shot rang out, then another. The windows rattled and a wave of terror silenced the crowd; then a firm voice said contemptuously, "The scoundrels!"

A third shot split the air. Again the windows shook. Zarubin uttered a loud cry, "Ugh!" His head struck the floor, making obeisance at someone's feet. Suddenly the tramcar was emptied and quiet. Klimkov, hiding in a corner, shrank on his seat, listless, thinking, "I might have been killed."

He looked around wearily. The man in the hat stood on the platform of the car. Melnikov advanced toward him past Yevsey while Zarubin lay motionless, face down, on the floor.

"I will shoot you down—everyone of you! Keep away from me!" was the loud, dry cry from the platform.

But Melnikov stepped across the body of Yakov, seized the fair young man round the waist, and threw him out into the street.

"Beat him down—!" he shouted in a frenzy, his voice savage.

Three revolver shots followed in quick succession. The sharp sounds echoed. Somebody howled in a long-drawn plaintive cry, like an infant, "Oh, oh, my leg!"

Another man shouted hoarsely, with all his might, "Ah, ah! Hit him on the head! D'you hear?"

And a thin hysterical voice pealed in ecstasy, "Tear him to pieces, my dears. Strangle him! Enough! Their time is past! Now we'll give it to them. Our turn has come . . ."

Suddenly the cries were drowned—by a single exclamation, heavy with mournful disdain, "You fools!"

In a daze, Yevsey had staggered to the platform and watched from there the tangled mass of humanity. With bent backs, swinging their arms and legs, groaning under the strain, uttering tired, hoarse sounds, they stirred busily on the street like large shaggy worms dragging over the stones the body of the fair young man, already crushed and torn. They kicked it, trampled its face and chest, pulled its hair, legs, and arms, and—tore it apart. Half-naked, dripping with blood, the corpse flapped against the stones, soft as dough, with each blow losing more and more its semblance to a human being. The people worked him over industriously. One thin, little peasant was trying to crush his skull; he stepped on it with his foot, and yelled, "Yes! Our time has come, too."

The work was almost done. One after another they left the middle of the street and retreated toward the pavement. A pock-marked lout wiped his hands on his short sheepskin overcoat, and asked, "Who took his gun?"

Now the voices sounded weary, reluctant. But on the pavement a laugh was coming from a small group of people standing next to the lamppost. An offended voice was arguing hotly, "You lie! I was the first. The instant he fell I gave it to him on the jaw with my boot."

"The cabman Mikhailo was the first to set on him, then it was me."

"Mikhailo got a bullet in his leg."

"If it didn't hit the bone, it's all right."

The taste of blood had given them courage. They looked about them with eyes hungry, greedy, and expectant.

In the middle of the street lay a dark, shapeless heap from which blood oozed into the hollows between the stones.

"That's the way they do it—" Yevsey thought, looking dully at the red designs on the stones. In the dark red mist quivering before his eyes appeared the hairy face of Melnikov. His voice sounded tired and muffled.

"There, they've killed him!"

"Yes, and it all happened so quickly!"

"They killed another one this morning."

"What for?"

"He was speaking. Chashin fired into his stomach."

Yevsey repeated, "But, what for?"

"They're deceivers—all of them! The manifesto is a humbug —the people don't get anything!"

"It's Sasha who invented all this," said Yevsey quietly, with conviction.

Melnikov shook his head, looking down at his large hands.

"There's always somebody who deceives," he mumbled in a seemingly drunken voice. "Is Yashka dead?"

He walked back to the tramcar, bent down, and lifted Zarubin easily, laying him on his back on the bench.

"He's dead. There's where it hit him. . . ."

Yevsey looked for the scar on Zarubin's face left by the blow of the bottle. He did not find it. Over the spy's right eye there was now a little red hole from which Klimkov could not tear his eyes away. His whole attention was concentrated on it; he felt a sudden stab of pity for Yakov.

"Have you got a gun?" asked Melnikov.

"No."

"There, take Yakov's."

"I don't want to. I don't need it."

"Everybody needs a gun now," said Melnikov simply, and slipped the revolver into Yevsey's overcoat pocket. "Yes. That's how it happens: here today—gone tomorrow."

"It was I who marked him for death," thought Yevsey, examining his comrade's face.

Zarubin's brows were drawn together in a stern frown. His little black mustache still bristled on his upper lip. He appeared to be out of humor and his half-open mouth looked as if at any moment it would pour forth a rapid torrent of excited chatter.

"Come away," said Melnikov.

"And he—what happens to them?" asked Yevsey, forcing his eyes away from Zarubin's face.

"The police will take them away. It's against the law to remove the bodies. Let's go somewhere, and pull ourselves together. I haven't eaten today. I can't eat—it's the third day that I've gone without food. And I don't sleep either." He sighed deeply and added with sullen indifference, "It's I who should have been put to rest in Yakov's place."

"It's Sasha who's at the bottom of all this killing," said Yevsey, through his teeth.

They walked along the street, muttering, observing nothing, each lost in his private thoughts. They were like drunken men.

"Where's the truth?" Melnikov asked, putting his hand in front of him as if to feel the air.

"There, you see, two have been killed," said Yevsey, trying hard to catch an elusive thought.

"Many people have been killed today, I should think. They're blind, all of them."

"Why did Sasha do this?"

"I don't like him either . . ."

"He's the one who ought to be killed!" cried Yevsey with fierce bitterness.

Melnikov was silent for a long time. Then suddenly he shook his fist in the air, and declared aloud, "Enough! I've taken enough sins upon myself. Over there beyond the Volga I have an uncle, a very old man. He is all I have in the world. I'll go to him. He keeps an apiary—when he was young he was tried for forgery." Then after another pause the spy laughed softly.

"What's the matter?" asked Yevsey, irritated.

"I keep forgetting . . . My uncle has been dead for three years."

They came to a public house they both knew well. Yevsey stopped at the door and looked thoughtfully at the lighted windows.

"People everywhere," he murmured with reluctance. "I don't want to go in there. I'm tired of people."

"Let's go in. Never mind the people," said Melnikov, taking him by the arm and leading him on. "I'd be bored there, alone. Besides I'm scared. It's not that I'm afraid of being killed for being recognized as a spy. It's just a general feeling of dread."

The two men did not go to the room where their comrades usually met in the public house, but sat down in a corner. There was a large crowd but nobody was drunk; the talk was noisy and loud, and one was aware of an unusual excitement in the air. By force of habit Klimkov began to eavesdrop; the thought of Sasha clung to him, however, and turned this way and that in his mind. He was overwhelmed by the impressions of the day but was revived again by the waves of fear of Sasha and of a poignant hatred of him. "He'll be my death . . . He's sure to be my death . . ."

Melnikov silently drank his beer without relish and scratched himself from time to time.

Three men were sitting at a table not far from them; apparently clerks, they talked with the speech characteristic of their class. They were young and fashionably dressed, sporting gay neckties. One of them, a curly-haired young man with a tanned face was talking with great animation, his dark eyes flashing.

"They profit by the savagery of starving beggars to prove to us that liberty is impossible because of the numbers of such barbarians. However—permit me—savages were not born yesterday. They have always existed and justice has always been able to cope with them; they could be held under the fear of the law. Why then are they permitted to perpetrate every sort of outrage and bestiality today?" He looked around the room triumphantly and answered his own question with ardent conviction. "Because they want to point out to us: 'You want freedom, ladies and gentlemen, well, here you have it.' Freedom for you means murder, robbery, and every kind of mob violence."

"Do you hear what he's saying?" asked Yevsey. "Isn't this Sasha's scheme?"

Melnikov looked at him sullenly but did not reply.

The curly-haired man rose from his chair and continued, gracefully waving a glass of wine in his hand. "But this is not true, and

I protest against it. Honest people want liberty, not in order to destroy one another, but so that each can protect himself against the prevailing violence of our lawless life. Liberty is the goddess of reason. And they have drunk enough of our blood. I protest. Long live liberty!"

The audience cheered and tramped with their feet.

Melnikov looked at the curly-haired orator and muttered, "What a fool!"

"But he is right!" rejoined Yevsey angrily.

"How do you know?" asked the spy indifferently; he began to drink his beer in slow gulps.

Yevsey longed to tell this uncouth man that he was himself a fool, a blind beast, trained by the cunning, cruel masters of his life to hunt down human souls. But Melnikov had raised his head and was staring into Klimkov's face with dark eyes wide with horror. In a loud whisper he said, "The reason I'm so afraid is that when I was in prison something happened one day."

"Wait a moment," said Yevsey. "I'm listening."

A thin, rasping voice cut triumphantly across the soft buzz of general conversation.

"Did you hear? He talks about a goddess, but there's only one goddess for us Russian people, and that's the Holy Mother of God, the Virgin Mary. That's the way these curly-headed youngsters talk!"

"Throw him out!"

"Keep quiet!"

"No, if you please! If we are to have liberty, then everyone has a right . . ."

"You see? These curly-headed youngsters can walk the streets, beat up the people who rise to support the Czar's truth against treachery, while we Russians, the true Orthodox Russians, don't even dare to open our mouths. Is this liberty?"

"They are going to fight," said Klimkov, shuddering. "Somebody will get killed. I'm going."

"What a strange fellow you are! Let's go, then. To hell with them! What does it matter to you what they say?"

Melnikov flung some money on the table and moved toward the

door, his eyes on the floor as if to hide his conspicuous face. But in the street, in the dark and the cold, the words poured out, though in a subdued tone, "When I was in prison—it was on account of a foreman who was strangled in our factory; I was hauled in, too . . . They told me I would get hard labor. Everybody said it, first the coroner, then the police joined in trying to frighten me. I was still young then and I didn't like the idea of hard labor. I used to weep." He coughed a racking cough, and slackened his pace. "One day the assistant warden of the prison came, Aleksey Maksimych, a good little old man. He was fond of me, and grieved for me all the time. 'Ah,' he said, 'Liapin'—my real name is Liapin —'Ah,' he said, 'brother, I'm sorry for you. You are such an unfortunate fellow . . .' "

Melnikov's speech ran on softly, evenly. Klimkov followed it like a narrow path leading down into the darkness, into something like a fascinating, terrible fairy tale.

"He comes to me and he says 'Liapin, I want to save you for a good life. Yours is a hard-labor case, but you can escape it. The only thing you need do is to execute a man. He was sentenced for political murder. He will be hanged according to law in the presence of a priest, he will be given a cross to kiss, so that you needn't be uneasy about it.' So I say, 'Why not? If it's with the consent of the authorities, and if I'm to be pardoned, I'll hang him for you. Only I don't know how . . .' 'We'll teach you,' he says. 'We have a man who knows how, but he's stricken with paralysis and can't do it himself.' Well, they taught me for a whole evening. It was in a cell. They stuffed a sack with rags and tied it with a string to pretend it was a neck. Then I had to learn how to pull it up on a hook. Early in the morning they gave me half a bottle of alcohol, and took me to the yard with soldiers carrying guns. I saw that a gallows had been erected, and there were various officials standing in front of it. They were all muffled up and shivering. It was autumn, you see, November. I climbed up the scaffolding and the boards shook and creaked under my feet like teeth. This upset me and I said, 'Give me more vodka. I'm afraid.' And they did. Then they brought him . . ."

Again Melnikov began to cough hoarsely, and he clutched at his throat. Yevsey pressed close to him, trying to keep in step with

him. He kept his eyes fastened on the ground, not daring to look
to the front or to either side.

"He was a sturdy young fellow. He stood firm, and all the time
kept stroking his hair from his forehead back to his neck, like that.
I began to put the face-cloth on him. I must have pinched or hurt
him in some way, for he told me quietly, without anger, 'Be careful.' Yes. The priest gave him the cross, and he said, 'You needn't
bother with that. I'm not a believer.' His face looked as if he knew
all that would happen after death, as if he knew it all for certain.
Somehow I managed to hang him; I was shaking all over. My
hands grew numb, my legs would not hold me. It was the way he
was so calm about it all, as if he were a master over death . . .'"

Melnikov fell silent, looked around, and began to walk more
quickly.

"Well?" asked Yevsey in a whisper.

"Well, I hung him, that's all. Only ever since, when I see or hear
that a man has been killed, I remember him. He was the only man
I've ever felt really knew the truth. That was why he was not
afraid. And the strange thing was, he seemed to know what would
come afterwards—and no one can know that, can they? I tell you
what, Yevsey, why don't you come and spend the night with me,
eh? Please!"

"All right," said Yevsey softly.

He was glad of the offer. He was unable to walk to his room
alone now, along the streets, in the darkness. He felt a tightness
in his breast and a heavy pressure weighing on his bones, as if he
were creeping underground and the earth were squeezing his back,
his chest, his sides, and his head while in front of him gaped a deep
pit, which he could not escape, into which he must soon descend
—a silent bottomless abyss down which he was going to plunge
for ever and ever.

"That's good," said Melnikov. "I would be bored alone."

"If only you could kill Sasha," Yevsey suggested longingly.

"Go on with you!" Melnikov waved away the idea. "What are
you imagining—that I enjoy killing? They asked me twice after
that to hang people, a woman and a student. Well, I said no. It
would make another two to remember instead of one, when the

occasion presented itself. The dead, you see, they come back and visit you. They come back."

"Often?"

"Sometimes, sometimes not. And how can you defend yourself against them? I don't know how to pray to God. Do you?"

"I remember my prayers."

They entered a courtyard and walked a long time before they reached the other side, stumbling over boards, stones, and rubbish. Then they went down a flight of steps, which Klimkov, feeling the walls with his hands, thought would never come to an end. When he found himself at last in the spy's lodgings and looked about him in the light of the lamp, he was amazed to see the mass of different pictures and paper flowers that almost entirely covered the walls. Melnikov at once appeared to be a stranger in this comfortable little room, with its broad bed in the corner behind white curtains.

"It was all set up by the woman I lived with," said Melnikov, starting to undress. "She ran away, the wretch! A gendarme, a quartermaster, lured her away. I can't understand it. He was a grey-haired widower, and she was a young woman, greedy for a male. But she left me all the same! The third one that's left me already. Come, let's go to bed."

They lay side by side in the same bed; it rocked under Yevsey like a tossing sea, all the while sinking lower and lower, and his heart sank with it. The spy's words weighed heavily upon his breast.

"One was Olga."

"What did you say?"

"Olga. Why?"

"Oh, nothing."

"A little thing, she was, thin and jolly. She used to hide my hat, or something or other, and I would say, 'Olga, where's my hat?' And she would reply, 'Search for it. You're an expert at searching, aren't you?' She liked to joke, but she was loose. Hardly was my head turned before she was with somebody else. I was afraid to beat her, she was so frail. Still I used to pull her hair, you've got to do something . . ."

"Oh, Lord!" Klimkov exclaimed softly. "What shall I do with myself?"

His comrade was silent for a while, then said dully and slowly, "That's the way I howl, too, sometimes."

Klimkov buried his head in his pillow to stifle the desire to scream.

Chapter 22

YEVSEY AWOKE with a strange, vague resolution which encircled his breast like a wide invisible belt. He felt the ends of this belt were held by an insistent being who obstinately led him on toward some unknown but inescapable destiny. He was inclined to submit to this force; his awkward, cowardly thinking cautiously groped for it, but at the same time he did not want to see the force take shape.

Melnikov had dressed and washed and was sitting with his hair disheveled at the table by the samovar, munching bread lazily like an ox.

"You sleep soundly," he said. "I drowsed a little, then awoke in the night, and suddenly saw a body beside me. I remembered that Tania wasn't here but I had forgotten about you. Then I suddenly thought it was that man whom I had killed lying there, who had come and lain down—just to warm himself." Melnikov giggled. "However, and this is not a joke—I lighted a match and looked at you. I think you're not well. Your face is blue like a . . ." He broke off with a cough, but Yevsey guessed the unspoken word, and thought gloomily, "Rayissa, too, said that I would hang myself."

The thought frightened him, clearly touching on something he did not want to face.

"What time is it?" he asked.

"Getting on to eleven."

"It's still early," Klimkov remarked.

"Yes," confirmed the host, and both were silent. Then Melnikov suggested, "Why don't we live together, you and I?"

"I don't know," replied Yevsey.

"What don't you know?"

"What will happen," said Yevsey, after reflecting a moment.

"Nothing will happen. You're a quiet fellow, you don't talk much, and I don't like to talk much either. Once you start talking, one says one thing, and another says another, and a third says something different again. Well, I can't be bothered with all that. All you have is a lot of words, and none of them is true."

"Yes," said Yevsey, for the sake of answering. "Something must be done," he thought in self-defense. Suddenly he decided, "First, I must settle Sasha." But he had no desire to envisage what would come afterwards. "Where are we going now?" he asked Melnikov.

"To the office," Melnikov replied unconcernedly.

"I don't want to," declared Yevsey drily and firmly.

Melnikov scratched his beard for a time in silence, then pushed the dishes away, and placing his elbows on the table, said in a thoughtful undertone, "Our work has become difficult. Everybody has started to rebel, but who are in fact the real rebels? You work it out, if you can."

"I only know who's the villain behind all the dirty work!" muttered Klimkov.

"You mean Sasha, I suppose?"

Melnikov started to dress, sniffing loudly. "So we'll live together, eh?" he asked.

"Yes."

"Will you bring over your things today then?"

"Perhaps."

"Will you sleep here tonight?"

"Yes."

When the spy had gone, Klimkov jumped to his feet and looked around in terror, shivering under the stinging blows of suspicion.

"What if he's locked me in, and gone to tell Sasha. They'll come and seize me now . . ."

He rushed to the door. It was not locked. Then he said to himself as if bitterly trying to convince someone, "Don't you see, it's impossible to live like this, trusting nobody."

He sat by the table for a long time without moving, straining his mind, exercising all his cunning to lay a snare for the enemy without endangering himself. Finally he hit upon a plan. Somehow he must lure Sasha from the office to the street and walk with him. Then if they would happen to meet a large crowd, he would shout, "This is a spy, beat him!" And then the same thing would happen as had happened to Zarubin and the fair-haired young man. If the people would not turn upon Sasha as seriously as they had yesterday upon the disguised revolutionary, Yevsey would set them an example. He would fire first as Zarubin had done. But *he* would *hit* Sasha. He would aim at his stomach.

Klimkov felt strong and brave and began to hurry. He wanted to do what had to be done at once. But the memory of Zarubin hindered him, confusing the pathetic simplicity of his plan. He found himself involuntarily remembering his own words. "It was I who marked him for death."

He neither reproached nor blamed himself. Yet he felt that a certain thread bound him to the little black-haired spy, and that somehow the thread must be broken.

"I didn't say good-bye to him—and where will I find him now?"

When he put on his overcoat he was glad to feel the revolver in his pocket; his resolve once again flared within him and he walked boldly out into the street.

But the nearer he got to the Security Department the more this bold mood melted and faded away. The feeling of power vanished; he saw the narrow blind alley and suddenly at the end of it the dismal three-storied building, felt an urgent desire above all else to find Zarubin and pay his last respects.

"It's because I wronged him," he explained his desire to himself, quickly swerving away from his plan. "I must find him . . ."

At the same time in some vague way he felt he could never escape from the idea that had seized his heart and now pressed him on toward the only way out of his terrible predicament.

The task of the day, the resolve to destroy Sasha, did not hinder the growth of the dark, dominant power which filled his heart, much as the sudden ardent wish to find the body of the little spy had hindered the carrying out of this resolve.

He emphasized this wish in every way, in the fear that it, too,

would disappear. For several hours he rode around in cabs to police stations, making eager and painstaking inquiries regarding
Zarubin. When at last he found where the body was, it was too
late to visit it, and he returned home secretly pleased that the day
had come to an end.

Melnikov did not come back to his lodgings that night. Yevsey
lay alone, trying not to stir. Every time he moved, the curtain over
the bed moved, a smell of dampness blew into his face, and the
bed groaned and squeaked. In the stillness a few wretched mice
scuffled around in the darkness, and the rustling sounds they made
ripped the thin thread of Yevsey's thoughts of Zarubin and Sasha.
He had glimpses of the dead, calmly expectant emptiness of his
surroundings with which the emptiness of his soul seemed determined to blend.

Early the next morning he was standing in the corner of a large
yard at a small yellow shed with a cross over the roof. A grey
hunchbacked watchman said as he unlocked the door, "There are
two of them here. One was identified, the other wasn't. The unidentified one is being taken to the grave at any moment."

Then Yevsey saw Zarubin's angry face. The only change it had
undergone was that it had grown a little blue. The small wound
in place of the scar had been washed, and had turned black. The
small taut body was naked and clean; it lay face upward, stretched
like a cord, the tanned hands folded over the breast as if Zarubin
were angrily asking, "Well, so what?"

Beside him lay the other dark broken body, swollen, and covered
with red, blue, and yellow bruises. Someone had covered the
face with blue and white flowers. But under the flowers Yevsey
could see the bones of the skull, a tuft of hair glued together with
blood, and the torn shell of the ear.

"This one cannot be recognized; there's hardly any head left.
Yet he was identified. Two young ladies came yesterday with these
flowers and covered up the human outrage with them. As for the
other one, we don't know who he is."

"I know who he is," said Yevsey firmly. "He's Yakov Zarubin. He
served in the Security Department."

The watchman looked at him and shook his head negatively.
"No, that's not the man. The police also told us he was Zarubin,

and our office inquired of the Security Department, but it appeared it was wrong."

"But I know it's true!" Yevsey exclaimed quietly, in an offended tone.

"In the department they said, 'We don't know such a person, no man of that name ever served here.'"

"It's not true," exclaimed Yevsey, grieved and dumbfounded.

Two young men came in from the yard and one of them asked the watchman, "Which is the unidentified man?"

"This one."

The hunchbacked watchman pointed to Zarubin and said to Yevsey, "You see?"

Klimkov walked out into the yard, pressed a coin into the watchman's hand, and repeated with impotent stubbornness, "It is Zarubin, I tell you."

"As you please," said the old man, shrugging his hump. "But if it is so, others would have recognized him. An agent came here yesterday looking for someone who had been killed and he didn't recognize your man either, though why shouldn't he admit it if he did?"

"What agent?" asked Yevsey.

"A stout man, bald, with a gentle voice."

"Solovyov," guessed Yevsey, watching dully the way Zarubin's body was being laid in a white unpainted coffin.

"It won't go in," mumbled one of the young men.

"Bend his legs, you fool!"

"The lid won't close."

"Lay him in sideways, then?"

"Have more respect for the dead, you boys," said the old man calmly.

The youth who held the head of the corpse sniffed, and said, "It's a spy, Uncle Fiodor."

"A dead man is nobody," observed the hunchback philosophically, walking up to them. They fell silent, continuing to squeeze the lithe tanned body into the short narrow coffin.

"You fools, get another coffin," said the hunchback angrily.

"It doesn't really matter," said one; the other added grimly, "Not as big as he'd like to be."

Yevsey left the yard, bitterly humiliated because of Yakov. He clearly heard the hunchback behind him say to the young men as they bore off the body, "There is something queer about that, too. He comes here and says 'I know who he is.' Perhaps he's the one behind it all? What do you think, boys?"

The two young voices answered almost simultaneously, "He's probably a spy, too."

"What do we care?"

Klimkov quickly jumped into a cab and shouted to the driver, "Hurry!"

"Where to?"

Yevsey answered in a low voice, after a moment's hesitation, "Straight ahead."

The offensive thoughts thudded dully in his brain. "They'll bury him like a dog—and me, too . . ."

The street rushed to meet him. The houses rocked and swayed, the windows gleamed. People walked noisily; nothing was real.

"I'll destroy Sasha . . . I'll go there now and shoot him . . ."

Dismissing the cabman, he walked into a restaurant which Sasha frequented less than the others, stopped in front of the door of the room where the spies gathered, and said to himself, "I'll shoot him the instant I see him."

Trembling, he knocked on the door softly, and feeling for the revolver in his pocket, stood rooted to the spot in cold expectation.

"Who's there?" asked someone on the other side of the door.

"I," said Yevsey.

The door was opened a little. The eyes and little pink nose of Solovyov flashed in the chink. "Ah-h-h!" he drawled in amazement. "There was a rumor that you had been killed."

"No, I have not been killed," Klimkov responded sullenly, removing his coat.

"I see. Lock the door. They said you were together with Melnikov."

Solovyov was carefully chewing a slice of ham which made his speech difficult to understand. His greasy lips smacked slowly and indifferently emitted the words, "So, it isn't true that you were together with Melnikov?"

"Why isn't it true?"

"Well, here you are alive, and he's in bad shape. I saw him yesterday."

"Where?"

The spy named the hospital from which Yevsey had just come.

"Why is he there?" Klimkov inquired apathetically.

"Well, the story is that a Cossack struck him on the head with a saber and then the horses trampled him. How and why—we don't know. He's unconscious. The doctors say he won't recover."

Solovyov poured some sort of green vodka into a glass, held it up to the light, squinted at it, and then gulped it down. "Where have you been hiding yourself?" he asked Yevsey.

"I'm not hiding."

A plate fell in the corridor. Yevsey started, and remembering that he had forgotten to remove the revolver from his overcoat pocket, rose to his feet.

"Sasha is raging at you."

The sinister red disc of the moon surrounded by a cloud of heady lilac-colored mist swam before Yevsey's eyes. He remembered the sniffling, ranting voice, the yellow fingers on the bony hands. "Won't he come here?"

"I don't know."

Solovyov's face was shining; he seemed to be very satisfied with something, and smiled more frequently than ever. His voice rang with the lofty affability of a superior. Everything about him sickened Yevsey. Incoherent thoughts tossed around in his mind, each one breaking up the one before. "Rascals, all of you . . . Sad about Melnikov . . . So this obese creature didn't want to identify Yakov—why? . . ." "You saw Zarubin?" he asked aloud.

"Who?" asked Solovyov, raising his brows.

"You know who."

"Yes, yes, yes. Of course I saw him."

"Why didn't you tell them that you knew him?" Yevsey asked sternly.

The old spy reared his bald head, and exclaimed with astonished sarcasm, "W-w-what did you say?"

Yevsey repeated the question, this time in a milder tone.

"That's not your business, my dear fellow. I'd like that to be quite clear. But I'm sorry for your foolishness, so I'll tell you this: we have no need for fools, we don't know them, we don't understand them, we don't recognize them. You should remember that, now and forever, to the end of your life. Mind what I say, and tie up your tongue with a string."

Solovyov's little eyes sparkled as cold as two silver coins; his voice rang with a promise of evil and cruelty. He shook a short thick finger at Yevsey and the greedy purple lips were pouting sternly. But there was nothing frightening about him.

"They're all the same," thought Yevsey. "They are all one gang—they all ought to be . . ."

He darted to his overcoat, snatched the revolver from the pocket, aimed at Solovyov, and shouted dully, "Now!"

The old man jerked and dropped from his chair to the floor. He seized the leg of the table with one hand and stretched the other toward Yevsey.

"Don't—you mustn't," Yevsey gasped. "My dear sir, don't touch me."

Klimkov pressed the trigger more tightly, and still more tightly. His head froze with the effort, the hair stirred on his scalp.

"I'm going to get married tomorrow. I'll never again . . ." The heavy, cowardly words rustled in the air. Grease glistened on the spy's chin, and the napkin over his chest quivered.

The revolver did not go off. Yevsey's finger hurt him and horror swept over him from head to toe and took his breath away.

"I can give you money!" Solovyov whispered rapidly. "I will say nothing . . ."

Klimkov raised his hand and flung the revolver in the spy's face. Then he picked up his overcoat and took to his heels. Two feeble shouts overtook him, "Hah, hah!"

The shouts stuck like leeches to the back of his neck, filling him with an insane horror, and drove him faster and faster. It seemed to him that a crowd was gathering behind him noiselessly, their feet never touching the ground, running after him, stretching out to his neck scores of long clutching hands that touched his hair. They played with him, mocked him, disappearing and reappearing again. He hired cabs, drove around for a while in them, jumped out of them, ran along the streets, and drove around again. But the crowd was close to him all the time, unseen and thus so much the more horrible.

He felt more at ease when he saw the dark patterned wall of trees and bare branches before him; they stretched out to meet him. He dived into the thicket and walked between the trees, moving his arms behind his back as if to draw the trees together more compactly behind him. He descended into a ravine, sat down on the cold sand, and then got up again and paced the length of the ravine, breathing heavily, perspiring, drunk with fear. Soon he saw an opening between the trees. He listened carefully, noiselessly advanced a few steps farther, and peered ahead. A railway track stretched in front of him; beyond the slope rose more trees, but these were small and far apart and the grey roof of a building shone through the network of their branches.

He quickly walked back up the bed of the ravine where the woods was thicker and darker.

"They'll catch me." A cold assurance pushed him on. "They'll catch me . . ."

A slow, soft noise traveled slowly through the woods. It rang nearby and shook the thin branches as it touched them. They swayed in the ravine in the dusk, filling the air with their rustling. The thin ice of the brook under his feet cracked drily; there was no water in it and ice had covered the dry, grey gullies with a white skin.

Klimkov, bending down, sat and put a piece of ice in his mouth. The next instant he jumped to his feet and clambered up the steep slope of the ravine. He then removed his belt and suspenders and began to tie them together, cautiously examining the branches over his head.

"I don't have to take off my overcoat," he reflected without self-pity. "The heavier, the quicker."

He was in a hurry, his fingers trembled, and his shoulders involuntarily rose as if to conceal his neck. A frightful thought kept pounding in his head.

"I won't have time. They'll be here any moment . . ."

A train passed. The trees hummed in displeasure and the ground quivered. White steam threaded its way between the branches.

Titmice flew by, whistling boldly. They gleamed in the dark

nets of the branches, and their quick bustle hastened the movements of Yevsey's cold, disobedient fingers.

He made a noose with his belt, threw it over a branch, and
tugged at it. It was firm. Then, just as hurriedly, he began to make
another noose with his suspenders which he had twisted together.
When everything was ready, he heaved a sigh.

"Now I must say a prayer."

But no prayer came to him. For a few seconds he stood lost in
thought.

"Rayissa knew my fate," he remembered unexpectedly and,
thrusting his head into the noose, said quietly, simply, and without a quiver in his breast, "In the name of the Father, the Son, and
the Holy Ghost . . ."

He pushed the ground with his feet, and jumped into the air,
doubling his legs under him. There was a painful tug at his ears;
a strange inward blow hit his head and stunned him. He fell. His
entire body struck the hard earth, turned over, and rolled down;
his arms caught the roots of trees, his head knocked against their
trunks. He lost consciousness.

When he recovered his senses he found himself sitting at the
bottom of the ravine, the torn suspenders dangling over his chest.
His trousers had burst, his scratched, blood-stained knees peeped
pathetically through the cloth. His body was a mass of pain, cen-
tered round his neck. The cold seemed to be flaying his skin.
Forcing his head back, Yevsey looked up the slope. There, under
a white branch of a birch, the belt swung in the air like a thin ser-
pent, beckoning to him.

"I can't," he said to himself in despair. "I don't know how
. . . There's nothing I can do . . ."

Tears of impotence and injury began to flow. He lay on his
back and saw through his tears the clean, pale sky above him, broken by the dry pattern of the dark branches.

He lay for a long time wrapped in his overcoat, tortured with
pain and cold. Without his willing it, his meaningless life passed
before him in a chain of dark, misty rings, leaving no spark of hope
in his heart.

Trains went past the grove several times, filling it with a rumbling noise, with clouds of steam and occasional flashes of light.

The rays of light glided along the trunks of the trees, as if groping among them, in search of somebody hidden there. And then suddenly, quivering and cold, with a last flicker, they were gone.

When Yevsey was found, he raised himself to his feet with an effort, and followed the men in the twilight of the woods. He stopped at the clearing and leaned against a tree, waiting and listening to the distant angry hum of the town. It was evening already; the sky had grown purple. A dim red light glowed over the town.

In the distance a faint drumming noise could be heard. The rails began to hum and ring. A train was coming, its red eyes blinking in the twilight. The dusk quickly swirled after it, growing thicker and darker. Yevsey walked as fast as he could to the railway tracks, sank on his knees, and lay on his side across the ties, his back to the oncoming train and his neck on one rail. He wrapped his head tightly in the folds of his overcoat.

It was pleasant to feel the burning contact of the iron for a few seconds. It soothed the pain in his neck. But soon the rail began to tremble and sing louder, more menacingly. It filled his body with an aching groan. The earth, too, seemed to quake as if it were moving, swimming from under his body, and pushing him away.

The train approached heavily and slowly, but the clanking of its couplings, the even clatter of the wheels over the joints was already deafening. Its snorting breath roared and pushed Klimkov in the back. Everything outside and inside him shook in a violent throb, and tore him from the earth.

He could wait no longer. He jumped to his feet, ran along the rails, and shouted in a high screeching voice, "I will do anything you say—I will, I will!"

Reddish rays of light darted along the smoothly polished metal of the rails, gaining at every second on Klimkov. They glared more and more fiercely. The two red strips of iron seemed to glow as they flowed impetuously on either side of him, directing his course.

"I will . . ." he yelled, waving his hands.

Something hard struck his back. He fell across the sleepers between the red cords of rail, and the harsh iron rumble deadened his feeble screams.